THE BRIDGE

B BASKERVILLE

HYEM BOOKS

PROLOGUE

Two years ago.

CAPTAIN JUDE MCDERMOTT RESTED a hand on the helm and peered out to sea from the sanctuary of the bridge. The space bore the marks of time, with outdated but well-maintained technology. The screens occasionally flickered, and the controls had a tactile feel, the kind that came from years of hands running over them. It wasn't cutting-edge, but it got the job done. Despite its age, the room was airy and ordered, unlike the raw, untamed nature of the North Sea churning outside.

Just as raw and only slightly more tamed, Captain Jude cut a formidable figure in a white polo shirt that strained against his broad chest and slight beer belly. It was dawn, the blood-red glow of sunrise barely breaking through the thick fog that engulfed the SOV, a service operation vessel.

North Star was the behemoth ship tasked with ferrying engineers and technicians back and forth from the Port of Tyne to Odin's Gale, an offshore wind farm almost 200 nautical miles from Northumberland. The deep-red hull of the vessel had earned North Star the nickname Rust Bucket. And Jude, with hair and beard a shade not too dissimilar, had heard some of the technicians refer to him as Rusty. He preferred Captain.

Jude inched the throttle forward, increasing speed to the maximum permitted for this visibility. The hour was still early, but his thoughts were already in The Masons, that dingy pub with sticky floors and cheap pints. God, he needed to unwind. Once they'd offloaded the turbine parts from their hold and returned to port, he'd down six, hell, maybe even seven, if today kept up like this.

Beside him, First Mate Hal Simpson had a geeky, scholarly air. He stood tall and slender. His wiry frame was still with focus as he monitored the radar and AIS displays, the bright lights of the bridge glinting off the glasses perched on the end of his nose.

"A bit of a pea souper, eh?" Hal remarked, peering into the dense fog before confirming their coordinates.

The radar beeped out a warning.

Jude grunted in agreement, his eyes scanning a blurry horizon. "Aye. The North Sea's hiding her secrets today."

The radar's beep sliced through them. "What you got?" asked Jude.

Hal shivered. "Something small on our port side. Nothing's showing on AIS. Probably a fishing vessel."

Jude pressed the horn, alerting whatever was out there of their presence. The resonant sound vibrated through the metal beneath his feet. He'd repeat the action every minute until conditions improved.

Suddenly, a small boat materialised from the gloom.

"Bloody 'ell," cursed Jude. "They aren't fishermen."

The tiny boat, dwarfed by the towering SOV, bobbed precariously on the waves. Compared to North Star, it was nothing more than a plastic toy in a bairn's bathtub. Its occupants brandished placards, holding them aloft, murky shapes in the grey.

A woman with unruly blonde curls under a woollen bobble hat lifted a megaphone to her lips.

"Stop the Slaughter! Save our Seas!"

Her voice hardly penetrated the bridge over the wind and waves.

Jude, spying their 'SAVE THE BIRDS! STOP OFFSHORE WIND!' signs, rolled his eyes. "Greenpeace wankers," he scoffed.

Hal, ever the diplomat, adjusted his glasses. "They look a little underfunded to be Greenpeace. More likely some bird group. Ornithologists Against Turbines, maybe?"

"I don't give a shit what they call themselves," said Jude, grabbing the throttle and putting the boat into neutral. "Those Chris

Peckham-loving hippies are playing chicken with a ship a thousand times their size.

The SOV was slow to stop, continuing through the water. This was no Ford Focus; one couldn't just slam the brakes. The old boat was ready for decommissioning. In a few months, it would be nothing but scrap metal.

The eco-protesters drew perilously close, ignoring the rules of the nautical road. Jude's ship had far less manoeuvrability than the small motorboat buzzing off their port. Both irritated and concerned, his hand moved instinctively to the ship's horn, sending five deep blasts into the fog. The blare would be deafening, echoing over the waves, yet it only spurred the protesters on. They jeered louder, shaking their signs defiantly.

"How'd these fucking tree-huggers even find us out here?" Jude wondered aloud. "Our transponder's on the blink, and the site's not even on the charts yet."

He gripped the helm in frustration. Odin's Gale was still under construction and wouldn't be functional for at least a year, but once up and running, 120 turbines would generate over 1400 megawatts of renewable energy. The new wind farm had brought a welcome boost of jobs and money to the region, but it had also drawn controversy.

"Go home, sea killers!" shouted the woman with the wild hair. "Leave our oceans alone!"

"It's a sea, not an ocean, ya pillock." Jude picked up the radio. "Unidentified vessel, this is SOV North Star. You are on a collision course, over."

No answer.

He handed Hal the radio. "Keep tryin' to raise those bloody fools. Tell the daft buggers to shift their arses before they get squashed."

Hal pressed the button. "Unidentified vessel. You are impeding safe passage. Advise you alter course immediately to avoid collision."

Tension knotted the air. The protesters didn't look to be wearing life jackets, and they weren't appearing on the AIS screen. Jude wouldn't be surprised if the idiots had come out in this fog without a radio or life-raft.

The smaller vessel zipped close to the hull of North Star, coming within a few feet. Jude swore and blasted the horn again. He edged to starboard but couldn't turn too quickly, or he'd risk the stern colliding with the protesters' boat. But just as quickly as they emerged, the small vessel backed away, blurring into the ghostly grey mist.

The radar's frantic beeping faded as the little dots tracing the boat's movements disappeared off the edge of the screen.

A collective sigh filled the bridge as Jude and Hal relaxed. The former waited several minutes for his heart rate to lower, then pressed the throttle again, edging North Star forward slower than before. The latter cleaned his glasses on a microfibre cloth, moved from the radar, and collapsed into a chair.

"You okay, son?"

Hal nodded, wiping his brow, soft chestnut curls bobbing. But as soon as he slumped in the chair, the beeping resumed, more urgently than before.

The little boat zipped out of the heavy fog once again, this time perpendicular to their course.

Jude's stomach lurched; the bloody idiots had no idea what was coming. He slammed the throttle into reverse, but the massive SOV's momentum carried it forward.

"Brace for impact."

The inevitable happened. The crash was slight for North Star but catastrophic for the tiny vessel. The smaller boat crumpled against the massive hull, fragments of fibreglass and wood flying.

Hal winced at the ear-splitting crunch of metal ringing through the bridge as the protesters were thrown about like peg dolls.

The young woman with the megaphone was flung furthest, her head cracking against the stern of her boat with a sickening thud. She tumbled limply overboard, her wild blonde hair spreading over the surface like the tentacles of a lion's mane jellyfish.

"No!" Hal gasped, his face paling in panic.

Jude, heart thumping, put the ship into neutral and seized the emergency alarm. The claxon blared as he shouted into the radio. "Man overboard! Begin rescue operations!"

He could picture crew leaping from their bunks, donning life jackets and running through the maze of corridors on the old rust bucket to their muster stations where they'd launch North Star's fleet of RIBs and transfer vessels.

The first mate, white as a sheet, raised the coastguard on radio channel sixteen. His voice was steady, but his hands shook with dread.

Keeping his eyes fixed on the spot where the woman had entered the frigid waves, Jude willed her to move, swim, show any sign of life.

Come on, come on...

His gut twisted as the seconds ticked by. He pressed his hands against the broad, reinforced window, eyes scanning for the rescue boats.

But the sea, unforgiving and cold, had already claimed its due. The captain's heart sank with the woman as he watched her disappear beneath the waves, her protest silenced forever by the very waters she sought to protect.

CHAPTER 1

Present day.

THE VAST WHITE TURBINES of Odin's Gale dotted the North Sea, ivory towers piercing a brilliant, cloudless sky of pink and orange, their blades rotating in a gentle, hypnotic rhythm. It was relaxing, thought Second Officer India Morgan, her gaze lost in the turbines' dance that, for a moment, calmed the constant churn of her mind. India stood by one of several portholes in the mess, her blue eyes reflecting topaz waters.

The early light of dawn cast a soft, golden hue on her tanned face, highlighting her high cheekbones and strands of blonde hair that had escaped her usually immaculate bun. She took a deep breath, the air tasting of salt and the promise of a busy day ahead. For there were no quiet days on Electron, the brand-new, state-of-the-art, fully-electric SOV that replaced that damn rust bucket, North Star. Electron had full-time chefs catering to every diet imaginable. Everyone on board enjoyed private accommodation with their own phone and television. Of course, not everyone slept in their own bunk. Not that it was any of India's business. Electron even had a gym, a cinema, and a helipad for crying out loud.

India liked Electron, but she didn't like being third in command. She was forty-four and not getting any younger. If she wanted to make captain by fifty, she'd have to make some changes. Still, the crew got on well, and they all knew their roles, both professionally and socially. Captain Jude played up to his part as the grumpy old sea dog. That was understandable, given what happened and what he'd been through since. Hal, the first mate, was the young, enthusiastic pup, full of youthful energy and positivity. Third Officer Graham Bell was more of a nervous stray, always so desperate for Jude to give him a pat on the head. Still, he was a great listener and the crew's unofficial psychologist. This left India, who, if she continued the canine metaphor, was the hard-nosed bitch. She'd earned the captain's wrath and respect on her first day when she refused to make him a cup of tea. She was the second officer; she was no tea maid. She'd handed him an iPad, quipping that surely a man of his qualifications knew how to work a kettle, but failing that, he was only three swipes of the tablet away from ordering one directly from the galley. He'd never asked India to make him a cuppa since.

Speaking of tea. Graham Bell – known to all as Gray – approached, brandishing two steaming mugs. India took one gratefully, cradling the warm mug between her hands as she sat at an empty table. Gray sat opposite, nursing his cup, the quietness between them a comfortable blanket. India didn't care for small talk.

The mess hall was slowly coming to life as technicians trickled in, each absorbed in their morning rituals of coffee, newspapers and social media. India caught the expression on one of their faces, saw the little nudge from his mate. And they say women like to gossip, she thought, turning away. Some of the blokes on Electron couldn't resist a rumour if their lives depended on it. Still, aside from juvenile glances, the ambience was one of subdued efficiency, a symphony of sleepy footsteps and muted conversation. It was a gentle buzz, underscored by the ship's hum, more akin to a purr than the old growl of diesel engines from ships past.

Gray leant back, his posture relaxed despite the early hour. "It's strange, isn't it? Not feeling the ship vibrate under our feet like the old days," he remarked, his baritone voice breaking the tranquillity.

India raised an eyebrow. "Surely, you don't miss being jolted awake by Rust Bucket's temper tantrums?" Her tone was dry, the hint of a smile showing her amusement.

"Nah," Gray replied with a shrug. He smelled of shower gel, his hair still wet from the shower. "Though I reckon it kept us sharp. All this," he gestured around them at the mess's sleek stainless steel and laminate surfaces, "it's easy to forget we're at sea. Feels like we're in a floating hotel."

India sipped her cup of English breakfast. "A *flotel?*"

"*Boatel?*" Gray's smooth, brown forehead creased as he looked beyond India at something over her shoulder. "Thought we were starting with A03 today?"

"We are." India turned back to the porthole, her eyes narrowing. "Or at least we were."

Odin's Gale was 200 miles offshore and covered an area larger than Greater London. When they set off from the Tyne late last night, they had instructions to head straight at twenty-five knots to OGA03, the third turbine in the northernmost row.

India pressed a small orange button on a handheld radio. "Has there been a change of plan, Captain?"

Nothing but static hissed back at her. They were off course, only by a few degrees, but over vast distances, a few degrees could take you miles from your destination. From where India was sitting, they looked to be heading towards the middle of the field rather than the northwest corner.

She shook her radio, wondering if it was faulty. "See if you can raise them," she said, nodding towards Gray's waist where his handheld was clipped to his belt. After trying the bridge three times, India's professional acumen kicked in. Something was off. She got to her feet. "Let's go check."

Gray looked longingly at his tea. "The captain doesn't like being checked up on."

India jiggled her radio. "And I don't like being ignored."

She turned and walked with purpose through Electron's corridors, her boots thudding on metal grates. She could feel Gray rolling his eyes behind her. People often mistook her distance for coldness, just as they branded Jude stubborn and gruff. But India knew that sometimes, being firm and direct was the only way to get things done. And they were both far too busy looking after a floating city to be bothered with sentimental nonsense.

"Captain," she said tersely, pushing open the door to the bridge. "I know I'm off watch, but I'd appreciate you telling me if—"

Blood. Everywhere. Spattered on controls and windows, a crimson mess on the floor.

She froze at the sight of Jude slumped against a workstation, still as stone, eyes glassy and vacant. Red rivulets streaked down his neck, chest and arms from countless brutal stab wounds. The room seemed to spin as India tried to make sense of the gruesome scene before her. Blood pulsed hard in her ears, drowning out the beeps and bleeps of various instruments.

Hal lay face-down nearby, a pool of blood surrounding him. India lunged for him, turning him over. Blood gushed from a deep wound in his left arm, staining her pristine white polo shirt. "Hal?" she called. "Hal?"

He was pale as ash, his glasses shattered.

"Oh, my God," Gray said weakly. He grabbed the wall for support before gathering himself and stumbling towards Jude, kneeling beside him.

"Captain? Can you hear me, Captain?" He grabbed Jude's shoulders, shaking him, willing him to answer.

"Who could do this?" Gray asked, his deep voice cracking.

India swallowed. "Someone on board."

She hadn't meant it to sound flippant, but it was true. She pressed two fingers to Hal's neck, finding the faintest pulse.

"What are we going to do?"

"First things first. Contact the medic. Hal's alive. But barely." The thought of someone on board Electron being capable of such brutality turned her blood to ice. "Then send everyone to their accommodation."

"Shit! India!" Gray's eyes were wide, staring not at Jude or Hal, but out the window of Electron's bridge. He pointed a finger as the turbines loomed huge, blades slicing the air. India's training took over. This was no North Star. Electron could turn on a sixpence and hold an exact position using thrusters and satellite technology. But she only had seconds.

Rushing for the controls, her boots slipped in a puddle of blood. She hit the floor hard; Electron hit the turbine.

The boat shuddered, 5000 tonnes and £90 million worth of steel screaming. The twenty-five-knot impact sent everything and everyone flying. Jude's lifeless body slid across the floor, leaving a thick, sickening smear of red in its wake. Gray was hurled against the navigation station, cursing through clenched teeth as his head hit the edge, a deep gash tearing open across his forehead.

"Medic! Now!" India barked, her voice filled with urgency as she jabbed her finger at the intercom. She struggled to her feet, her hands shaking with adrenaline as she took control of the vessel. "I want the senior engineers out inspecting the damage. Everyone else is to get to their quarters immediately. No exceptions." Her eyes narrowed, the gravity of the situation taking hold. "No one else comes in here besides you, me and the medic. This is a crime scene."

CHAPTER 2

DCI ERICA COOPER LET the hot water cascade down her neck, the sound of the shower drowning out the tinny echoes of metal music playing from her phone. Listening to Judas Priest at such a low volume felt criminal, but at this hour, she had little choice. There was a sleeping infant in the next room, though, in fairness, of everyone in the house, he was the least likely to have a tantrum about being awoken early. The familiar tune had aggressive undertones but was a comforting distraction to the routine check she performed with a practised hand. Two years clear, and every shower was still a battleground, her fingers tracing her lumpectomy scars and floral tattoos with a mix of defiance and dread.

Check completed: no new lumps or changes. Two years cancer-free, but the relief still felt as fragile as glass. It could shatter at any moment.

Some days she wondered what she was playing at, working long hours, mingling with murderers and rapists when she could be home with her seven-month-old son or spending time with her teenage daughter. During her more vulnerable moments, Cooper wondered whether she should give it all up and do something crazy, live off-grid or travel the world. Build memories and savour every moment. But those moments were fleeting – CID was as much her home as the house in Tynemouth.

Danny's father, Justin Atkinson, had stepped up. His enthusiasm for becoming a father again in his forties was infectious, his bookish manner giving way to a tenderness she hadn't always given him credit for. He reduced his hours to work only two days a week, spending the other days at home with Danny while she chased the demons of the northeast. It was his time, he'd said, to be the parent he couldn't be to his twins years ago. And Cooper? She was no homemaker; she could barely manage scrambled eggs without setting fire to something. Being a detective was her bloody redemption. She'd go mad if she had to stay home all day. But the guilt, societal or otherwise, clung to her like the stench of smoke on clothing.

She turned off the water and towelled herself dry, avoiding the mirror. With hair as short as hers, there was no need for hair products, a hair dryer, or even a brush. She threw on a smart pair of jeans and a jumper before heading for the kitchen.

The house was still, the rest of her family enjoying the luxury of a lie-in. Tina had a free period and wouldn't need to be at school until ten. Atkinson would sleep as long as Danny did. *If the baby's sleeping, Daddy's sleeping.* Cooper relished the silence, appreciating the rare moment of solitude before the day's demands beckoned.

In the kitchen, she prepared toast and tea – something even she couldn't screw up. Or so she thought, the toast burning while she checked her emails. She ate in the living room with the news on the television turned low. A chipper woman on a windswept dune reported the number of gulls and guillemots washing up on northeast beaches. Though the report was interesting, Cooper's thoughts were in CID, running through possible leads in an unsolved carjacking and an armed robbery. Then there was the ruthless vigilante who'd been dubbed the Masked Mackem.

Cooper's phone chirped, jolting her from her mental to-do list. She finished her culinary masterpiece of burnt toast and dusted her hands on her jeans before answering.

"Cooper."

Cooper recognised the hacking cough that greeted her before the man even spoke. Chief Superintendent Howard Nixon was full of flu but refused to take a day off. The stubborn old fool would infect the entire station within a fortnight.

"Homicide," he said, voice like gravel. "Stabbing victim on one of the boats working the wind farms. You're the SIO, Cooper."

"Any witnesses?" she asked, rinsing her cup and plate and leaving them in the sink. Cooper made a

B BASKERVILLE

mental note to apologise to Atkinson later for the unwashed dishes.

"Yes. But he was gravely injured in the same attack. He's being flown to the RVI now. How soon can you be there?"

"Grabbing my keys as we speak." Cooper stepped out into the crisp October air, the cold biting the back of her neck, her breath visible in small clouds as she locked the door behind her. It was late in the month, and fallen leaves, the colour of turnips and pumpkins, filled Tynemouth's streets. "Has DI Singh been informed?"

"He'll meet you there with a couple of sergeants," Nixon told her.

Cooper hung up, a ripple of anticipation washing away the remnants of domestic guilt. This was her element, where burnt toast and school schedules paled compared to the urgency of a new case. The thrill wasn't like her colleague DS Paula Keaton's – she wasn't an adrenaline junkie – but the allure of a fresh investigation, especially in the golden hour, was undeniable. When evidence was still raw, and suspects hadn't had time to align their lies, that's when the real dance began.

CHAPTER 3

CHECKING HER BREASTS IN the shower that morning, Cooper hadn't expected to pass by the Breast Screening and Assessment Unit in the Royal Victoria Infirmary, yet there she was. The sign pointing patients in the right direction still hit her in the gut with the same anxiety she'd felt when she'd been referred to the unit by her GP. She took a moment to centre herself, raised her chin, and continued to the escalator.

When she emerged on the roof, she could hear the thudding of helicopter blades somewhere nearby. Three figures stood ahead, their conversations muted by the noise of the chopper. As Cooper approached, DI Daljit Singh flashed a brief smile, his solemn eyes hinting at the seriousness of the situation.

"Good morning, DCI Cooper," he greeted.

"Morning, Daljit." She gave him an appraising look. Singh's pale grey three-piece suit was pressed to perfection. "Looking dapper as usual."

Beside the DI, two detective sergeants searched the sky, waiting for the helicopter to appear.

"There it is," DS Paula Keaton announced, pointing east. "Right on time." Keaton was built like the rugby pro she once was, broad in stature and confident in posture. She was the sort of woman who considered *thunder thighs* to be a compliment.

DS Elliot Whyte, hands shoved into the pockets of his long, black coat, merely nodded. The reserved type, he doled out words as if they cost him a quid a time. Still, there was a warmth in his dark eyes as Cooper neared.

Across the helipad, hospital staff waited by a gurney, ready to receive the injured party. Cooper noticed an older man in office attire speaking on a phone. The sound of the chopper muffled his words, but the tone was unmistakably angry.

As the helicopter descended, it stirred up the morning's dust and debris, sending gritty particles swirling through the air and stinging Cooper's eyes. Singh placed a protective hand on his turban, dipping his head into the gust. Keaton's tight ponytail refused to budge, but the wind whipped Whyte's brunet locks into a frenzy. On days like this, Cooper didn't miss having long hair.

The pilot lowered the craft further, settling it onto the helipad. The older man in office attire strode quickly towards them. He was lean, the suit expensive – a picture of corporate efficiency and image consciousness.

"DCI Cooper," Singh shouted as the helicopter landed, "meet Sean Hargreaves from VāyuVolt Renewables. They operate Odin's Gale wind farm."

Hargreaves pocketed his mobile phone, his face pinched with annoyance as he shook his head.

"Bloody journalists," Hargreaves spat, echoing the sentiment on Cooper's own tongue most days.

Cooper arched an eyebrow. "They're onto the incident already?"

The corporate representative shook his head, irritation evident. "Not the murder. It's the damn birds. They're trying to stick every avian death from the Forth to the Humber on Odin's Gale."

"Right," Cooper said, her mind already racing ahead. Bird deaths were a nuisance; murders were a crisis. Either way, someone was always looking for a scapegoat.

Heads lowered, the hospital staff raced forward, swarming the helicopter. In a coordinated motion, they lifted a stretcher carrying a pale, wounded man swaddled in blankets. The sight triggered a tension in Cooper's jaw.

"Hal Simpson," Hargreaves told Cooper. "First mate onboard Electron. He's alive but barely. They're taking him straight in for surgery."

"Keaton," Cooper barked over the noise without looking back, knowing the DS would be within earshot. "Go with him. I want updates on Hal the minute he's out of surgery. As soon as he can talk, get a statement out of him. Timeline, description, anything he can remember."

"Got it, boss," Keaton said, already stepping forward to liaise with the medical team.

"And the other victim?" Cooper asked Hargreaves. "The gentleman who didn't make it."

"Jude McDermott. He was Electron's captain," Hargreaves told her, voice straining against the din."

"Electron's the boat?"

"Correct. The absolute state-of-the-art. The best of the fleet."

"And Odin's Gale?"

Hargreaves straightened his tie. "Odin's Gale is a marvel of modern engineering. If the renewable energy sector had a *Seven Wonders of the World* list, Odin's Gale would top it. 200 nautical miles offshore, OG is a Colossus. The field's bigger than the size of Greater London. A real beast of engineering."

His pride was palpable but seemed inappropriate given the circumstances.

Hargreaves' voice took on the rehearsed quality of a well-practiced pitch. "With its cutting-edge turbine technology and state-of-the-art monitoring systems, Odin's Gale represents the pinnacle of green energy innovation. VāyuVolt Renewables is proud to harness the power of the prevailing winds in the North Sea, generating enough electricity to power 1.2 million homes annually, all while reducing carbon footprints, promoting environmental sustainability and bringing hundreds of jobs to the region."

He paused, seemingly expecting some form of admiration or acknowledgement, then launched into the next part of his spiel without missing a beat. "Our commitment to corporate social responsibility is unwavering. Our Odin's Gale initiative has set new industry standards for ecological stewardship and community engagement. By integrating the latest advancements in turbine efficiency and marine life safety measures, we're not just leading the charge in renewable energy, we're redefining it."

The pitch was slick, the kind of talk that would no doubt play well in boardrooms and industry conferences. But to Cooper, it rang hollow, almost tone-deaf.

She cut him off. "I'm sure the specifications of Odin's Gale are impressive, but we're here to investigate, not to invest. We need to examine the scene as soon as possible. I assume they're bringing Electron into the Tyne or Blyth, given it fell on my desk and not my Dutch equivalent's."

"I'm sorry—" said Hargreaves, though his tone suggested he was confused rather than apologising. He dipped his chin, brows lowered. "You weren't informed?"

Cooper bristled. "Informed of what, exactly?"

"The SOV is registered to the Tyne, but she's not coming into port. Not yet, anyway. Electron sustained some damage during the collision."

"What collision?"

"The incident," Hargreaves began, quickly slipping back into his corporate veneer, "was minor. It is negligible in the grand scheme of operational difficulties and the safety protocols we uphold. Such occurrences are, of course, rare, and it's a testament to our top-of-the-line design that—"

He caught himself, perhaps noticing the frustrated look on Whyte's face.

Cooper was equally unhappy. The golden hour was slipping away from her. Each second wasted was evidence lost. "This is a murder investigation. My team and our forensic investigators need to view the scene right away. You need to get Electron back in the Tyne now."

The corners of Hargreaves' mouth turned down. "I don't have that authority. Besides, it would take eight hours to tow her back into port. That said, it doesn't mean you can't view the scene."

"Excuse me?" asked Cooper, raising her voice as the chopper's rotors roared back to life.

Hargreaves gestured at the aircraft. "If the mountain won't come to Muhammad..."

CHAPTER 4

SINGH COULD BARELY CONTAIN his excitement. "I've never been in a helicopter before."

"Keaton's going to be sick when she hears," Whyte said.

Cooper managed a tight smile despite her nerves. Keaton would be positively green with envy when she found out they'd boarded the chopper while she twiddled her thumbs waiting for Hal Simpson to come out of surgery.

"You first, sir," called the pilot over the din, pointing Singh towards his seat.

Cooper was next. She stepped onto the skid, gripping the frame like a vice.

"Mind yer head, luv." The pilot's northern accent was as thick as pease pudding.

Cooper ducked instinctively, settling into her seat, her body tense. Whyte followed, sandwiching Cooper between the two men. The

25

close quarters were cramped and claustrophobic, forcing Whyte's thigh against hers. She could feel the warmth of his leg through her jeans. It was a touch that sent an unexpected jolt through her. Memories flooded back to the previous month when Whyte had arrived just in time to save her, their eyes locking in a shared moment of vulnerability. A look that had lingered too long. Cooper shifted subtly, crossing her legs away from him, creating a fraction of space in the cramped cabin.

The safety drill was a blur. Ear protectors were handed out, straps pulled tight across their chests.

"My colleague is flying your forensic team out as we speak," the pilot told them. They'll be there shortly. We have a cruising speed of 160 miles per hour, so sit back, relax and enjoy the view; I'll get you to Odin's Gale in around ninety minutes."

Cooper managed a terse nod, her hands clasped in her lap to stop them from shaking. She felt far from relaxed. Singh, however, beamed as he fiddled with the volume dial on his headset, eyes twinkling with anticipation.

The blades roared louder as the helicopter lifted, then surged forward, leaving the roof behind. Cooper's stomach knotted as their bubble of plexiglass and metal ascended into the crisp expanse of clear sky.

Below them, Newcastle dwindled, a sprawl of miniature houses and toy-sized cars. The architecture shrank further as they climbed, the Tyne weaving through the city like a slender silver stream rather than the vast river it was.

"Scared of heights, boss?" Whyte asked.

"No," said Cooper dryly. "I'm scared of falling. There's a subtle but important difference."

Whyte chuckled. "I think it's cool. It's like playing on Google Earth."

"Geek," she teased, faking levity.

As they crossed the coastline, the last sliver of familiar landscape gave way to the immensity of the North Sea. Cooper had seen the view several times from aeroplanes, but the fragility of the chopper and the sight of endless water stretching before them amplified her unease. She worked to maintain a neutral expression, aware of Singh's curious glances and Whyte's mute observation.

The water shifted from a brilliant azure at the coast to darker shades of sapphire and ink as they headed further offshore. An undulating swell rose and fell beneath them, and within half an hour, the pilot's voice crackled through their headsets.

"Odin's Gale. Two o'clock."

Whyte pressed his Roman nose to the window. Specks of white emerged on the horizon like ivory matchsticks. As the chopper continued its steady journey, the specks slowly grew into distinct shapes. Towering metallic structures glinted under the sun, row after row surfacing in the distance. Hargreaves hadn't been overplaying it when he said the field was bigger than Greater London.

"It's quite a sight, isn't it?" Singh remarked, leaning over, trying to take in the scale of the operation.

"Incredible," Whyte added, his tone carrying a rare note of awe.

Cooper, however, was focused on the task at hand. As impressive as it was, she couldn't forget why they were there. The captain was dead, and by the end of the day, the first mate probably would be too.

Her headset crackled with static again. "If you look to your right, you can see our destination. That's Electron. Can't miss her."

The service vessel was a vibrant shade of green. Along with the turbines, it looked almost out of place in the rugged enormousness of the sea. Cooper wondered if there weren't a place on Earth humans wouldn't conquer.

Singh peered out the window. "Well, this is an unexpected adventure. The biggest boat I've been on is the Shields Ferry."

"Not sure which is scarier," Whyte said. "Being all the way out here or risking the Shields Ferry at half ten on a Friday night?"

"I'd pick the ferry any day," Cooper said, eyeing Electron's sleek, modern lines. As far as she was aware, no one had killed anyone on the Shields Ferry. Not yet, anyway. "That ship's a crime scene, and someone on it is a murderer. Keep your heads on a swivel. Both of you."

The two men nodded.

"Right you are, boss," Singh agreed. "Eyes peeled, minds sharp."

Whyte nodded solemnly, then tapped the window. "I can see a helipad."

Thank heavens. Since they took off, Cooper had been plagued with images of being winched down. At least one fear had been nullified. No mid-air heroics today.

Whyte suddenly brightened, straightening up, a smile on his lips as he pushed his hair back. "Check them out," he said, pointing out the window.

Cooper followed his gesture, spotting the seals. Tens of them. They bobbed in the water by a turbine, slick, grey bodies gleaming in the sunlight. For a fleeting second, she smiled.

"They're watching us," Whyte said as they started their descent.

The landing onto Electron's helipad was smooth, the pilot expertly navigating the gusts of wind that rattled the cabin and flogged cold air against their faces. The roar of the blades seemed to crescendo before finally yielding to silence as the craft touched down and its engines turned off.

Singh was first to alight, unfolding his tall body from the cramped space. He offered a hand to Cooper, who took it gratefully. She unbuckled and stepped onto Electron's helipad.

"Ah, solid ground," breathed Whyte as he jumped from the chopper with an irritating amount of energy.

Cooper's boots felt good against the platform. Still, as she took in her surroundings – a steel island in an unending expanse of water – the reality hit her hard. Water stretched endlessly in every direction, with no land in sight, just the sea, the sky, and the towering turbines of Odin's Gale. And waiting on this floating fortress was a murder victim and, somewhere nearby – the one who'd done it.

Cooper gulped. "Solid ground, my arse."

CHAPTER 5

THE WIND BELLOWED ACROSS Electron's helipad as a hulking, broad-shouldered man strode towards the detectives. With tanned skin, blonde hair and a square, strong jaw, he could have played an action hero. He assessed the three detectives before extending his hand towards Whyte.

"DCI Cooper?"

The three shared a look, but Singh was the first to speak. He made a buzzing noise reminiscent of the gameshow Family Fortunes. "I'm afraid that's incorrect. You have two guesses remaining."

The action hero wore a spotless white polo shirt and navy trousers. His giant feet sported blindingly white trainers. There was an awkward pause while he looked between the dark-skinned man in a turban and the skinny, white woman with a shaved head.

"My apologies," he said, shifting his handshake toward Cooper this time. "Cliff Longacre. Bosun."

31

His voice was deep and authoritative, carrying over the clangour of the wind, the sea and the chopper.

"No harm done," Cooper said. "Are you in charge?"

"Negative. That's Second Officer India Morgan. She's acting captain for all intents and purposes. She and Gray found the captain and first mate. She has control of the ship now."

"And Gray is?"

"Third Officer Graham Bell. He's not doing so well. He sustained an injury during the collision. The medic's also treating him for shock."

"I was informed another helicopter would bring the forensics officers."

"Yes, they're already here," Cliff told her. "They're on the bridge with India. I appreciate time is of the essence, but I can't take you to them until we've been through some basic safety instructions."

Cooper nodded, understanding. She quickly glanced at her phone: no signal. "Fair enough," she said. "Please make it as quick and painless as possible. And if we could go via a bathroom, all our bladders would appreciate it."

Whyte and Singh nodded.

BLADDERS EMPTIED, CLIFF LONGACRE TOOK the detectives to their muster station and told them where to locate their life jackets if instructed to wear one. He demonstrated how to put one on and showed them how to board the life raft. Although well intended, it only served to increase Cooper's anxiety.

"This is all precautionary," Cliff assured her. "Just in case. Electron's a tank; there's nothing to worry about."

"What about the crash?"

"A minor incident."

"You sound like Sean Hargreaves."

Cliff grimaced, his strong jaw tightening, clearly insulted. "That bean counter's never been on an SOV in his life. Look," he held up his palms in surrender, "we hit a turbine. It's a bit of a mess, which is putting it lightly, and a lot of people were hurt, but everything is in hand," he said before repeating, "Nothing to worry about."

Singh smoothed his waistcoat. "Sounds like an unstoppable force hit an immovable object."

"You can say that again," said Cliff. "The hull is intact, which is the important thing. But we need to ensure all our systems are working as they should before we head back. We don't want to get halfway home and find there's a gas leak or the bilge pumps have gone."

Cooper didn't know what a bilge pump was, but it sounded important.

"And a tow is out of the question?" she asked, once more checking her phone, feeling cut off from her family.

"We have Wi-Fi," Cliff said. "We'll get you all connected soon. And yes, a tow isn't an option. Right now, the only tug big enough to bring

Electron back in is busy off Shetland. Would take forever to get here, then another eight to ten hours on top. Flying you in was far quicker."

"Right then," Cooper said, wanting to waste no more time on logistics and protocols. "Let's not dawdle. I need to view the scene and speak with India Morgan."

Cliff nodded and turned, leading the way through Electron's corridors. Cooper followed, with Singh and Whyte shadowing her, tension palpable. Once at the bridge, Cooper observed the scene from the door, watching SOCOs in protective overalls document the chaos. Shattered screens blinked erratically, throwing eerie light across consoles and walls. A first aid kit lay gutted on the floor, its contents scattered.

"Christ..." Whyte muttered. Beside him, Singh took a long, slow breath.

Bloody footprints, smeared and overlapping, trailed through the room. Crimson clues that would be analysed for days or weeks. The SOCOs laid metal plates like stepping stones across the bridge, creating a path through the gore. India Morgan stood rigidly on one by the helm, her eyes tracking the SOCOs' movements, her expression unreadable. She was a slim woman: thin arms folded over her chest, blonde hair pulled back in a professional bun. Cooper noted the rose-coloured blood stains on her white polo and light brown boots.

Flashes from a SOCO's camera caused the detectives to blink as it illuminated the captain's corpse, which lay at unnatural angles.

A considerable man with thick red hair and a matching beard, the captain's white skin was paler in death. Frenzied stab wounds peppered his bare torso. His shirt was cut wide open where someone had attempted to use a defibrillator, the loose fabric hanging into the red puddles of blood pooling by his side.

"Someone didn't hold back," Whyte whispered behind her.

"Reminds me more of a domestic," Singh said.

Cooper agreed. This wasn't the average single stab wound you might see after a drunken argument between strangers. The sort of cold, detached violence expected from someone who carried a knife because they were too cowardly to use their fists, too stupid to use their wit, or too bloody egotistical to walk away.

"This was personal," she said. "Impassioned. We're looking for someone who felt betrayed, wronged in some way."

Whatever happened on the bridge early that morning was fuelled by deep-seated anger or resentment. Cooper wondered who had it in for Jude McDermott and where Hal Simpson fitted into it. Did he disturb the killer, or was Hal the intended target? Did the captain rush to defend his first mate only to become another victim? Cooper's mind flooded with questions. Would Hal survive his injuries? Who would be motivated to kill them both? And who would benefit from their deaths?

Next to the captain, an officer unrolled a black body bag. Cooper turned to Cliff, "The helicopter?"

The bosun's deep voice cracked as he spoke. "Waiting to transport Captain Jude back to shore."

Whyte pulled out his phone. "I'll contact Dr Swanson. Let her know to expect the body." He frowned at the lack of signal.

"There's a phone in the office you can use," Cliff told him. "I'll take you there. Get you hooked up to the Wi-Fi while we're at it."

Cooper watched the two men go while forensics manoeuvred the deceased into the bag and zipped it closed. It took four of them to hoist it. Cooper and Singh moved aside, allowing them to pass into the corridors that led back to the helipad. There was a silence that followed, both sorrowful and respectful. After a minute, Cooper had no choice but to break it. She pulled on protective clothing and stepped carefully across the metal plates towards the second officer.

"India? I'm DCI Erica Cooper, Northumbria Police. I understand you and the third officer were the ones who found Jude and Hal and that you're now in command of the vessel."

India nodded but said nothing.

Cooper eyed the bridge, trying to catalogue every broken control and blood smear in her head. Her gaze landed again on the footprints, willing the puzzle pieces to fit together. "Other than my colleagues, who has been in this room?"

India pressed two buttons on her console. They beeped quietly. "Just the three of us. Third Officer

Graham Bell, our medic Georgie Peters, and myself."

That was good. Despite the stress India must have been under, her quick actions in shutting down the crime scene would make the forensics work a whole lot easier. At least there hadn't been umpteen people wandering through, contaminating everything.

"And you never left?" Cooper asked. "No one could have come in between you finding the scene and the forensic team arriving?"

"Absolutely not. I've been here ever since."

"And where are Gray and Georgie now?"

"In the medical bay," India explained. She tugged at her left earlobe, rotating a tiny anchor-shaped earring. "Gray hit his head and needed stitches. They both did their best to keep Hal alive while we waited for the chopper, but Gray was trembling badly. He was acting confused, fearful. Georgie suspects some kind of psychological shock. I asked for him to be kept in the medical bay for now, but Georgie has his hands full. Gray wasn't the only one injured during the impact – there were a few broken bones, some concussions. Georgie needs to get the injured to hospital."

Cooper took this all in, making notes on a small notepad. She looked behind her to Singh, still standing by the door, quietly observing his surroundings. "Daljit, act as crime scene manager until we assign it to someone else. Start a log book."

"I'll need stationary," he said, addressing India.

India spoke into her radio for a moment. "Cliff's bringing some up for you."

"Most appreciated," he said. "You said the medic, Georgie Peters, wants to get some people to hospital. Has anyone other than Hal been airlifted to shore?"

"No, not yet. I know what you're asking, and no, no one other than Hal – and now Jude – has left the ship. Cliff took two engineers in one of our daughter craft to assess the external damage. They returned within the hour. Everyone who was onboard at the time this happened..." She gestured around the bridge at the pools of sticky blood on the floor. "...is still on board. Anyone not working on fixing this mess is holed up in their bunks."

Cooper was impressed. India seemed stern and standoffish, but she'd done everything Cooper would have done. She was a skilled leader.

"I assume you have a list of everyone onboard."

"A manifest? Yes, of course we do." She checked something on a tablet. "I'll print a hard copy. Let me know your email, and I'll send a digital copy, too."

"Thank you, India. I'd like to compare it to everyone who disembarks when we return to port. Make sure no one stowed away."

"Knock yourself out," India said. "But it'll be your time you're wasting. Everyone here knows each other. Electron might be massive, but there's nowhere to hide. We'd notice a new face."

Cooper bristled. "That might be so, but I'd rather waste my time than miss a vital piece of evidence."

"I concur," said Singh. "I'll contact the port authority, have them pull up their security footage and send it to Martin. We can count how many people boarded."

"Great idea. Thank you, Daljit. Speaking of port," she said, turning back to the second officer / acting captain. "How soon can we head back? You've done an excellent job preserving evidence, but I need to get specialist equipment in here."

India's lips thinned. "I understand your frustration. It's difficult being all the way out here; not many people can handle it. But we have repairs to finish first. I'm sure our bosun explained to you that our nav lights are shot. Even if we leave now, some of the journey will be in the dark. I can't permit us to go until the lads have sorted them."

"Like driving without headlamps?" Cooper asked.

"Not exactly. They make us visible to other vessels. Without them, we'd be invisible. Not to mention we'd be breaking international collision regulations. We can't risk hitting another boat, not a—" Her radio crackled and India listened into a conversation about some wiring. "Sorry about that. As I was saying, we'll fix the lights and then link to the substation to charge Electron's batteries."

Cooper must have looked confused because India, looking irked, went on to explain. "There's a reason you can't smell any diesel fumes, detective. Electron's fully electric; the longer I have our four thrusters operating to hold our position, the lower our batteries run. We'll need to fully recharge before heading back."

Cooper checked her watch. "And how long does that take?" she asked. It was Family Friday, and she wondered what the chances were of her making it home in time for tea.

"Depends on about fifty different factors."

Outside the sweeping window of the bridge, turbine blades rotated slowly in the sunshine.

Zero, Cooper thought. Her chances were zero.

CHAPTER 6

KEATON SLOUCHED IN A HARD plastic chair in a sterile corridor of the Royal Victoria Infirmary, her gaze occasionally drifting towards the double doors through which Hal Simpson, the stabbing victim, had disappeared hours ago. The image of his arrival by helicopter on the hospital roof lingered in her mind – pale and fragile, his pained whimpers more like a child than a grown man. From what Keaton had seen, Hal was slim with smooth, youthful skin. He reminded her of her younger brother.

A WhatsApp message came through from Whyte, distracting her from her boredom. It was a black-and-white selfie, his dark hair swept off his face with a bloody great big wind turbine behind him. She read the accompanying message: *Guess where we are?*

Lucky git.

Keaton shifted in her chair, pushing her jealousy down. She called him a poser and closed the app, opening a dating app instead. Seeking refuge in the distraction of her phone, Keaton thumbed through potential partners. *Swipe left, swipe left. Ugh.* She sighed and looked back at the doors, but no surgeon or nurse came to update her. Boredom gnawed at her until she couldn't stop herself, and she typed in the familiar name: April Davis. The ex.

The Instagram page loaded – all perfect food shots and beaming smiles. Keaton's chest tightened. She scrolled through pictures of a new restaurant: Saffron & Sage. Exposed brick, driftwood furnishings, Edison bulbs and fresh herbs in retro soup cans. All very quirky and yet the same as every other Insta-friendly place popping up in the *Toon*. She remembered lying in bed one lazy Sunday morning with sunbeams illuminating their bed as April rested her head in Keaton's chest and told her about her dream of owning her own restaurant. Well, there it was, the dream come true in all its shabby-chic, organic glory. A few steps up from the catering company April ran from their home, or what was their home, until Keaton kicked her out.

The bitterness churned in her stomach, a familiar, self-inflicted ache. Why did she always end up here – staring at a life she was no longer a part of.

"Masochist," she muttered, looking up as a nurse emerged from the double doors but walked straight past her. And yet, she didn't put the phone away. She lingered on a picture of April in her chef's whites, arm around a svelte brunette. Keaton's jaw tightened. A colleague? The sous-chef, maybe? Or something more? She shook her head, but the thought clawed at her.

Around her, hospital life ebbed and flowed – nurses in scrubs moved with purpose, families huddled in anxious clusters. She tapped on the mentions tab, her eyes scanning a heated exchange between April and another chef, each accusing the other of culinary plagiarism – a fancy term for recipe stealing.

When another photo arrived from Whyte, Keaton locked her phone and stood abruptly. A walk would clear her head. Besides, it didn't look like Hal Simpson would be going anywhere in a hurry. She strode down the sanitised corridor, boots squeaking on the polished floor. But each step took her closer to April's new restaurant. Keaton hesitated at the exit. Curiosity warred with bitterness. Curiosity won out.

"ERICA, I TRUST YOU grasp the severity of the situation," India began, her tone laced with a hint of condescension. "I won't move Electron until she's fully charged. I can't risk us being set adrift in the middle of the North Sea."

Aboard Electron, the strain was showing. Cooper wanted the vessel to return to port; India would allow no such thing. Cooper was unaccustomed to being told what to do by anyone other than Superintendent Nixon, and even then, it was fifty-fifty whether she'd actually follow his advice. Being addressed by her first name only added to Cooper's irritation. The only ones who called her Erica were her boyfriend and the plump-lipped pathologist, Margot Swanson. That was another alpha female Cooper sometimes found herself locking horns with. Why was it always this way?

She knew the answer stemmed somewhere from the days when there was only ever a single seat at the table for women in the workplace. Times when if one wanted said seat, they'd have to trample on their fellow females to get it. Be smarter, be prettier, be more willing to put up with sexist shit. Laugh it off like one of the boys. Women pitted against women. Those days might be over, but the ingrained competition from that toxic time still lingered.

Cooper's response was a tight-lipped smile and a decision to play nice – for now.

"I understand the stakes, India," Cooper finally said. "You want to preserve the vessel, and I want to preserve evidence, but above it all, we have the same goal – to ensure the safety of everyone on board. Someone in your crew is a murderer..."

India flinched, but Cooper continued. "India, your knowledge of the ship and crew will be invaluable. Can we count on your cooperation?"

"Of course. I want this resolved as much as you do. Hal doesn't deserve this. And the captain, he was a good man."

She looked at her feet.

"But?" guessed Cooper.

"He wasn't everyone's cup of tea. But he was a good man."

Their conversation was cut short by the arrival of Singh and Whyte, both men looking slightly out of their element. The brisk sea air seemed to invigorate Singh, who stood tall and carried his notepad like a shield.

"Shall we divide and conquer?" asked Whyte.

Singh patted his jacket, where a slight bulge suggested something was filling his inside pocket. "I've brought enough sweets to bribe the truth out of anyone."

That got Cooper's attention. "What you got stashed away in there?"

"Love Hearts and Chewits."

"I haven't had a Chewit in donkey's years," said Cooper, holding her palm out and salivating in anticipation.

Whyte took a Love Heart, looked awkward as he read the inscription, then threw it in his mouth like an aspirin. "Thought I'd start with the technical logs and crew schedules. See if I can get a handle on who was supposed to be where and when. Someone's routine might give us a lead."

"Good thinking," said Cooper. "Unaccounted time is going to be crucial with this one. Daljit?"

"Crime scene manager," he said, brandishing the notepad. "I'm not going anywhere. Though,

I would like to speak with Mr Graham Bell." He turned to India. "He was with you when you discovered the scene?"

"That's right."

"Can he come and speak with me here?"

"Gray's just left the medical bay for his quarters. I'll send for him," India said, her voice lowering. "He's in bits, really shaken. Go easy on him."

Singh bowed his head. "Of course."

"And you?" India asked Cooper.

"I'd like to speak with the medic."

India nodded. "Georgie Peters. I'll have someone take you to him." She spoke into her radio. "What else can I do to help?"

It was a welcome olive branch. "Keep doing what you're doing. We're all in this together. Have a think about this morning and the past few days. Let me know if anyone seemed out of character or if anything didn't seem right."

As India returned to her workstation, Cooper followed the crew member who would lead her to the medic, Georgie Peters. She walked briskly down the narrow corridors of Electron, breathing in the faint smell of saltwater.

The infirmary lay below deck in a cold, white room with a desk, a couple of chairs, a bed and numerous filing cabinets. Knocking on the open door, Cooper was greeted by a weary but tough-looking man in his fifties. He had kind eyes, an earring in one ear, and a shadow of stubble over his jaw and neck. He wore the same white polo, dark trousers, and brown boots as the rest of the crew, but his polo bore a green cross above

Electron's logo on his left breast. With practised skill, he wrapped the last of a roll of gauze around a woman's misshapen finger.

"DCI Erica Cooper," she introduced herself as she stepped inside. "I hope you don't mind me dropping by for a chat."

"That'll do you for now," Georgie said to the injured woman. He patted her shoulder, adding, "Keep it elevated, yeah?"

As the sturdy-looking blonde with a wrist tattoo shuffled out, Georgie washed his hands in a small sink, lingering over the stream before splashing his face and holding a towel over his eyes for several seconds. He looked like he needed more than just a physical cleanse.

"You've had quite a day," Cooper observed, noting the tension in his shoulders.

The medic slid an X-ray into one of the filing cabinets, the metal drawer clanging shut. He sank into his chair, the leather creaking under his weight, and pointed to the other chair with a slight nod. "Slight understatement. Please, take a seat."

He typed quickly on a keyboard. "Sorry, just updating my records. There, all done. Yeah..." His voice trailed off, eyes distant. "I've had worse."

"You have?"

"Helmand for one. Battle of Nad Ali."

"You were in the military?"

"Army medic," Georgie said, his voice gruff as he pushed the keyboard aside. He sat back, folding his arms across his chest. "Caught the tail end of the Bosnian War, then served in Iraq with Operation

47

Telic. I was stationed near Basra for a while. Then it was Afghanistan before I retired from active duty in 2012." He looked down at his hands: fat knuckles, rough palms. "I've seen plenty of dead bodies before. I've seen mates literally blown to smithereens. Had to amputate limbs, had to shove a bloke's guts back inside him and staple him back together after some shrapnel disembowelled him, but..."

Georgie's voice faltered, and he reached for a nearby cup of something brown, taking a sip before grimacing and setting it back down.

"But you thought you'd left that all behind?"

Georgie looked her dead in the eye, and Cooper saw the haunted expression of a man who hadn't come to terms with all he'd been through.

"I knew I'd face death in this role. I just thought it would be from a fall or a heart attack. Not fucking murder." He shook his head slightly. "You've seen it up on the bridge. I haven't seen that much blood since..."

Cooper felt terrible for him. "You've spent all morning making sure everyone on board is okay. Has anyone stopped to ask if you're okay?"

"No." He rubbed the back of his neck. "And nor should they. That's my job. Have you heard if Hal made it? Is he okay?"

Checking on everyone else again.

She shook her head, apologising. "I haven't heard."

"He's a good lad. I liked the captain as well, mind. He was all right, you know? Not everyone's cup of tea, like—"

"You're not the first person to say that," Cooper said, forehead creasing.

"Aye. I'm not surprised. He was rough and abrasive, shall we say? On the spectrum most likely, not that he knew it. He was one of those people who, if he had a thought or something needed saying, he'd just say it, didn't matter if it was rude or if it upset anyone."

"Can I have an example?"

Georgie looked up and gave a long sigh. "Like, Gray might walk in the room and the captain wouldn't say hello, good morning, or owt. He'd just come straight out with his orders. And things were *always* orders, never questions. Never '*Can you sort this out for me, please?*', just '*Sort this out.*' That got people's goat up. But I saw what was done to him and Hal. Nee one does that over someone forgetting their manners."

Cooper agreed. "I know this will be difficult, but I need to ask you while your memories are fresh. Can you go over what happened this morning?"

He hesitated momentarily, his gaze flicking to the door as if making sure they were alone. Finally, he took a deep breath and looked up at Cooper.

"The impact woke me up at six thirty-seven. I practically fell out of bed. I knew something major had happened, so I started getting dressed. I was about to call the bridge when Gray called me first. That was six thirty-eight. He said it was an emergency but didn't say what. I remember being a bit peeved because I could have done with the information; I didn't know what kit to grab, so I assumed someone was badly hurt from hitting the turbine. I see now why he didn't say. He didn't want to have it all over the airwaves. Everyone was panicking as it was."

Georgie paused, swallowing hard. "When I got to the bridge, it was chaos. Pure chaos. And I say that as someone who was at the Siege of Sarajevo. Gray was bent over Jude, giving him chest compressions. I have this vivid recollection," he said, tapping his temple, "of blood dripping out of the gash on Gray's head directly into one of the stab wounds on Jude's neck. Jude's injuries were catastrophic. I grabbed the defibrillator, of course, but it was pointless after that much blood loss. I wiped the blood off his chest, but there was so much I couldn't even get the damn pads to stick. It was useless; he was long gone."

"And Hal Simpson, the first mate?"

"Hal was different. He was alive. Barely conscious, but he was hanging on. He had cuts everywhere. Deep ones too. It looked like someone had gone after him with relentless fury. I had Gray apply pressure to some of the wounds while I stitched up the worst of them. I got a tourniquet on his left leg to try to stem the bleeding until we could get him to shore, but the amount of blood... It was like whoever did this wanted to ensure there was nee chance of survival."

Cooper pitied the man. He, like her, had a job that involved doing things and seeing things the average person couldn't fathom. The sort of things that didn't leave you alone, even in your sleep.

"Georgie, I know you've had to treat plenty of injuries today, and I know you're going to want to think well of your fellow crew and passengers on board Electron, but has anyone presented to you wounds which may suggest they'd been in a fight? Has anyone come to you with more blood on them than is consistent with their own personal injuries? Has anyone presented with cuts or bruises they can't explain?"

Georgie seemed to sit with his thoughts for a while, his eyes moving over the table between them. Eventually, he said, "Sorry, my mind's all over the shop. I can't think straight." He entered a password on his computer, getting it wrong twice before accessing his notes. "Let's see, I've treated broken limbs, a broken collarbone, broken thumb, couple of concussions. A few of the guys cut their heads when they fell during the collision, and aye, the people with cuts had a bit of blood on them but nothing to suggest – in my opinion – that they'd been in a fight. The ship hit a turbine. People fell over. People were hurt. That's it. I just feel bad for the captain, like. After all he'd been through with the tribunal and the HR shit—"

"What tribunal?"

Georgie shook his head like it was a sore subject. "It was a couple of years ago now. You might have seen it on the news. Jude was cleared of any wrongdoing, of course. He was completely innocent."

"Innocent of what?"

"There was a collision back when they were building Odin's Gale. A group were out here on a small boat protesting the installation of the wind farm." He rolled his eyes. "It was foggy. Jude did his best, you know? It was all there in the records. He did his best to save that poor lass's life, but..." His voice trailed away.

Cooper sat still for a moment. There was something familiar about what Georgie had just told her. "Two years ago?" she asked, remembering lying in bed, weak and nauseous, the TV flickering in the background as she drifted in and out of sleep. The news had been on, reporting the tragic incident at sea. She recalled the footage of the dense fog enveloping the lifeboats as they returned into the Tyne and the reporters standing outside the courts where environmentalists called for the captain to be charged with murder.

"I do remember. I was off sick; it was on the news all the time. What was the girl's name? Victoria?"

"Violet."

"Violet," repeated Cooper. The details were hazy in her memory, blurred by the fog of medication. Still, they began to clear as she remembered the image all the papers used of a pretty blonde woman with rosy cheeks chained to a tree, staring defiantly at men with chainsaws. "And it was Captain Jude who—"

"It was Captain Jude who did everything he could to avoid the collision in the first place and Captain Jude who launched rescue efforts despite the danger it put his own team in."

"Of course. I wouldn't imply otherwise. What about Hal?"

Georgie nodded. "First Mate then too. Newly promoted, but he knew his shit. He tried to contact the protesters over and over, but they didn't even have a radio. It was all in the report."

Cooper leaned back in the chair, her mind racing with new information. Could there be a connection between the tragic accident two years ago and the murder and attempted murder on the bridge? It could all be a horrid coincidence, but the only way to find out was to dig deeper.

"I felt sorry for the pair of them," Georgie said. "Having to go through all that. They raked through Jude's personal life. The press tried to paint him as an alcoholic, tried to get his missus to give interviews and all that. Disgusting. All the stuff with HR as well. They put him through the wringer."

"Thank you, Georgie," Cooper said, rising to her feet. "I'll leave you in peace. But please, look after yourself. Get some rest." But as she said it, an alarm pierced the air, causing them both to flinch.

CHAPTER 7

THE SCREAM OF THE fire alarm drilled Cooper's ears. The cold sea air stung her cheeks. Her heart rate doubled as the chaotic crowd of bodies jostled and shoved her toward the assembly point. Beside her, two men looked relieved when Cliff Longacre, the big bosun, announced that it was just a drill. False alarm. Test over. Still, Cooper's pulse continued to hammer in her head, fueling her growing restlessness. She hadn't even considered how they'd get off the ship if a fire raged through it. She was more preoccupied with thoughts of the bridge. If Singh, India, and the forensic team had stayed to preserve the scene or left it unattended. Had the fire been real, she wouldn't hesitate in telling them to get out of there as fast as possible, but knowing it wasn't, she hoped Singh at least stayed.

"Cooper!" Whyte called out, weaving through the dispersing crowd. She nodded at him, and they slipped into a narrow corridor. "You reckon someone set that off on purpose?"

"Crossed my mind," said Cooper. "I've just been with the medic. Do you remember a case in the news two years ago? A service vessel hit a boat full of protestors out here. A young woman died?"

Whyte wrinkled his nose. "Not ringing any bells. Do you think the two incidents are related?" he asked, lowering his voice and glancing around as people bustled past them, grumbling about the drill and observing the detectives with suspicion-laced curiosity.

"We'd be stupid to rule it out. The woman who drowned was called Violet. I remember the news stories; she was only twenty-two, twenty-three."

Whyte moved closer – too close – as another group pushed past.

"Christ," he whispered, his breath warm on her cheek.

Cooper felt the familiar coil of tension tighten in her gut. She edged away, but her back met a cold metallic wall. She turned her head and rubbed the bridge of her nose, trying to focus.

"Give me your phone," she said. It was time to phone Boyd.

DC SAFFRON BOYD ANSWERED on the third ring. Her desk was tidy, and her notes on a case dubbed the Masked Mackem were arranged in perfectly aligned piles and adorned with colour-coordinated annotations, highlights, and stickers. A glass of sparkling water caught the fluorescent lights of Northumbria Police HQ, casting an effervescent glimmer over her delicate features. Across the other side of CID, her boyfriend and fellow DC, Oliver Martin, sat with his foot elevated on a small stool. His Achilles tendon would heal with time, but as for his nerves, Boyd didn't know how long they'd remain frayed after that lunatic had attacked him with a machete. Still, it wasn't long ago that she was the nervous one, jumping at every slamming door and scared of her own shadow. Thanks to the support of Whyte and Martin, she'd found some of the courage that seemed to have abandoned her. She could do the same for Martin.

While Cooper talked – first about the Wi-Fi signal, then about the case – Boyd took notes, glancing up occasionally to smile at Martin. She listened intently to Cooper's recount of an event two years ago, tapping her pen against the desk as she processed the information. She could hear background noise, the hum of a busy environment.

"I agree," Boyd said, underlining the name Violet, "we need to explore it. I'll dig up some articles from the time."

"Great. See if you can find anything from the tribunal," Cooper added. "Court transcripts, anything from the HSE. I'll look over it all when I'm back at the office."

"Any idea when that'll be?" Boyd asked.

"Your guess is as good as mine. Find out why exactly Violet was there. What was her motivation? Was there anything more specific than stopping the wind farm? I want to know who else was on that boat and who Violet was closest to."

"Will do, boss," Boyd replied, neat handwriting filling her notepad.

When Cooper hung up, Boyd finished her water and put the Masked Mackem file in a drawer.

"What was that about?" Martin asked.

"Grab your crutches," she told him. "Time for a new project."

SATISFIED, COOPER TURNED BACK to Whyte, moving her gaze from a portlight showing nothing but a clear horizon, a reminder that they were miles from land and surrounded by unseen depths. She clenched her jaw, trying to will away the unease that crawled up her spine.

The corridor had quietened, and the once-bustling crew had now scattered to their quarters or respective duties. Whyte shifted uncomfortably beside her, his gaze flicking between her face and the floor. "I wanted to speak to you about something," he finally said, his tone hesitant.

"Is it about the case?" she asked.

"No," he admitted, cheeks colouring.

"Then let's stick to business," Cooper said, avoiding the subject. "What have you found out?"

Whyte wavered for a moment before launching into his report. "Right," he began, dark eyes serious. "I sent the manifest to the office and started reviewing the crew and passenger timetables. The turbine engineers mostly work during daylight hours unless something comes up, but just about everyone else is on a watch system. Crew, housekeeping, chefs... there's always someone awake."

Cooper frowned, already sensing where this was going. "And?"

"Problem is, the estimated time of death is bang in the middle of the switchover," Whyte continued, his voice tinged with frustration. "Jude and Hal's shift was coming to an end. India and Gray were set to take over at seven. They were up and having a pre-shift coffee when they discovered what happened."

"Everyone was up?" Cooper asked, the implications sinking in.

He sighed. "Pretty much. Either getting up for their shift or chilling out after finishing work."

"Great," Cooper muttered, massaging her temples again. "Narrows it down, then."

"Actually," Whyte said hesitantly. "There might be something. Besides the turbine engineers, the scientists are the only ones not on shifts."

"Scientists?" Cooper's interest piqued despite her headache.

"VāyuVolt Renewables commissioned marine biologists at Newcastle University to research marine life around the wind farm. They tag and track mammals and birds in the area, that sort of thing. They're all accounted for in the manifest and have been on several trips to the wind farm. They're known to the crew."

"Interesting," Cooper mused.

"I didn't think so. Not until you mentioned this death two years ago. Now, it's got me thinking. It might be a PR move to show how the protesters were wrong. If they can get data supporting the idea that wind farms are good for marine life, they'd have carte blanche to build even more."

Cooper stared.

"Yes, I said *carte blanche*. No, I did not get a dictionary for my birthday."

Down the corridor, a door opened, and a gust of cool air swept over Cooper. Cliff Longacre closed the door, nodding as he passed, his white trainers leaving salty footprints.

Cooper waited until they were alone again before saying, "Let's get the names of all the scientists."

"All on the manifest," he said. "I've put a red asterisk next to them all."

"Perfect. Could you forward them to HQ? Have them run background checks. I want to know if any of them have connections to environmental activism or our dead protester."

Whyte's face hardened. He looked around and then at Cooper. "Did you feel that?"

"Feel what?"

Whyte turned to the portlight, the sun illuminating half his face. "We're moving."

CHAPTER 8

AN IMPOSING SILHOUETTE DOMINATED the end of the corridor. Cliff Longacre's action-hero physique was instantly recognisable. He'd returned, radio in hand, calling over to Cooper and Whyte. "Word from Second Officer Morgan. Our checks are complete. We're headed to the substation to charge the batteries."

Good news, Cooper thought, glancing at her watch. She might make it home for Family Friday after all. Dinner with Atkinson, Tina, her mum and baby Danny was a weekly tradition that seemed miles away now. She crossed her fingers, hoping to make it back on time. Failing dinner, she might manage a late supper.

The two detectives followed Cliff to the bridge where India was in her element. Despite the bloody scene and forensic workers shuffling around her, India concentrated, her fingers tapping against the controls.

"How did it go with Graham Bell?" Cooper asked Singh.

"Too traumatised to be interviewed," Singh replied, his usual smile replaced with a look of concern. "I suggested he go back to bed."

"And I agreed," India said without looking back. "He needs rest."

Cooper took Singh's logbook from him and looked around at the SOCOs. A forensic photographer was finishing up. Given five minutes of training, he'd be a suitable crime scene manager, she thought. It wasn't protocol, but out here, their options were limited. Cooper needed Singh working the case and conducting interviews, not tied up with box-ticking. All the SOCO had to do was log the comings and goings of anyone permitted to be on the bridge. Besides, Cooper was sure if anyone tried to blag their way in, India would sharp put a stop to it.

"I've assigned you a meeting room," India said, swiping on an iPad. "Office Three. Cliff will show you the way. It should have everything you'll need."

Cooper thanked her, then turned to Cliff, lowering her voice. She wavered for a moment, choosing her words carefully. "I hate to bring it up, but with no captain, no first mate, and the third officer out of commission... Will India be okay bringing Electron back into the Tyne by herself?"

"Excuse me?" India snapped, overhearing Cooper's question.

The woman had the hearing of a bat after a double espresso.

India's eyes narrowed. "What kind of car do you drive, Erica?"

"Erm... A BMW 5 Series," Cooper answered coolly, sensing an impending argument.

"What? And you can park that big ol' car all by yourself?" India shot back, her voice laced with sarcasm.

"All right, point made," Cooper conceded, raising her hands in surrender. "Apologies."

To be fair, the 5 Series could basically park itself, but Cooper knew now wasn't the time to bring up the Parking Assist feature.

"I can handle docking the vessel if you can handle your internalised misogyny."

Cooper felt her face bloom with embarrassment. "That's not what I was implying, I can assure you. But again, I apologise." She took a deep breath. "Right," she said, snapping her focus back to the investigation. No time to let bruised egos get in the way now. "Singh, please show that young SOCO how to fill in the logbook and then join us. Cliff, if you wouldn't mind showing us to Office Three. And India, sorry again. Let me know when the vessel is charged and you can take it back to port."

"*She*," said India, lips pursed, eyes narrowed. "Not *it*. I'll let you know when *she's* charged, and I can take *her* back to port."

"Right."

Cooper had the good sense to turn away before rolling her eyes. *Now who had the internalised misogyny?*

CLIFF LED COOPER AND Whyte down a narrow passageway, Cooper's boots clattering on the metal floor. Pipes snaked along the walls, interspersed with bold warning signs: *Danger: High Voltage. Caution: Low Headroom. Fire Door – Keep Closed.*

Cliff stopped at a door, entered an access code, and held it open. "Here," he said, scribbling the code on a Post-it and sticking it near the printer. "Printer's there, stationery's in the cupboard, tea and coffee by the window."

"Thank you," Cooper replied, stepping into the room. It was small but well-equipped, with a long table and several chairs. A window overlooked the wind farm, white blades carving the blue sky.

Whyte placed his tablet on the table before silently making them both strong coffees. Singh joined them soon after, opting for a turmeric tea. As the three settled into their makeshift incident room, Cooper felt a growing sense of urgency. The clock on the wall ticked relentlessly while she brought Singh up to speed with what the medic, Georgie Peters, had told her. In return, Singh gave an overview of his brief time with the third officer. Gray Bell's story perfectly matched India's.

By the time the clock struck one, Cooper's stomach was growling. The calories from her meagre breakfast of a single slice of toast had long worn off, and she was pleasantly surprised when the chef on board appeared with a plate of fish and chips for each of them.

"Thought you were veggie," said Whyte, watching Singh tuck in.

Singh shook his head. "Mostly plant-based, but not fully vegetarian." He examined the crispy batter on the haddock before taking a bite, nodding with satisfaction. "Mmm, can't say no to fish and chips. Even the best intentions have limits."

"I'll drink to that," Cooper said, sipping a Coke Zero. The meal was warm and tasty, the batter just on the right side of greasy. It was a morale-boosting meal if ever she'd had one.

Finally connected to the Wi-Fi, Cooper's phone buzzed. She wiped her mouth and hands on a napkin and checked the message. "Margot Swanson," she said, referring to the pathologist at the Freeman Hospital.

"She received the body?" asked Whyte.

Cooper nodded. "Captain Jude McDermott's autopsy is scheduled for Monday."

Whyte shrugged. "I'll be surprised if it comes back with anything other than catastrophic blood loss from umpteen stab wounds."

Cooper agreed, but she'd seen stranger things: Gunshot wounds disguising poisonings, strangulations staged as suicide hangings, severe burns covering the hallmarks of domestic abuse bruises.

"You never know," Cooper said quietly.

"You never know," echoed the two men.

———————————

BACK AT THE STATION, Saffron Boyd glanced up from her computer as Oliver Martin's laughter filled their shared office. She raised an eyebrow in curiosity. Leaning over to catch a glimpse of his phone, he quickly tucked it away in his pocket.

"Fine," she muttered, seeing nothing but the green backdrop of a WhatsApp chat. She turned her attention back to the task at hand, inclining forward in her chair, the glare from her computer screen casting a ghostly pallor over her pale face. The quiet office was punctuated by the intermittent clicking of her mouse as she navigated between two digital documents – the accident report from two years ago and the manifest of the service vessel Electron. The HSE had ruled the accident just that – an unfortunate collision at sea, claiming the life of Violet Sinclair.

Boyd repeated the name aloud, her finger tracing down the computer screen. "Sinclair..." It wasn't an unusual surname. *Click, click, click.* Opening three new tabs, she toggled between LinkedIn, Facebook, and a news article covering Violet's funeral.

Boyd rarely swore, but with a pinched expression, she whispered, "Shit." As Martin almost fell off his chair, Boyd grabbed the phone.

"COOPER."

"You're not going to believe this," Boyd said, skipping introductions and cutting to the chase. "The woman who died in the collision two years ago, Violet Sinclair, her immediate family included her parents, June and Dustin Sinclair, and her siblings Sean and Luna Sinclair."

"Go on," Cooper said, stacking her crockery on top of Whyte's as he gathered their lunch plates into a neat pile.

"I thought I recognised the surname. I know it's not uncommon, but it felt like too much of a coincidence. I've checked various sources, and I'm certain."

"Certain of what?" Cooper asked, impatience growing.

As Boyd spoke, Cooper's body temperature seemed to drop a degree. When she hung up, she gestured for Singh and Whyte to stand. "Find Cliff Longacre. I need him to locate someone."

"Who?" asked Whyte, already at the door.

"A turbine technician." Cooper pushed her hands into her pockets. "Captain Jude McDermott was at the helm when Violet Sinclair died in that collision two years ago. According to the manifest, on board right now," she paused, letting the weight of her words settle, "is Luna Sinclair – Violet's sister."

CHAPTER 9

WHYTE CALLED THE BRIDGE using the office phone. He asked India to radio Cliff Longacre and send him their way. The bosun didn't appear in a hurry, showing up after ten minutes. Though chiselled, his tanned face seemed paler than before – probably the LED lighting, Cooper concluded.

"We need to see Luna Sinclair," Whyte told him. "Can you take us to her accommodation?"

"Luna? Sure, I can." Cliff's jaw worked while he thought. "Sinclair? I only ever knew her as Luna. She's not... I mean, she's not related to that poor lass, is she? The protestor?"

Cooper avoided the question. "We'd just like to chat with her regarding our inquiries."

He nodded slowly and ran a hand through his hair before leading them back down the narrow corridor to the stairs to the accommodation deck.

The muffled sounds of life filtered through cabin doors: television shows, music, the tinny sound effects of a smartphone game – the din of mundane distractions. Cooper caught snippets of phone conversations as they passed some cabins, workers' hushed conversations to loved ones on land about what had happened that morning. In one room, she heard boisterous laughter and the shuffling of cards.

She raised an eyebrow. "I thought India told everyone to stay in their own rooms?"

He shrugged, unapologetic. "They're nervous. Some of them are seeking safety in numbers."

Fair enough, she thought, reminding herself she would do the same thing. None of these people were under arrest. She could hardly enforce their solitary confinement.

When they reached the final door on the row, Cliff dipped his head. "This is Luna's room."

Cooper rapped her knuckles against the door. No response.

Her mind raced as she considered the legality of the situation. Could she force entry? Did she need a warrant? She wouldn't need a warrant if she was arresting Luna, but simply being related to someone wasn't grounds for arrest. Did the rules she played by on dry land even apply here? Way more than twelve miles offshore, they were technically in international waters, but this was a British-flagged vessel at a British/Dutch wind farm installation.

Before she could untangle the bureaucratic web, Cliff dangled a key in front of her, eyebrows raised. "Want me to open up?"

A loophole. Cooper loved a loophole. She knocked one more time and called for Luna by name. When there was still no answer, she turned to the bosun. "Go for it."

The door swung open, revealing a small cabin bathed in a natural glow from two round portlights. Cooper asked Cliff to wait in the passage while the other three stepped inside, careful not to touch anything. The cabin was meticulously organised, with barely a trace of Luna's personality peeking through. A neatly made bed sat against one wall with a folded green hoodie at the end of it. A sparse desk was screwed to the opposite wall; a hairbrush and a bottle of perfume were the only items on display.

Cooper tapped her foot, glancing about until something caught her eye. Speaking quietly to Singh, she said, "Small red smudge on the drawer handle."

"Yeah, I see it," he whispered back.

"Take some photos, then get forensics in here. See what they make of it." Then, turning to the door, she addressed Cliff, "Where else could she be?"

He hesitated. "Knowing Luna, maybe the gym or the mess."

So much for staying in their accommodation.

"Fine. Let's find her," Cooper said, stalking off down the corridor, gesturing for Whyte to follow her and for Cliff to lead the way.

They found Luna Sinclair with four men at a hexagonal table in the mess, laughter echoing around the room. Cooper recognised her immediately as the woman medic Georgie Peters was treating for an injured finger. She was short but solidly built with a round, friendly face. Her Geordie accent rang out clearly above the racket, punctuated by the occasional guffaw from one of the men.

"Mate, you're shitting me!" Luna was almost crying with laughter.

"Nah, I swear it's true. The Wi-Fi back then was so crap that there was only enough bandwidth to stream one thing at a time. So all the lads would get off shift, gan to their cabins, and the bloke in the first cabin would gan straight on Pornhub. He'd watch what he needed to watch to do what he needed to do. Then he'd disconnect from the Wi-Fi and bang on the wall of his cabin so the bloke in the next room could do the same. And down the corridor it went, one room at a time."

Luna was red in the face, wiping her eyes on her sleeve. Up close, Cooper could get a better look at her wrist tattoo, a ban the bomb symbol peeking out from beneath a friendship bracelet made of purple thread. Or was it violet?

"Like a Mexican wave of masturbation?"

The man nodded. "Exactly. You younguns don't know how good you've got in on here with Starlink. Stream whatever you want for as long as you want. We used to call it the Dogger Bank Wank."

The technicians fell into fits of hysterics, clutching their sides as laughter overtook them.

Having heard enough, the detectives moved in. The technicians' glee came to an abrupt end. A few uneasy eyes glared at the bosun, perhaps wondering if Cliff would report them up the chain of command for ignoring India's instructions.

There was a tense silence until Luna coughed, wiped her eyes again, and asked, "May I help you?"

"I'm DCI Erica Cooper. I'm here investigating the murder of Captain Jude McDermott."

The men shifted uncomfortably. Cooper presumed they felt guilty for laughing and joking around when something so terrible had happened that morning. She didn't judge them; people used laughter all the time to cope during troubled times, and the police were no different.

The smallest of the men spoke up. He had a pointed chin and wide-set eyes, which gave him a child-like expression. "Does that mean Hal's okay?"

"I'm sorry, I haven't heard," Cooper said truthfully.

He looked saddened, diverting his gaze to the table.

"Luna Sinclair," Cooper continued. "We'd like to speak with you. Privately."

Around the table, the men shared confused glances, brows lowered, shoulders shrugging.

The tiniest flicker of a smirk passed over Luna's lips. She pushed her chair back, rising to her feet, sizing Cooper up. "Thought you might," she said, nonplussed. She took her phone from her pocket and glanced at the time. "To be honest, I'm surprised you didn't find me sooner."

CHAPTER 10

ELECTRON GLIDED THROUGH THE WATER towards the substation.

"Steady," India muttered to herself.

The substation always reminded her of an industrial tree. A thick yellow trunk covered in pipes that climbed the cylindrical base like vines. The trunk branched in four directions to support the five-storey structure. Green railings wrapped around each platform like leaves, with orange life rings as fruit.

India kept her eyes on the substation, still far off in the distance, well aware of what she'd see if she looked anywhere else: blood. The blood of her colleagues smeared over every surface. The metallic stench of death lingered in the air while she twisted a silver anchor-shaped earring in her left lobe. The earrings were a gift from Captain Jude on her forty-second birthday. A rare show of affection from the big man.

Her chest tightened, thinking of him. She felt like her ribs would crush her heart at any second. She stood up taller, breathed slower.

"Damn it, Jude," she whispered. "Who'd you piss off this time?"

She shook her head, trying to focus. The detectives – Erica, Elliot, and Daljit, was it? – had asked to see Cliff. That was twenty minutes ago and she needed him for docking.

She tried the radio. "Bosun. Bridge."

No response. What did they want with him? She had one theory, but she pushed that aside, instead concentrating on manoeuvring the massive vessel.

"Bridge. Bosun."

Finally.

"We're fifteen minutes out. Prep the daughter craft and transfer team."

"Copy."

Cliff would launch a smaller boat from Electron and transfer crew onto the substation, where they would lower the charging cable to him. The daughter craft would then bring the cable back to Electron and connect it. It sounded easy but required everyone to know exactly what they were doing. Which was difficult – laughable even – given Electron was the first of her fleet. No one knew the safest way to charge a fully-electric SOV the size of Electron, because no one had made one before. For all their safety procedures and high-viz clothing, they were essentially making it up as they went along.

The noise of a forensic officer sneezing made India turn. Without thinking, her gaze swept over the grim scene behind her. Blood streaked the floor, evidence markers scattered like morbid confetti. Her stomach churned.

She had to keep it together. She was responsible for everyone on board; their safety was in her hands. The responsibility rested heavily on her shoulders, and she reminded herself that this was what she wanted. She wanted to be captain.

Not like this.

The radio crackled. "Bridge. The transfer crew are suited up. Daughter craft is ready when you are."

"Thanks, Cliff. I'll let you know when we're in position."

"Standing by."

India straightened her shoulders, forcing steel into her spine. She turned five degrees to starboard and began decelerating for the approach. Images plagued her thoughts: Jude's lifeless body in a bag, Hal's pale face as he was stretchered to the helipad, Gray being ushered to the medical bay, blood streaming from his forehead.

She picked up the phone and dialled for the medic. She couldn't do anything for Jude or Hal; she could at least get a status update on Gray.

Georgie picked up straight away.

"How's our patient?" she asked.

Georgie's voice was tired. "Which one?"

"Fifty Shades."

"Gray's asleep. I just popped by his cabin. I had to sedate him."

India thanked the medic and hung up, thinking of Gray tucked up in his quarters, blissfully unconscious. His face swam before her – soft-spoken, eyes darting nervously whenever Jude approached. India winced, recalling Jude's booming voice.

"Dammit, Gray! Can't you do anything right?"

She'd intervened once, early on. "Easy. He's doing his best."

Jude had sneered but backed off. With her, at least. But Gray...

India tugged her earring till it hurt, remembering Gray's trembling hands, the constant mistakes under Jude's watchful eye.

He had seemed distracted, mentioning problems at home. What problems? She had never asked. None of them had. Gray was a good listener, the one they all went to for a bitch and a moan, but none of them had been there for him.

India put the ship into neutral and activated the thrusters. Gray was no use to her in bed. She really was alone in getting this floating city back to the Tyne in one piece. Cliff was all she had. She hoped she could rely on him.

"Transfer crew. You're clear to launch."

THE TURBINES REVOLVED LEISURELY in the darkening sky, their blades like the second hands of clocks earnestly rotating in time with one another. It was late October, and the sun was dipping toward the horizon. Cooper watched the scene for a minute before reminding herself that the sun wasn't actually going anywhere. It was just the rotation of the Earth that made it appear so. She wondered how the crew and technicians felt about being out of sight of land for two weeks at a time. Was it worse at night? Did they ever get used to it? In all this forced proximity, how much did personality play a part in the recruitment process? Sure, skills and qualifications were essential, but so was the ability to get on with the people they'd share a ship with for weeks on end. Cooper knew how people felt about Captain Jude – decisive, stubborn, abrasive. Still, she was curious as to how they felt about Luna.

Cooper's phone buzzed with a WhatsApp message. It was Atkinson asking why she wasn't replying to his texts.

> No phone signal out here. WhatsApp works fine, though.

> Out where?

No one had told him. She assumed the forensic team would have updated him.

> On a boat. Long story, but looking forward to telling you all about it later.

She added a string of kisses to the end of her message.

Does that mean you'll be back in time for dinner, or will I be reheating it in the microwave?

Again?

Cooper ignored that one and put her phone in her jacket pocket. With a deep breath, she lowered her shoulders and lifted her chin before joining the others in Office Three, their makeshift incident room turned interview suite.

Luna Sinclair sat uneasily, her earlier bravado depleted now her mates weren't around. Her round face flushed while she twisted the purple friendship bracelet on her wrist, the threads rubbing against her tattoo.

Whyte stood by the window, half his face in shadow. Singh was by the kettle making hot drinks. He served Luna a cup of Tetley with three sugars. "You look tense," he said, placing the cup on a coaster.

"Can you blame me?" Luna replied.

"No," he said, "But I was talking to DCI Cooper. Everything okay?"

Cooper nodded, but part of her mind remained at home. Atkinson chose to be a stay-at-home dad, and part of that deal meant playing house husband. It wasn't like she was out drinking with friends; she was a senior detective on a murder case.

Singh offered Luna a strawberry Chewit. She declined.

Sitting opposite Luna, Cooper got straight to business. She unlocked her phone, turned it to aeroplane mode to avoid any more passive-aggressive messages from flashing on her screen and began, "Interview with Luna Sinclair onboard SOV Electron. Present are DI Daljit Singh, DS Elliot Whyte and myself, DCI Erica Cooper. Today's date is October twenty-seventh, and the time is two thirty-seven p.m."

"Don't I have the right to a lawyer?" Luna asked, sitting low in her chair.

"You do," Cooper assured her. "But you're not under arrest. This is nothing more than a chat, but we're recording the conversation in case we need to fact-check anything later on. It's for your protection as well as ours. You are well within your rights to seek legal representation and meet us at the station when we get back to port. You're also within your rights to tell us to go and jump if you don't want to chat at all."

Luna smiled. "But that would look pretty sus, wouldn't it?"

"It would," said Cooper, returning the woman's smile. She opened a notepad and slid it to Singh, who already had his pen poised. "But it's completely up to you."

Luna paused, weighing her options. "Nah," she said finally, "let's just get it over with."

"Very well," Cooper said. "When we approached you in the mess, you seemed to be expecting us. Why was that?"

"Because of Violet." Luna tugged against the friendship bracelet. It was only now, up close, that Cooper appreciated the craft that went into it. A chevron design of tightly knotted threads in a range of purples, some with a metallic hue, all secured with a silver clasp in the shape of a crescent moon. Cooper wondered if Violet had a matching one. Had she been wearing it at the time of the accident?

"Your sister? Correct?"

"Aye."

Luna sucked her lips in and looked away. Sadness radiated out of her, but she quickly shut it away and steadied herself.

Singh pressed his fingertips together. "Tell us about her."

"There was less than a year between us," Luna breathed, her voice heavy. "Irish twins, our mam used to call us. Can you say that now? Irish twins? Anyway, we were very alike, very different too."

"How so?" asked Singh.

"We were both environmentalists," she said, holding up her wrist, displaying the ban the bomb tattoo. "But we went about it in different ways. We both wanted to save the world, but she was always a bit more extreme. Like, I'm a vegetarian, but she had to be vegan. She used to give me shit all the time for not going vegan. Would roll her eyes every time I had milk in my tea or ate a bit of cheese in front of her."

"Sounds annoying," Cooper said.

"Yeah, it was." Luna hugged her mug of tea. "But I'd give up dairy and honey in a heartbeat if I thought it would bring her back."

"You mentioned saving the world," Cooper said. "Is that why you work in renewable energy?"

"Exactly!" Luna pointed at Cooper. "Exactly that. I feel like I'm actually doing something, you know? But Violet... Jeez, her way of saving the world was just to yell and scream at everyone. Nothing was ever good enough for her. If a new technology promised to make safe drinking water in Africa, but it used a tiny amount of rare Earth metals, well, she'd want it banning, wouldn't she? Or if a country came up with a carbon capture device, she'd poo-poo it because of their human rights violations. She never had an idea of her own, of course, just wanted to rubbish everyone else's."

"Like Odin's Gale?"

Luna sighed. "Like Odin's Gale," she echoed. *"Wind power's bad. Some birds might die,"* she said, imitating her sister. "So what then? We should just keep burning coal? You know what else kills birds? Cats! And guess what? She had three of the furry bastards."

"Are you okay to talk about the day she died?"

Luna shrugged, her strong shoulders coming right up to her ears before relaxing. "It's been two years. Still hurts, but aye, I can talk about it."

"Were you working that day?" Cooper asked.

"Not on North Star. I was working on London Array back then. Down in Kent. I got buzzed to go to the bridge, and the captain told me what happened. I think I was in shock. I don't even remember them transferring me back to shore or the train journey back north. It's a complete blind spot in my memory."

"Did you blame Captain Jude McDermott?"

Luna's eyes widened. "No. Never." She swallowed. "I blamed Violet for being so bloody stupid. She shouldn't have been out here in those conditions. She should have known better."

"Was it upsetting working with Captain Jude?" Singh asked.

Luna pouted for a moment. "Not really."

"Did you get on okay?"

"We never really interacted, to be honest. He was part of the ship's crew: him, Hal, India, the others. They all work on the vessel. Electron is their job, and the turbines are mine. The technicians and the crew, we're totally different entities."

"Okay, let's move on," Cooper said, not entirely sure that she believed Luna. Hypothetically, if Tina died in an RTA and someone Cooper worked with had been the one driving, she could never see herself working with that person again, no matter how sure she was it had been an accident. It would be too painful, even after two years.

"Talk me through this morning, please, Luna," she continued.

"You mean my alibi?"

"Like I said, if you'd rather do this at the station—"

"I got up early. I wanted to fit in a workout before starting my shift."

"Where did you work out?" asked Singh.

"In the gym. There's one on board. A really good one, too. Weights, cardio machines, stretching mats. It's nice. The music they have on is shite, but the gym's good. And before you ask, yes, someone saw me there. Billy Cameron was in there on the elliptical trainer going about half a mile an hour."

Singh scribbled down the name. "What did you do next?"

"Went back to my cabin to shower and dress. Then I went straight to the mess for breakfast. I was there when we hit the turbine." She held up her bandaged finger. "Might be broken. Hurts like hell. And that turbine will take some fixing, I can tell you that for nowt."

"There were others in the mess at the time?" Cooper asked.

"Yeah, plenty of people. We all fell like bowling pins."

There was a knock on the door. Whyte went to deal with it.

"And can anyone vouch for your whereabouts between when you were in the gym and when you got to the mess?"

Luna's brows shot up into her forehead. "Like when I was in the shower, you mean? No. I don't tend to let people watch me shower and dress. I'm sure some of the blokes on here would jump at the chance, but no, to answer your question, I was alone."

"Okay," Cooper conceded, although she couldn't help but make a mental note of the gap in Luna's alibi. It wasn't much, but it was something, and it coincided with the time of the murder.

Whyte reentered the room. "That was Cliff. India wants you to know that Electron needs another two hours to charge before they're ready to leave the substation and head back to the Tyne. They've arranged paramedics to take the more seriously injured straight to the RVI."

"Thank you, Whyte." Cooper nodded, her thoughts flickering between work and home: Hal in the hospital, Jude in the morgue, Atkinson in the kitchen, Danny in his crib.

"All right, Luna," Cooper said, returning to their interviewee. "We'll wrap this up for now. I'd like you to write down everything you told me about your movements this morning. DI Singh will help you. Please include timings and the names of anyone you saw."

While Luna sank deeper in her chair, sighing, Cooper rose to her feet. She picked up her phone and said, "Interview terminated," before hitting the red *stop recording* button. She left Singh and Whyte to it and decided to get some fresh air.

The clear sky of the day was giving way to a bitterly cold night. Shivering, Cooper pulled her jacket closer around her, the biting breeze gnawing at the base of her skull. Atop each of the turbines, lights glowed orangey-red – warning beacons to aircraft and seafarers. She counted the hours on her fingers, calculating that she could be home before midnight, but only just.

She unlocked her phone to send a text, the frosty air making typing difficult.

Looks like I'll be reheating dinner in the microwave.

Don't wait up.

CHAPTER 11

IT WAS PAST HALF-ELEVEN when Cooper stepped onto the cold quayside. She felt the fatigue of a long day settling in her bones. Wrapping her arms around herself, she tucked her hands into her armpits for warmth. Cooper glanced at Singh, noticing his breath clouding in the frigid air. The DI bid her a good night, departing in a waiting taxi.

Whyte stood by her side, hands deep in his jacket pockets. "I could do with a caffeine hit? Do you want to grab a coffee before we call it a night? I know a twenty-four-hour place near here."

Cooper considered it for a moment, the awkwardness of her silence stretching between them. Once upon a time, when they were both new to the force, Whyte had asked her out for a beer. About ten minutes later, she'd decided never to speak to him again. There was more to the story – there always was – but they'd found a way to work together these days. The past had a funny way of lingering, though.

"Thanks, but I'd better head home," she replied, forcing a tight-lipped smile. "Justin will have my head if I don't show up soon."

"Right, Family Friday, isn't it?" Whyte said with a nod.

"It was. It's almost Saturday now."

"If only murderers and rapists stuck to office hours, right? Monday to Friday, nine to five?"

Cooper allowed herself a small laugh. "That would be nice." Criminals hardly considered the impact they had on victims and their families; they weren't going to give a flying proverbial about the social lives of the officers sent to investigate them.

"See you Monday, boss," Whyte said.

With her car still in the city centre, Cooper hailed a taxi. She climbed into the backseat and gave the driver her address, bracing herself for what awaited at home: an annoyed Atkinson and a quiet house.

COOPER ENTERED THE DARKENED living room. Her mother, Julie, had already left, and Tina and Danny were nowhere to be seen. Danny was presumably asleep, and Tina would be the same or would have her head in a book. Cooper heard the ping of the microwave before stepping into the kitchen. Hunched over the microwave, Atkinson retrieved Cooper's reheated leftover shepherd's pie.

"Sorry," she said. "Double stabbing on one of the boats that services the wind farm. I assumed they'd bring the boat straight into port, but they flew us out instead."

"Sounds very exciting," he grumbled, handing her the steaming dish.

She sighed, peeling off her coat and draping it over a chair. "One man is dead, and another man's fighting for his life in the RVI."

He opened the fridge, pulled out two beers, and handed one to Cooper. A peace offering, perhaps.

"Sorry," he said, wiping his forehead. "It's just been a long day, and two hours of your mum's gossiping didn't help."

"She's a widow. She's lonely... This is delicious."

"It was better fresh. But Julie's your family—"

"*Our* family."

He didn't respond. Cooper ate silently for a few minutes. The shepherd's pie worked the same wonders as the fish and chips she'd enjoyed earlier in the day. It was warming and satisfying, with plenty of carrots, peas, and onion. The mashed potato top was crispy, buttery and perfectly seasoned.

"You know as well as I do murder investigations don't stop at five on a Friday. Being late home is part of the job description. It's part of *your* job description. If you were scheduled to work today, you'd have been there with me."

Atkinson collected her plate and rinsed it in the sink. "You're right," he placed a hand on her shoulder. "I'm just tired and grouchy. And somewhat jealous. You got to fly in a helicopter."

Cooper rested her palm on the back of his hand, feeling his warm skin against hers. "Singh and Whyte enjoyed the ride out. I felt like I was in a gravity-defying tin can. And I'm not surprised you're cranky. Looking after a baby and running a household is hard work."

She finished the beer. It was a small bottle, but the few mouthfuls of bitter IPA were welcome. Standing up, she wondered if Whyte had gone for a coffee alone.

"Come on," she said, her voice softening. "Let's go to bed. Maybe we can figure out some plans for the weekend."

But even as she said it, Cooper wondered if they'd find the time. Or the energy.

THE MORNING AIR WAS brisk, punching a chilly hole in Cooper's chest as she and Atkinson stepped outside. She glanced at the front wall, where three crows perched ominously. "Were those there yesterday?" she asked, a flicker of unease creeping in as the nearest one fixed its beady eye on her.

"Yeah," Atkinson replied with a shrug. "They've been there all week."

"Odd," she muttered, shaking off the spooky feeling. Today was about making amends, not worrying about beady-eyed little birds and Atkinson's mood swings. They drove into Newcastle via the A1058, residential suburbs morphing into university campuses and commercial hubs.

"I thought we'd try that new exhibit at the Great North Museum," Cooper suggested, trying to inject some enthusiasm into the day. It's about the flora and fauna around Hadrian's Wall and how the landscape would have looked in Hadrian's time compared to now."

Atkinson merely nodded, his mind elsewhere.

Cooper parked on Claremont Road, and they completed the rest of the journey on foot, arriving at the museum a few minutes later. As they wandered through the exhibit, the vibrant colours of the interactive digital displays couldn't break through the friction between them. She repeatedly tried to converse with Atkinson, but his responses were short and clipped.

She sighed. "Listen, I'm sorry again about last night," she finally blurted out in front of a picture of a peat bog. "I'll make it up to you, I promise."

Atkinson put his arm around her shoulders. "It's not that. Ignore me. I'm just an old grump."

"You always said I made you feel young."

"You do." But before he could elaborate, his phone rang – his ex-wife's name illuminated on the screen. Elspeth.

"Can't this wait?" he snapped into the phone, rolling his eyes.

Cooper watched him walk away through engraved stones and Roman weaponry. When he returned, his face was one of controlled fury, hiding his emotions for the sake of societal norms. They were in a museum, after all, not exactly the place for ranting and four-letter words.

"What's wrong?" Cooper asked in a hushed voice as a family in matching hoodies shuffled by.

"The twins have burned through their student loans. They're not even halfway through the semester. Elspeth wants me to lend them more money."

"Lend?"

He gave a dry chuckle. "*Donate* would be a more accurate term. The last time I loaned them money, it was never mentioned again, let alone repaid."

Cooper had yet to meet Atkinson's sons from his now-dissolved marriage. They were studying at Edinburgh, and from the sounds of things, they'd inherited their mother's impulsiveness rather than their father's studiousness.

He paused by a display of Roman coins. "How much do you think these are worth?"

"You thinking of robbing the place?"

"If it'll cover their rent and rum fund."

Cooper eyed a silver coin depicting the profile image of an empress. She nudged him playfully. "Unfortunately, you live with the one and only DCI Erica Cooper." She patted her chest. "Who would solve the case in a heartbeat."

Atkinson relaxed and cuddled her back. "Unfortunately for the one and only DCI Erica Cooper, the perpetrator is a renowned expert in all things forensic. He'd cover his tracks. Not a whisper of DNA."

"Damn," she said, laughing. "I've met my match. How about we skip the Great Museum Heist and go to lunch instead?"

"A much tastier idea."

———

MONDAY MORNING CAME WITH a vengeance. While Cooper lay in bed wondering why Atkinson had turned down her advances after they seemed to be on the right track again, Saffron Boyd, blonde hair messy from sleep, scowled at the phone screen in her hand as Oliver Martin stirred beside her. The incessant beeping had woken her up, and she couldn't ignore it any longer.

"What you doing?" Martin grumbled, rubbing his eyes.

"Your phone," Boyd said, sitting up in bed and pulling the covers over her chest. "It's been buzzing non-stop all night."

"Pass it over," he said, reaching for the device. "It'll just be my mum."

Instead of handing it over, Boyd showed him the screen. "It's not your mum. It's that stupid WhatsApp group."

"Ah."

"Ah, indeed. Do you know how far back through these messages I've scrolled?"

Martin's cheeks reddened. "That's private correspondence."

"It's a police scandal, is what it is."

From what Boyd had seen, the group chat started innocently enough with childish memes and short-form videos of dogs on skateboards and people falling over. Then, someone changed the group's name to *The-Not-So-PC-PCs,* which seemed to give the green light for more politically incorrect posts. From then on, the chat took a darker turn.

"Look at this crap." Boyd's finger stopped on a series of messages where the PCs and DCs had taken to rating female witnesses and victims out of ten, even going so far as to take covert photos of them.

Martin ran a hand through his brown hair and stifled a yawn. "I didn't partake in any of that. You know I wouldn't."

"Christ, Oliver," Boyd said, her voice shaking. She recalled the news stories about those police creeps, the ones who'd harassed and exploited their positions. And her old DCI – the one who'd always made her feel like prey. The thought of Martin being part of this sickening behaviour churned her stomach. "You need to leave the group."

He hesitated, glancing away. "I can't, Saff."

"Can't? Or won't?" she challenged. "Remember what happened with the Met officers during the Sarah Everard investigation? Their careers were practically over after those messages came out."

"I know, I know. But it's just a bit of banter, nothing serious—"

"Banter? That's what those guys from Cheshire Police thought, too. Racist and homophobic jokes got them sacked, not just a slap on the wrist. Is it really worth risking your badge over a few laughs?"

Martin got out of bed and pulled on some boxers. "Look, I don't agree with what they're doing, but if I leave the group, it'll look bad. They'll think I'm not one of them."

"You're *not* one of them," Boyd said, reaching for her robe. She wrapped the thin fabric around herself, feeling her hands shake as she tied the cord. She tossed his phone onto the bed. "At least I hope you're not," she added before storming out of the room.

CHAPTER 12

KEATON STRODE INTO THE meeting room with her short, pristine ponytail swinging. Singh, Whyte, Boyd, and Martin were already gathered around the table.

"Morning." Keaton grabbed a brew and plopped into a chair. "What's the tea?" she asked, holding up her mug before taking a sip. The hot drink scalded her throat. She liked it. She needed a jolt.

Whyte sat back and folded his legs, resting his left foot on his right knee. "I was just telling Martin to take Saff to that new restaurant in town – Saffron & Sage, seeing as it's her namesake. I've heard good things."

Suddenly, Keaton's brew tasted bitter. She snorted. "I wouldn't, mate. I heard they already failed a health inspection." The lie slid smoothly off her tongue.

"Really? Cheers for the heads-up," said Whyte. "I was thinking of giving it a whirl myself. Thought

Amy might like it. Guess I'll find somewhere else then."

Keaton coughed to suppress a guilt-laced smirk. Lying about her ex-girlfriend's new business venture was catty and frankly pathetic, but she didn't care.

THE NORTHUMBRIA POLICE HQ in Wallsend was already alive with the clamour of Monday morning when Cooper pulled into a free parking space. She paused, adjusting the collar on her coat while a brisk wind swirled amber leaves across the lot. She glanced up at the modern glass facade reflecting the brightening sky.

Taking a deep breath, Cooper headed towards the revolving doors, her shoes clicking against the concrete. As she passed reception, she was greeted by the smell of ink and the sound of swearing. The printer had gone rogue, spewing ink over a civilian office worker.

She climbed the stairs to CID and entered the meeting room where the team were assembled around a table discussing a new restaurant. They paused their chatter as she sat down.

"Happy Monday. Right, let's get to it. Saff, update on the Masked Mackem case?"

Boyd sat up in her chair. Usually quiet and reserved, she had a tense edge to her that morning. "Nothing for a fortnight now," she reported. "No new victims."

The Masked Mackem was the nickname given to a vigilante who'd not only caught several sexual predators in the act but had killed them for good measure. He was both a dangerous man and a new folk hero.

"Serial killers don't just stop," said Cooper. "They don't retire. They don't get bored. They don't suddenly grow a conscience or see the error of their ways. So, why the pause?"

Boyd fussed with the cuff of her white blouse. "I have a few theories. First, he might have been hurt. He could have met his match and is either in hospital or at home licking his wounds."

Cooper nodded. It was a good suggestion. "What else?"

"A situational change," Boyd continued. "Something might be keeping him from attacking. He could be locked up for a different crime, or he could have moved away for work, or his shift patterns might have changed."

"Have you checked the hospitals and jails?" Cooper asked.

Nodding, Boyd assured Cooper that she had. "I have one other theory."

"Go ahead."

"I know you said serial killers don't retire, but reports of assaults across Tyne and Wear are massively down. In Sunderland City Centre, there's been an eighty per cent drop in stranger rape and assault allegations. Perhaps he's not killing anyone because no one's attacking women."

Silence fell over the room as they digested Boyd's words. Had the Masked Mackem stopped because he'd achieved his objective? Had he done what campaigns and policing had failed to do?

"Bloody hell," Cooper said eventually. "You might be right. I can't condone him running around handing out the death penalty, but really, eighty per cent?"

"Eighty-three per cent, to be precise," Boyd said.

Cooper took a drink of water. "Well, the case is still active. Keep looking for witnesses, CCTV and other evidence. Regardless of his motives, we still need to find him."

"Be easy enough tomorrow night," Whyte said.

Everyone turned to look at him.

"Halloween. I've heard half of Sunderland are dressing up as him."

Cooper's lip curled in disgust. "Right, well, keep—"

Whyte's mobile buzzed loudly, cutting Cooper off. She glanced at the screen: it was a Newcastle 0191 number. "Sorry, gotta take this."

Cooper waited for Whyte to leave the room, then steered them back on track. "The SOV case. Captain Jude McDermott's murder. Where are we on Luna's alibi?"

Singh cleared his throat. "I spoke to the gentleman Luna said was at the gym at the same time as her. William Cameron – prefers to be known as Billy. He remembers seeing Luna in the gym. However, the timings aren't quite as Miss Sinclair implied. Billy arrived there just before Luna left."

"Meaning?" Cooper arched a brow.

"Meaning her unaccounted time is longer than we first thought." Singh grimaced. "More time to commit murder. Potentially."

Cooper pursed her lips at Luna's unravelling alibi. "Right, we'll put that to Luna and see what she has to say about it." She turned to the rest of the group. "Anything else to report?"

Keaton raised a biro in the air. "Yeah, it all kicked off in Craster over the weekend."

Craster, a fishing village on the Northumberland coast, was not far south of Dunstanburgh Castle.

"Apparently, there was some argy-bargy at a market. Someone was supposedly selling counterfeit Craster kippers."

Chuckles of disbelief filled the meeting room. "Seriously?" asked Cooper. "Counterfeit kippers? I've heard it all now."

Singh snickered. "Sounds a bit fishy if you ask me."

Groans echoed around the room.

"I *sea* what you did there," Boyd joined in.

"Oh, cod," added Martin.

Cooper held up a hand. "Enough. Keaton, why is this our problem?"

"Reported as fraud," Keaton answered, still giggling.

Cooper rolled her eyes. "We have a murder at sea and a masked vigilante. The kippers are low-priority. Pass it on or shove it to the bottom of the pile for now—"

Whyte's return calmed down the fish-based humour. He held up his phone. "That was the RVI. Hal Simpson's ready for visitors."

CHAPTER 13

COOPER AND WHYTE ARRIVED at the Royal Victoria Infirmary via the main entrance. The cold, clinical atmosphere felt hygienic, but the familiar aura weighed heavily on Cooper. She pushed her personal memories of the place aside, concentrating on work instead.

Whyte held the door for her as they entered the intensive care unit. He was unshaven, which suited him, and his new cologne smelled of cedarwood and leather.

"I read an article last night. Thought you might find it interesting—"

"The desk's this way," said Cooper, cutting off the small talk and introducing herself to a nurse.

They were led to a room at the end of the corridor. Hal Simpson, Electron's first mate, lay propped up in bed, surrounded by a jungle of tubes and wires. His ashen face was drawn tight with pain, and every shallow breath seemed like an effort. Hal's eyes flickered open. A brief look of fear subsided before he swallowed hard and spoke in a hoarse voice. "I couldn't stop him."

Cooper approached the bed; Whyte remained by the door.

A rotund doctor in his fifties, wearing a white coat two sizes too big for him, extended a hand to Cooper. "I'm Dr Thompson. Hal here is lucky to be alive. He lost twenty-five per cent of his blood, leading to a massive drop in blood pressure." He checked an IV before continuing. "He suffered several stab wounds, but the one to his left leg is the worst. If it were a few centimetres to the right, it would have severed his femoral artery and you and I would not be here having this conversation."

Cooper glanced at Hal, who winced at the mention of his injuries. "How are you feeling?"

"Like I had a run-in with Freddy Kruger," Hal replied, attempting a weak smile. "But I'll live, thanks to this lot." He gestured at the medical staff around him.

"Dr Thompson gently patted Hal's shoulder. I'll be nearby. If you need anything, just push the button."

Once the doctor and nurses left, Cooper pulled a chair to Hal's bedside. Both of Hal's hands were bandaged. Blood seeped through, staining the white gauze red, suggesting deep gashes and a brutal struggle.

What struck Cooper most about the room was the smell. It wasn't the disinfectant so much as the lack of fragrance – no flowers, no fruit.

Whyte picked up the only card on a set of drawers. It was from VāyuVolt Renewables.

"Have your family been to see you yet?" he asked.

Hal looked away. "They're on holiday," he replied. "The nurse said she had trouble getting hold of them while I was under, and I told her to stop trying now I'm through the worst of it. They're getting older, and my dad's heart's not the strongest. I don't want to ruin their good time or cause them any worry."

Whyte nodded, moving further into the room. "I get that. My dad's got dementia. He gets stressed easily, so I try not to cause him any more worry than necessary."

Cooper glanced at Whyte, surprised by his vulnerability. She'd never heard him mention his father's illness before, only his love of a Sunday lunch.

"But this is a bit different, Hal," Whyte said. "I'm sure your parents will want to know."

"I know. I'll give it a few days," he said. "I can't have them see me like this. I'll call them once some of these bandages are off, and I don't look quite so much like death."

Cooper redirected the conversation towards what happened on Electron. "We need to know what happened to you, Hal. I know it will be hard to discuss, but can you walk us through it?"

Hal's feet twitched under the covers as he relived the nightmare. "I'd nipped out to my cabin. I'd left my glasses case there. I was only gone five or six minutes, but when I came back onto the bridge, I saw... I saw someone. He was on top of the captain. They were fighting. There was blood all over. Is it true? Is it true Jude's dead?"

"I'm afraid so," Cooper said, pausing while Hal processed the news.

He bit his lip hard and pressed his hands together in prayer, but the pain in his palms caused him to grimace. Hal's gaze dropped to the bedsheets, eyes unfocused, as though searching for some alternate reality where this wasn't true. His lips parted, but no words came out, just shallow, uneven breaths. He gripped the edge of the blanket tightly before letting out a shaky sigh.

Cooper didn't want to push him, but she had to. The longer they left it, the more Hal's memories would distort and fade. "When we came in here, you said you couldn't stop him."

"I tried." His voice faltered. "But he was a big man. Bigger than Jude. Me and my pathetic, skinny little arms couldn't do much." Shame crept into his voice. "I've always been scrawny."

"Did you recognise him?" Cooper asked".

Hal shook his head. "No. But he was tall. Taller than you," he directed at Whyte. "Six feet something. Broad, too."

"What was he wearing? Do you remember?"

Hal wiped a tear away. "Will never forget it. He was dressed in black with a black balaclava over his head."

Cooper softened her voice. Hal was breathing rapidly, and she didn't want to cut her questioning short because of his distress. Gently, she asked, "Do you remember his eye colour?"

"No. But a little hair was poking out the back of the balaclava. Blond."

"Thank you, Hal. That's really helpful. Are you okay to keep going?"

He nodded, the corners of his mouth pointing down. "Yeah. Just about."

"You came onto the bridge and saw this man attacking Jude. Did he say anything?"

"No. Not a word. They were both grunting and that, because the captain was fighting back, but the other man had a knife. It was only ever going to end one way."

"What kind of knife?" Cooper asked.

"A small one, like a kitchen knife, like the ones you'd use to peel potatoes." He held his hands up, the distance between them less than four inches.

"What happened next?"

"I was an idiot, that's what. I should have run for help or raised the alarm, but I wasn't thinking. I jumped on him, tried to grab the knife off him, but—" He gestured to his bandaged hands. "Permanent nerve damage, apparently. Good job I'm not a pianist." He gave an empty laugh and looked towards the window. "He punched me in the face, knocking me down. Then— Then—"

"Take your time," said Whyte.

"He got on top of me. Stabbed me here and here. Then— Then I gave up. Played dead like a fucking coward."

Hal's shame was palpable, tears streaming from his eyes.

"I mean, it worked. I lay there doing nothing, and he left me alone. Left me for dead and finished off Jude. I passed out shortly after, but maybe... Maybe I could have done something."

"Surviving is nothing to be ashamed of," Cooper assured him firmly. "You're alive, and that's what matters."

COOPER AND WHYTE STEPPED into the empty corridor, the heavy hospital door muffling Hal's pained breathing as it closed behind them. Cooper glanced at the DS, thinking about Hal's description of the attacker.

"Large, well-built male with blond hair," she said.

"That rules Luna out," said Whyte. "I still say we keep an eye on her."

"Agreed. Her sister's death is still motive enough for her to be involved somehow."

"Right," Whyte agreed, frowning. "An accomplice, maybe? I'm going to meet Singh this afternoon. We'll chat with the rest of the crew and technicians. See if anyone saw anything suspicious. I also want to know more about that research team."

"Good idea," Cooper nodded as they walked towards the exit. "I'll get in touch with the SOCOs and let them know we're looking for a balaclava and a paring knife."

As they neared the main doors, a violent retching sound filled their ears. A patient just ahead of them doubled over, sick splattering across the linoleum floor. In an instant, Whyte grabbed Cooper's arm and pulled her away from the vomit's trajectory.

"Christ!" Cooper exclaimed, flinching at Whyte's touch and wrinkling her nose at the stench of bile. She looked up to see him staring at her intensely, concern etched on his face.

"Sorry. Did I hurt you? I didn't want you stepping in that."

"No," she said, stroking her arm, cheeks hot. "And no need to apologise. You saved my favourite boots."

She moved back, creating distance between her, the spew, and Whyte.

"Erm...I thought we were good?" Whyte muttered, his voice low, unsure.

"We are," she replied quickly.

He rubbed his stubble. "Right. It's just... I feel like you don't want me around. Did I do something wrong?"

"Not at all." Cooper's tone was clipped, and Whyte wasn't buying it.

"Okay," he said, his jaw tightening as he shifted on his feet. "Singh's expecting me. I'll... see you later." He turned abruptly and walked away, his footsteps echoing down the corridor.

Cooper's throat tightened. She crossed her arms, biting the inside of her cheek. With a deep breath, she steeled herself. *Get it together, Erica.*

CHAPTER 14

HALLOWEEN MORNING AND DAYBREAK WAS STILL an hour off as Colin Finch made his morning rounds through the Poison Garden at Alnwick. A chill hung in the foggy air, and Colin shivered slightly, the cold seeping through his short-sleeved uniform shirt. The black wrought iron gates, adorned with twisting, creeping vines and foreboding skull-and-crossbones, creaked ominously as he passed through, torch in hand.

He'd been the night warden here for nearly a decade after retiring from his job as a school caretaker. The plants here might be deadly, but at least they didn't answer back like the workie-tickets at the local C of E primary used to. Alnwick had always been home – a place where he and his late wife had raised their children. Memories of football matches, family picnics, and Christmases were a bittersweet comfort in the cold dawn.

Belladonna, hemlock, monkshood, and oleander – some of the world's deadliest botanicals – grew behind the sturdy gates and stone walls, a necessity to keep out meddling trespassers who only came because there was a cannabis plant in a cage. Of all the deadly leaves, berries and blooms in the place, it was the *Salvia divinorum* that needed a licence from the Home Office.

Politicians, Colin thought, tutting to himself. Meddling in anything that brings the average person joy. Taxing the crap out of booze and fags. Criminalising a plant and hoying folk in jail for daring to use it to soothe their arthritis and MS symptoms. Everyone knew who the real criminals were.

He sighed, autumn leaves crunching under his green wellies as he wove through the toxic flora. The garden, with its sinister beauty, had always fascinated him, even before he took on the job. He admired the intricate patterns of the plants, their deceptive allure hiding lethal potency. As he neared the hemlock, he angled his torch, inspecting the plant. Its distinctive white, umbrella-shaped clusters were gone now, replaced by seeds that were beginning to dry and turn brown. His torch illuminated two reflective green eyes. A hiss and the cat scarpered up the nearest wall. Colin jumped, pressing a hand to his heart before laughing at himself.

Another noise. Behind him this time. Was it the wind? Another cat?

His breath caught in his throat as he turned slowly, the torch beam scoring through the fog. A dark figure in black crouched near the aconite, leather-gloved hands clutching something. Stolen cannabis leaves? A weapon? Colin had no idea, but the air felt tinged with danger.

"Oi!" he shouted with more bravado than he felt. "Stop right there. I'm calling the police."

The intruder leapt up, kicking soil and fallen leaves. Colin darted after him, torch bobbing. His heart hammered against his ribs as he lunged, tackling the intruder around the legs. They crashed in a tangle of limbs, grunting and cursing. Colin's old knees hit the concrete hard.

He was too old for this shit, he thought while the thief snarled beneath him.

"Gerroff me, old man!"

"Not bloody likely!"

Colin wrestled to pin the bastard down, but he was stronger than he looked. A knee rammed Colin's privates, knocking the wind out of him. Wheezing, he staggered back, losing his footing and falling onto a glass case. The pane shattered, and he toppled arse over tit into its contents.

Gympie gympie. *Dendrocnide moroides.*

The innocent fuzzy leaves concealed a cruelty beyond comprehension. Fire erupted across his skin – hot, burning needles stabbing deep into every inch of exposed flesh. It burned like acid. Like lightning zapping his bones. It wasn't pain; it was a living nightmare. He screamed, writhing.

Oh God, oh Jesus, make it stop. Please, I can't, I can't—

The pain hijacked every nerve, every synapse. Neurons shrieked. Colin arched and rolled, scrabbling to escape, but the movement only worked the tiny trichome hairs deeper.

His stomach spasmed, bile rose in his throat, head swimming. Sweat drenched his body. Colin clawed at his chest, gasping for air that wouldn't come, his heart galloping out of control.

He tried to roll to his knees, but a savage cramp seized his guts, and he collapsed, curling into a fetal ball. Tears and snot streamed down his face. He lay there in a nest of the world's most venomous plant, immobilised by the sickening pain.

Through watering eyes, he saw the indistinct black shape of the lowlife escaping out the sinister gates. His vision blurred, the blackness rising fast. The intruder and the garden all swam out of focus.

"H— Help," he managed to stammer. "Someone..."

But there was no one. Just the plants.

CHAPTER 15

COOPER CLOSED THE FRONT door behind her, a steaming cup of tea in hand. It was Halloween morning, and eight crows perched on the front wall looked at her with beady eyes, following her every movement.

"Don't get too comfy," she told them.

It was all her daughter's fault. Apparently, Tina had been feeding the black-winged troublemakers, and now, five to ten of them could regularly be seen waiting for her or bringing her small gifts. A piece of red ribbon, a glass bead, a pretty shell and a shiny fifty-pence-piece were lined up on the front wall as offerings to Tina. Cooper shook her head, remembering the time Tina raised a baby seagull in their kitchen. Why birds? Didn't most teenage girls want a puppy or a kitten?

Cooper knew the answer already. Tina had never been ordinary. Worryingly bright, a netball star, and now – apparently – queen of the damn crows. What did that say about her daughter? She didn't know whether to be proud or terrified.

Tina's feathered flock ruffled their feathers, cawing as Cooper shuffled past, unlocking her car. She selected a Metallica playlist, clicked on *Disposable Heroes* and put the car into gear. She was at HQ within fifteen minutes.

As she entered the glass-fronted building, the duty sergeant greeted her with ghoulish cupcakes, the smell of freshly baked goods flooding the foyer. Cooper took one, admiring the white icing shaped into a ghostly peak, its wobbly, jiggling eyes completing the look.

Removing the plastic eyes, Cooper ate the treat on the way to the incident room, taking care not to smear icing all over her face. Knowing the team, they'd let her conduct an entire meeting before telling her she had a frosted nose.

"Morning, crime fighters," she announced, entering the department and scanning the faces of Whyte, Singh and Keaton. Singh giggled, glueing a fifth pair of googly eyes onto Keaton's forehead. Noticing Cooper, he coughed, putting on his professional persona once more.

"Morning, boss," Keaton replied, peeling the plastic eyes from her face and sticking them onto a coffee mug.

Young Oliver Martin and Saffron Boyd were also present, the former's crutches propped up against the table while he rested his injured leg on a chair. They were locked in a whispered disagreement, their expressions tense. With no time to play relationship counsellor, Cooper got down to business.

"Right, let's get started." She sat at the table opposite Keaton, the murder board behind her. "The murder of Captain Jude McDermott. We now have a description of the perpetrator: a tall male over six feet, with a broad build, possibly blond, dressed in black. If Luna Sinclair didn't stab the captain, who did? And why? What other motives could we consider?"

She looked at their faces in turn, waiting for one of them to speak. Whyte was the first to break the silence.

"I spent the remainder of yesterday with DI Singh talking with crew and technicians. Everyone I spoke to had only good things to say about Jude. Hal too."

He opened a notepad, pointing his pen at notes as he read them aloud. "A father figure... Gruff exterior but a heart of gold... A walking encyclopedia of maritime knowledge... Learned more from him in a month than I did in years of training."

Cooper turned to Singh. "You agree?"

"I do, DCI Cooper, with one exception." Singh interlaced his fingers, resting them on the table. "One woman referred to Captain Jude as Captain Judas. Now, I'm no Christian – though I must say I love a nice Christmas jumper – but even I know Judas is not a compliment."

"It certainly is not," added Cooper, hoping they'd found a crack in Jude's diamond-in-the-rough facade. "Judas usually means a traitor. Did she elaborate?"

"She regretted it the moment it slipped off her tongue. She tried to play it off as mispronunciation at first. I pressed her, and she told me to speak to HR."

Cooper recalled speaking to the medic, Georgie Peters. She was sure he'd said something along the lines of, "*all that stuff with HR.*" She'd assumed it was connected to the inquiry into Violet's death, but perhaps not. Was something else going on?

"Who was this woman?" Cooper pressed, instincts kicking in.

"Kay Longacre," Singh replied, checking his notes.

"Any relation to Cliff Longacre?"

"She's the bosun's wife. She works in the galley as a chef."

"Interesting," Cooper said, picturing the bosun in her mind.

"I'll be speaking to HR today," Singh said. "I'll keep you posted."

"Brilliant. Thank you, Dal—"

Cooper's phone chirped so loudly that Boyd jumped in her seat. She gave a nervous laugh and looked at the floor.

The screen illuminated with Atkinson's name. Not his personal number, but his work phone. "SOCOs," she told the group, standing to answer. "Hey, it's me... Okay... I'll come straight over."

Hanging up, Cooper picked up her coat and bag. "I'm heading back to the port. We might have a lead."

WITHOUT ANOTHER WORD, COOPER strode out of the room, leaving an awkward silence in her wake.

Whyte stood, grumbled something about paperwork and headed for a free desk. Singh buttoned up his suit jacket and left for his appointment with the human resources department for VāyuVolt Renewables. Keaton peeled the eyes from her mug and pressed a pair onto Martin's nose. "I'll catch you losers later. Off to take a statement from an armed robbery victim."

Martin watched her go, removed the eyes from his nose and turned his attention back to Boyd, who had now crossed her arms defensively. He could feel her disappointment gnawing at him.

"Look, Saff, I don't like the group either. Not now that it's got all weird. But if I report it, I'll be outcast by the others. You know how this place works."

Boyd's big, doe-like eyes narrowed. Her voice was barely audible as she hissed, "So you're just gonna let it slide? You know they've been taking pictures of female victims and witnesses without their consent. It's voyeurism. It's sick. It's completely out of line."

He couldn't deny it; he'd seen the pictures himself. But dealing with it meant facing the ugly truth about his colleagues – and himself.

"I know," Martin replied, frustration creeping into his tone. "I'll— I'll try to talk some sense into the other constables, alright? But reporting it will just make pariahs out of us."

Boyd undid her bun and finger-combed her hair. "Fine," she said wearily. "But if nothing changes, I won't stand idly by, Oliver. You know I can't."

He knew she meant it, and that terrified him. It wasn't just about the group anymore; it was about their relationship and the trust they'd built.

"Alright," he agreed quietly, nodding. "Let me handle it my way first. If that doesn't work, we'll figure something else out. Together."

"One way or another, this group's gonna be found out," Boyd insisted, her eyes pleading with him to understand. "And when it is, everyone in it will cover their own arses and start pointing fingers. You need to get out now. Before the press gets wind of it and you all lose your jobs."

"I'll be blacklisted by everyone," he said, aware his voice was cracking.

"I was blacklisted by everyone," Boyd whispered, her cheeks paling as she reminded him of what she went through at her previous posting. "And it was the best thing that ever happened because it meant I got to meet you."

His heart clenched at her words. He reached out and took her hand, squeezing it gently. She was right, as always, and he couldn't bear the thought of losing her because he sacrificed his integrity to stay in the good graces of a stupid WhatsApp group.

Boyd gave him a weak smile as she tidied her notes. "You're better than those idiots, Oliver. You'll do the right thing. You're a good man."

But as Boyd kissed his cheek and left for her workstation, the question left ruminating in Martin's mind was, *Am I?*

CHAPTER 16

THE GREYISH-GREEN WATER OF the Tyne swelled with the incoming tide, the low autumn sun casting a shimmering path across its surface. The river's murky depths held many secrets for the city of Newcastle. For Cooper, it held the secret of who had pushed her friend Cindy to her death. It was the reason she'd joined the force, and though she'd failed to solve the occasional case here and there, it was Cindy's unsolved murder that followed her like a sorrowful shadow.

Cooper stood at the dock, watching three herring gulls screech and tussle over a discarded mussel, the briny scent of the river filling her nostrils and making her crave *moules mariniere.*

Electron's vast green hull towered above her on the north side of the Tyne, the shade so bright it evoked memories of summer days spent in grassy fields. Sadly, summer was many months away, and Cooper had to turn up the collar of her coat to keep the cold off her neck. Though Hal Simpson had been there and seen it all before passing out from fear, blood loss or a combination of the two, his description of the attacker had left them with nothing solid. Still, Hal wasn't their only witness; Electron was a witness, too: One who held the answers and knew for sure who had murdered Jude and left Hal for dead. And though Electron couldn't speak, the SOCOs could translate her knowledge into words and, through their reports, would take her witness statement.

A long, lean figure strode down the gangway towards Cooper, throwing elongated shadows over the dock.

"DCI Cooper," greeted Justin Atkinson with mocking formality.

"Mr Atkinson," she joked back. "Fancy seeing you here. Welcome to the case."

"And what a doozy it is too."

The tension that had plagued them over the last few days had dissipated with a night in front of the television and tender cuddles that continued to the bedroom. His classic looks still worked wonders on her, but the dark bags under his eyes told a story of fatigue. She knew the strain of balancing a career, parenthood, and their personal lives was catching up to him, just like it was to her.

"Turns out the suspicious death in Washington wasn't as suspicious as it first appeared." He extended an arm towards the gangway. "I managed to wrap up my work, meaning I'm free to join you on the Electron case. Well, for two days a week."

Together, they walked towards the bridge of Electron, the once-bustling hub of activity now weirdly silent. Gone were the beeps and bleeps of the instruments, the humming of illuminated screens, and India's stand-offish but professional energy that had dominated the space the last time Cooper was here.

"So why have I been summoned?" Cooper asked, looking around the room and taking in every detail. She felt the familiar knot forming in her stomach, her mind working in overdrive to piece together the events that had transpired here. She'd been to countless crime scenes over the years, yet each one still managed to unsettle her.

"Because we have something interesting to share with you," Atkinson replied. He pointed to gruesome, bloody footprints smeared across the bridge floor. "Take a look at these."

He handed her an iPad showing photographs of the same prints, organised into folders. He swiped the screen, and a bird's eye view of the bridge appeared, displaying the various boot prints, all colour-coordinated.

"They all look identical," Cooper said with a frown.

The prints were scattered across the floor, some closer together, others further apart. They led towards different areas of the room, creating a disorderly pattern. While some were blurred and smudged, others were more defined with distinctive tread patterns.

"That's because they are. They're all the same style of boot – crew standard-issue – but different sizes."

"Go on," Cooper prompted, her stomach twisting as she scanned the crimson mess around her. Blood stained the surfaces in long, erratic streaks, telling a tale of the violence that had unfolded.

Atkinson pointed at his colour-coordinated diagram. "Captain Jude's prints are all coloured red. He was a size eleven," he explained, pointing out the partial prints clustered around a single spot. "Didn't move far once he started bleeding out. Poor soul."

"Right," Cooper murmured, filing away the information in her mental catalogue, glancing between the illustrated prints on the screen and the real-life ones before her. "And the others?"

"Blue. Hal Simpson, the first mate. Size eight." Atkinson tapped the screen, indicating a handful of prints scattered throughout the bridge but clustered near where he fell. "India Morgan wears a size five-and-a-half. Green. They're all over the place since she had to take command of the vessel and try to attend to Jude and Hal before forensics got here."

"Gray and Georgie?" Cooper asked, already anticipating the answer.

"Both size ten," Atkinson confirmed, highlighting a few key areas where their prints were visible: near the helm, close to Jude's body, and by the VHF radio. "Apart from a small defect on Georgie's left heel, the prints are hard to differentiate. I've left them all yellow."

Cooper knew she hadn't been asked back to the scene so Atkinson could show off his detailed diagram. "Jude, Hal, India, Gray and Georgie," she recited, looking at the red, blue, green and yellow logos on the screen. "Which leaves the black prints."

"The mysterious sixth set."

She raised an eyebrow, waiting for him to continue.

He pointed at distinct, dark-red prints in the middle of the bridge. "There, there and over there. Crystal clear, and the only prints that don't belong to the victims or the three crew we knew were in here." He took the iPad back from Cooper. "Say hello to your size-fourteen-wearing killer."

CHAPTER 17

SARAH-BETH GRIFFIN SHIELDED HER hazel eyes as she strolled through Alnwick Gardens. Dappled patches of crisp morning sunlight streaked through the autumnal canopy of orange, rust and gold. She loved this time of the day before the visitors arrived and disturbed the peace.

The Poison Garden, hidden behind wrought-iron gates adorned with skull-and-crossbones, held a haunting allure. The plants inside, lethal and exotic, shimmered with dew, the tiny droplets enhancing their deadly beauty. Leaves rustled softly in the breeze, whispering toxic secrets to each other.

Sarah-Beth shivered as the iron gates creaked shut behind her. At twenty-seven, she was young but already a seasoned botanist, her passion for plants evident in the careful way she tended to even the most dangerous specimens. She wore a practical, albeit slightly worn, pair of work trousers and a thick sweater, her dark hair tied back in a loose ponytail.

She'd always found solace in the world of plants. Raised in a stormy household where her father's temper was as unpredictable as the weather, she sought refuge in their neglected garden. Among the flowers and herbs, she discovered a passion that would shape her future. Her role at the gardens was more than a job; it was a lifestyle. She loved the exquisiteness of her surroundings here, the quiet, the order, and the sense of control she could exert over her environment. Here, she felt at peace, her mind focused on the intricate dance of photosynthesis and soil chemistry.

But this morning, something felt off. Her day had started in the usual manner: Radio One, tea, toast and honey. But as soon as the gates closed behind her, Sarah-Beth knew something wasn't right. Signs of a struggle were evident: overturned pots, broken branches, disturbed soil. She crept carefully down the stone path, frosted cobwebs glistening on the stone walls.

Then she saw it. A leg peeking out from behind a shrub that, if ingested, could kill a man ten times over. *Oh God.* She edged closer, the body revealing itself a limb at a time.

It was Colin. Lovely, sweet Colin. His body lay sprawled in the dirt, eyes frozen open, his hand gripping his chest.

Heart pounding, Sarah-Beth knelt beside him, her hands trembling as she checked for a pulse. Nothing. Her mind spiralled, but she forced herself to stay calm, to think. She pulled out her phone and dialled 999, turning on speaker phone so her hands were free to begin chest compressions.

The dispatcher's tinny voice echoed around the garden. "What's the nature of your emergency?"

"Ambulance. Quick." Sarah-Beth said in time with the compressions. "He's not breathing. I can't find a pulse."

But as Sarah-Beth gave the address and described what she had found, she once again took in the trampled plants, overturned pots and signs of a fight.

"And police," she added. "Send the police too."

PC JAMIE THOMPSON SIGHED as he adjusted his uniform in the rear-view mirror. Standing at five feet nine inches with a slim build, his sandy blond hair and baby blue eyes gave him a boyish charm that belied his ten years on the force. He had hoped for a quiet day – perhaps some routine patrols, a few traffic stops, nothing more. But it wasn't even half nine, and already he was being called to babysit a body until the doc could confirm death.

He arrived quickly, taking a moment to appreciate a tiered water feature with pristine hedges. He'd lived in Alnwick all his life and hadn't visited until today. It was quite something, he thought before he was shepherded to his left by a manager who was holding back tears.

"Colin was such a genuine bloke," she said, sniffling. "Sarah-Beth's with him. She's the one who found him. Bless her."

Two black gates stood before Jamie, skull-and-crossbones seemingly staring straight through him.

On bloody Halloween of all days.

He saw the body first, then the young woman sat beside it, arms hugging her knees, sobbing softly.

"Sarah-Beth?"

Startled, she jumped to her feet, wiping her hands on her trousers, then dabbing her wet eyes. She was pale and shaken, her dark ponytail dishevelled and clothing stained with mud.

Jamie flipped open his notepad. "You found the deceased?"

"Yes," she said, nodding, her voice barely above a whisper. "I found him lying here. He wasn't breathing, so I tried CPR... I tried..."

"You did your best," he said, reassuring her. "And you knew the deceased?"

"He's called Colin. Colin Finch. He worked nights doing security. I didn't know him well, but he always made a point to say good morning to everyone when he was heading home after his shift. He was nice. A gentleman."

There was a lull in the wind, hushing the rustling of plants as if the hemlock and aconite were holding a moment of silence for their guardian.

"You told the dispatcher you thought there'd been a fight," Jamie said, looking around and agreeing with the assessment. There were definitely signs of a struggle. Close to Colin's body, a glass case was broken, jagged fragments of glass littering the ground. He reached his hand towards the plant it housed.

"NO!" Sarah-Beth snapped, slapping his hand away.

Had she just slapped him? He was about to give the young woman the mother of all warnings when she added, "Sorry. That's gympie gympie, and it was in a case for a reason. Touch that, and you'll be in more pain than you can possibly imagine. People have been known to take their own lives to escape the pain of..."

Her eyes flicked away as she spoke, her voice trailing off. Jamie followed her gaze to a gap in a flower bed.

"Something wrong, pet?"

She mumbled, almost speaking to herself. It sounded like, "Europa. Belle and Donna. Gone."

Jamie cocked his head. "Who are Belle and Donna? Coworkers?"

Sarah-Beth snapped back to attention. "No, no. I said *Atropa belladonna's* gone. It's a plant," she clarified, her voice steadier now.

Jamie flipped to a new page of his notepad before shaking his hand. She'd slapped him really bloody hard. "You're saying someone nicked a plant?"

"Not just any plant," Sarah-Beth replied, breathing deeply. "Someone stole deadly nightshade."

CHAPTER 18

DI DALJIT SINGH'S FINGERS danced over the stack of dusty HR files. He pulled out a worn manila folder marked *Captain Jude McDermott* in faded ink. Cradling a piping hot cup of coconut tea, he settled into his chair. The sweet aroma reminded him of the desiccated coconut his mother used when baking sweet treats. The nostalgia was welcome. He'd call her later, he decided, get the recipe, and whip up a batch for his girls. But first – work.

"Right then," Singh muttered, starting with the reports from two years ago that detailed North Star's collision with the protestor's boat and Violet Sinclair's tragic death. His eyes scanned each document, perusing the particulars, but they offered nothing he didn't know already. He was hunting for something unrelated, something that stood out like a sore thumb. And after an hour, he found it.

Six months ago, Captain Jude reported Cliff Longacre to HR for bullying. Singh stroked his beard, his black brows peaking. From what he'd heard about the captain, Jude didn't seem the sort of person who was easily bullied. Not by his own crew. Singh made a copy of the report, retrieved his favourite pink highlighter from his desk and began colouring anything he found interesting. According to Jude, Cliff mocked him for being ginger, called him tubby, and made fun of him for supporting Hartlepool.

Singh couldn't help but chuckle as he highlighted the words *Monkey Hanger*. It all sounded like playground tattle tales, the kind of pettiness only a five-year-old would be bothered by. *He called me poo-face. She said her dad could beat up my dad.*

"Come on, Jude. HR? Really?" Singh shook his head, taking a sip of his tea. Still, he knew one man's banter could be another man's bullying.

He clicked the lid back on the pink highlighter and switched to a shade of aqua blue. Opening a new folder and flipping to Cliff's account of events, he said, "Let's see what you've got to say for yourself, Mr Longacre."

OLIVER MARTIN'S CRUTCHES CRUNCHED through the gravel as he and Paula Keaton arrived at Alnwick Gardens to investigate a suspicious death.

"Can't you hop any faster?" Keaton teased.

"Sadly not."

"Want a piggyback?" she asked with a wink.

Keaton could easily carry his weight. Hell, she could probably bench-press him, but his ego would never allow it. Besides, it wouldn't look very professional.

"Want clipping round the head with one of these?" Martin joked back, brandishing one of the crutches.

"You wouldn't dare."

He smiled. "You're right. I wouldn't."

They were met by local PC Jamie Thompson who quickly brought the pair up to speed before saying, "Mind if I take off now? Dispatch want me to attend a shoplifting incident at Morrison's."

"Aye, no bother," Keaton told him. "We can take it from here."

They began by chatting with Sarah-Beth, the gardener who discovered the body. She was being comforted by another member of staff and looked visibly upset.

Martin introduced himself and Keaton before asking about Colin.

"He wasn't a gardener," Sarah-Beth told them. But he loved plants and knew quite a lot about them, too. In his previous job, he tended flowerbeds and a small vegetable garden. He said it was the best part of his job."

"What did he do before working here?"

"He was a school caretaker. He always joked about preferring plants to children." Her voice was tinged with sadness. "He never meant it, of course.

One of the kids from that school works here now. They got on like a house on fire."

She stopped and turned to bend over and pick up a bottle of water. Martin immediately thought of *The-Not-So-PC-PCs* WhatsApp group. At least one of its members wouldn't have hesitated to take a quick photo of the woman's backside.

While Sarah-Beth continued to talk about Colin, Martin refocused, listening to how Colin was a beloved member of staff, how working there helped him move on after losing his wife.

"Can you tell us more about the plant that was taken..." He checked his notes. "Atro— Atrop—"

"*Atropa belladonna*. Deadly nightshade." Sarah-Beth bit her lower lip and glanced at the empty spot of earth where the plant had been. "Very toxic," she explained. "It's rumoured the juice of the berries was used to poison Augustus Caesar. It's a beautiful plant with dark purple flowers and almost black berries. Belladonna literally means beautiful woman. Women used to make drops out of it to dilate their pupils, which was considered attractive. Of course, it also causes blindness."

"And I thought people who got Botox were stupid," Keaton said under her breath. "Are those gates the only access?" she asked Sarah-Beth.

"Yes. And they're usually locked."

The sides of the garden were lined with high walls topped with spikey railings or thick privet hedges. It would be difficult to descend, but not impossible, given the right motivation.

"How many people had keys?" Martin asked.

Sarah-Beth shrugged. "You'd have to ask management. But Colin and the other night warden had keys, some of the gardeners too." She held up her own key, attached to her belt.

Thanking the botanist for her time, Martin told her to go home and get some rest. They'd contact her if they needed anything else. Once she left, he turned to his colleague.

"One for Margot?" he asked, taking out his phone, ready to call the pathologist.

"He was an older gent, and it looks like there was a bit of rough and tumble. He might have had a heart attack, but we should rule out anything more sinister." Keaton stood by the body, head bowed respectfully. "If he disturbed a thief, things might have got violent. I can't see any blood, but he could have been hit round the head, and given where we are, we'd better make sure he wasn't poisoned."

"I'll call it in."

When Martin ended the call, Keaton was reading a plaque on the wall about Lakhvir Singh – the Curry Killer – who was jailed for life for poisoning her former lover.

"Unless," Martin mused aloud, "unless Colin was the intended target and his killer took the plant to throw us off."

Keaton shrugged. "Perhaps. We'll know more once Margot's done her magic. But you're right, Grasshopper, we should speak to some more of Colin's co-workers and his family. See if anything comes up to suggest this was anything other than him stumbling across a thief."

Martin finished scrawling some notes. "We'll do that as soon as the body's collected."

"Nope. Once the body's collected, we need to get some lunch. I'm starving. Fancy a curry?"

For some inexplicable reason, he did. "Yeah, a biryani would hit the spot."

"WELL, WELL, WELL."

Singh sipped a fresh coconut tea as he perused Cliff Longacre's version of events. "Looks like someone was trying to cover their own derriere."

He dialled Cooper's number, wanting to update the DCI.

"I know why Kay Longacre referred to Captain Jude as Captain Judas," he said when she answered.

"Happy days, Daljit. Tell me more."

Singh could hear the soft whistle of the wind from Cooper's end of the call.

"It seems the captain was a naughty boy. Jude, a married man, was having an affair with a junior member of his crew: a lady called Mandi."

"Tut tut," said Cooper.

"Tut tut indeed." Singh pointed the nib of his pen at his notes as he continued the story. "Cliff Longacre found out about the affair and rightfully called Jude out on his behaviour, saying it was inappropriate and an abuse of power."

"How did the captain take that?"

"Not very well," Singh told her. "Instead of taking it on the chin, admitting fault and promising to get his act together, Captain Jude reported Cliff to HR."

"On what grounds?" asked Cooper.

"Bullying. According to Jude's report, Cliff mocked and teased him about his weight and hair colour. According to Cliff's report, he did no such thing and accused the captain of deflecting to cover his own posterior."

Singh heard Cooper chat quietly to and thank someone at her end of the call before turning her attention back to the DI. "Who did HR side with?"

"The captain. Cliff almost lost his job over it." Singh doodled a picture of a jigsaw piece while he spoke. "I believe that gives Mr Longacre a sizeable motive, and when we consider Hal Simpson's description of the attacker – a large man possibly with blond hair – I think that makes him our chief suspect. He's a strong man in a physical role; he could easily overpower the first mate."

"Good work, Daljit."

The compliment made Singh smile.

"I have something as well." Cooper went on to describe her morning on Electron, the various footprints the SOCOs had identified, and the one crucial size-fourteen print they couldn't pair to an owner. Singh doodled another jigsaw piece next to his first one. He could feel the pieces falling into place.

"I've just got off the phone with the officer in charge of issuing crew equipment," Cooper continued. "Only one member of the crew wears size fourteens. Any guesses who that might be?"

Singh coloured in the jigsaw. "That would be our strapping bosun, Mr Longacre."

CHAPTER 19

WIPING A SMEAR OF curry from the corner of her mouth, Keaton listened to her voicemail. Office staff had identified the night watchman's next of kin: his eldest son. Colin Finch had three children. One lived abroad, and one died in an RTA. That left Andrew Finch, who still lived locally in Alnwick. Keaton jotted the postcode onto a napkin, opened Google Maps, entered the address, and brought up driving directions.

Fifteen minutes later, with a morsel of curried chickpea stuck between two of her back teeth, Keaton and Martin sat opposite Andrew Finch.

"My girls love their grandad," he said. "They're going to be devastated when I tell them."

"How old are they?" asked Martin.

"Four and five," Andrew replied, fighting back tears. He stood and began pacing. "Sorry. I'm all over the place. I don't think I took in what you said. You said he was attacked?"

Andrew's square face was darkening as angry blotches of red spread over his cheeks and neck. He was medium height, and his light brown short-back-and-sides needed a trim.

"We don't know that, Andrew," Martin answered softly. "We think he disturbed someone stealing plants. There are signs of a struggle, but we won't know how he died until the autopsy is completed. Even then..." His voice trailed away while Andrew paced across his green carpet.

"His heart wasn't great. But still, even if this bastard thief didn't hurt him, he still killed him, didn't he? Still gave him enough of a shock to drop him."

Andrew's jaw tensed, and he spoke through gritted teeth, his breathing becoming laboured.

"He didn't even need that job. Could have retired years ago."

Andrew swiped his phone from a side table and jabbed away at the keyboard on the screen. When he found what he was searching for, he showed the detectives the screen.

"He was on Dragon's Den. Invented a gardening tool for people with bad wrists and elbows. Meant people could still garden if they had arthritis. The Dragons didn't think it would be a big earner, but one of them, the woman, I forget her name, she wanted to invest. Thought it was a nice product to get on the market. It turned out to be quite popular. Dad didn't get massive royalties, but it was a decent nest egg."

Keaton watched Andrew as he spoke. He seemed to relax as he told the tale, pride beginning to rise to the surface, but it was quickly replaced by more anger.

"So yeah, he didn't need to work. If he hadn't been there, he'd still be alive."

His eyes welled up, but he swatted the tears away, taking a deep breath. "I'm sorry. I don't mean to get emotional."

"It's understandable, Andrew," Keaton said. "I'm sure your father worked because he enjoyed it."

"Aye. I suppose he did. It gave him a routine. After my mam died, he didn't sleep well, so the night job was a decent distraction. Gave him purpose. Sorry, I can't believe I'm angry at him for going to work. As if I'm blaming him for dying there. What sort of dickhead son am I?"

Martin leant forward in his chair, a hand resting on his crutches to stop them falling. "It's a natural part of the grieving process."

Andrew shook his head, eyes distant, as if he hadn't heard a word. "Have you spoken to that useless cousin of mine yet?"

Keaton and Martin shared a look. Keaton spoke first. "No, Andrew. You're the next of kin. Why would we need to speak to your cousin?"

Andrew sat in a striped armchair, folded his arms, then immediately stood back up.

"Andrew?"

He drummed his fingers against his arm as if tapping a rhythm helped organise his thoughts.

"Look, I feel like a right snitch, but if I didn't say owt and it turned out... He used to ask Dad for money all the time. Turned up at his house at unsociable hours more than once. He's got a gambling problem. The problem being he's shit at gambling. He'd take out payday loans, put the money into those gambling apps, burn through it, then ask Dad to bail him out."

Keaton's tongue worked to loosen the chickpea stuck between her teeth. If Colin's nephew would turn up at his house to ask for money, would he turn up at Colin's place of work to do the same thing? It was a possibility. Colin refused and turned Daniel away; Daniel got angry, and things got out of hand. That wouldn't explain the missing nightshade, though. Not unless Martin was right at it was nothing more than a red herring. She freed the chickpea, savoured the curry flavour and swallowed, thinking how she hoped Martin was right – the lad deserved a break.

"And did your father regularly give Daniel money?" Martin asked.

"Aye. He used to. Until about a year ago."

"What happened a year ago?"

"Dad got sick of being taken for a mug. Told Daniel he wouldn't help pay off his debts unless he went to rehab. Daniel refused and went in a huff."

Two phones sounded at the same time. One was Andrew's.

He checked the ID on the screen. "It's my wife," he said, sadness clouding his feature. "She loved Dad. Excuse me."

While Andrew left the room, Keaton checked her own phone. It was a local 01665 number.

"DS Paula Keaton."

Keaton listened to the caller on the other end while Martin stood and stretched his Achilles tendon, rotating his ankle a few times.

"That was the gardens," she said, hanging up. "Sarah-Beth found something. She wants us to pop back in."

Martin grabbed his crutches.

"Not so fast. One of us needs to stay with Andrew until his wife arrives." She nodded towards Martin's injured leg. "And seeing as you can't drive... Make the man a tea and get an address for Cousin Daniel. I'll be back in half an hour to pick you up."

She left before he had a chance to protest, and it wasn't like he could chase her.

SARAH-BETH WAS WAITING FOR Keaton at the entrance when she arrived. She'd changed her jumper and washed her face since Keaton last saw her.

"I know I shouldn't touch anything until the forensic people get here..."

"But..."

"But it might have blown away in the breeze, so I put a rock on it. "

"Put a rock on what?" asked Keaton, following the young gardener to the east.

When they entered the Poison Garden, Sarah-Beth pointed to a spot in the corner where some autumn leaves had gathered. Keaton approached and crouched down for a better look. Nestled between the leaves was a small slip of white paper.

"A receipt?"

"For Barter Books," Sarah-Beth said. "For yesterday at two p.m."

"Right," Keaton said, feeling a little annoyed about the wasted journey. She stood, allowing the silence to grow.

Sarah-Beth, eyes wide, was practically pleading with Keaton for her to get the point she was making. When Keaton didn't oblige, she exclaimed, "It might be a clue. It might belong to the man who killed Colin."

Keaton wanted to calm the situation. Terms like *killing* and *murder* could spread like flu, and they didn't actually know how Colin had died yet.

"Until we've established how Colin died—"

"But what if he was murdered? What if that receipt belonged to his murderer?"

"It could equally belong to Colin."

Sarah-Beth deflated. She turned away, running her fingertips through the foliage of a plant Keaton couldn't identify.

"Or it could belong to anyone who visited the gardens in the past few days," Keaton continued.

The gardener paused at a different plant, crouching, examining its stem and leaves. She let out a sigh of defeat. "It could have blown in on the breeze. I just wanted to help. To help Colin. Sorry to waste your time."

"Not at all." Keaton pulled out an evidence envelope and bagged the receipt as much to make the young woman feel better as anything else. "You did the right thing calling."

She didn't look up from the plant, pulling large green leaves back and forth, peering closer.

Barter Books was a stone's throw from the gardens. Even Martin on his crutches could cover the distance in six or seven minutes. Popular to the point of fame, the bookstore was loved by readers, writers and tourists alike.

Keaton labelled the envelope. "I'll follow up on it," she said to reassure the woman, "but if someone made the journey to Alnwick to visit the gardens, they'd probably pop into the bookstore while they were here. Or vice versa."

She moved towards Sarah-Beth, who was still staring intently at a plant, her face frozen, lips thin. Keaton placed a hand on Sarah-Beth's shoulder, and when the latter jumped with fright, it was enough to make the former flinch, too.

Deathly pale, Sarah-Beth's mouth opened, but she was unable to speak.

"What is it?"

"'Scuse me," she said, pushing past Keaton and mumbling about risk assessments and procedures.

"Sarah-Beth?"

The plant had a sturdy reddish-brown stem and palmate leaves, which spread like green fingers, turning brown at the edges. Keaton read the small plaque next to it: *Castor Bean Plant.*

Hurrying to catch the gardener, Keaton repeated herself. "What is it?"

"Er— Erm," stammered Sarah-Beth before she managed to gather herself. "Whoever was in here took more than belladonna. They've harvested all the castor seed pods. Every last one of them."

Keaton knew the answer by the look on the gardener's face, but she asked the question all the same. "Are you saying that's worse than deadly nightshade?"

"Much worse," she said, swallowing. "It's used to make ricin."

CHAPTER 20

FEELING LIKE A SPARE part, Oliver Martin gingerly gathered his crutches and politely excused himself from the company of Andrew Finch and his newly returned wife. He slowly navigated to the front door, carefully avoiding any bumps or obstacles that could cause him further discomfort.

The narrow street was lined on either side with modest terrace homes built with large, square, sandy-coloured stones. Most of the houses sported modern double glazing with UPVC frames, but some still retained the old sash windows with flaking, wooden surrounds. There were no front gardens, and cars mounted the kerb to park on the pavement.

The street was on an incline, and he chose the downhill option for ease. He swung his crutches, then hopped carefully forward. Martin was sick of the damn things and could walk without them for short bursts, but the risk of falling or injuring himself again wasn't worth it. When he was out and about and had to be on his feet for any length of time, it was best to use them. Didn't mean they didn't drive him up the wall, though. They weren't just crutches; they were a constant reminder that he couldn't keep up, that he was a burden. And the look people gave him when he wobbled or winced, he was sick of that too.

At the next crossroads, he turned right and found a park bench in the shadow of a Catholic Church with a square belfry and lichen-stained walls. He slid onto the cold wood and leaned back, tilting his head toward the heavens, where clouds were starting to gather. It was a moment's peace, a rare commodity in his line of work.

Sending his location to Keaton, he wondered what was taking her so long. The DS wasn't the sort to dilly-dally and rarely broke a promise. He made himself comfortable and watched a woman walk by with an old Scotty dog in a pushchair. Considering the case, Martin pondered what Sarah-Beth, the gardener, had wanted, what had changed for her to call Keaton. He thought about this cousin Andrew Finch had mentioned and if he was capable of hurting his uncle over money. Humans hurt each other over far less.

As the church bell emitted two loud chimes, Martin's phone chirped and buzzed against his thigh. He should have known the quiet wouldn't last. It never did. He drew the device from his pocket, expecting a message from Keaton saying she was on her way. Instead, he was disappointed to see a notification from the *Not-So-PC-PCs*. His thumb hovered for a moment before he clicked *view*.

A photo appeared of a Southwick DC dressed in a red-and-white striped Sunderland shirt and a black mask. He was wielding a foam baseball bat.

Deano 14:00

Check out my Halloween costume for the neet.

Whyte had said people would dress as the vigilante known as the Masked Mackem, but Martin was surprised to see a detective donning the costume. Immediately the group became alive with the ping-ping of replies.

Alex the Great 14:01

Belta.

Johnnie red n white 4 life 14:01

Fucking class.

Little Nix 14:02

Sad Mackem Bastard.

Johnnie red n white 4 life 14:03

You're just jealous Newcastle doesn't have its own superhero.

Little Nix 14:03

He's not a superhero. He's a dickhead.

Bobby Dazla 14:04

> Aye. Probably only saves those lasses coz he wants to shag 'em.

Frustration and anger prickled under Martin's skin. These idiots weren't worth losing his job over, and they definitely weren't worth losing Boyd over. With a deep breath, he tapped *settings* and then pressed *mute*, silencing all notifications for the next week.

He needed guidance from someone older and wiser than himself. Keaton would call him an idiot and tell him to grow a pair, and while he respected Cooper, he feared her reaction. It was times like this when he really missed Tennessee. Scrolling through his contacts list, Martin finally settled on a name and pressed the call button with a mix of hope and apprehension.

Chapter 21

Cooper was at the wheel as she and Whyte drove through the autumnal gloom of Wednesday morning, leaving HQ in Wallsend behind. The road stretched west toward Prudhoe, the river a grey companion to their left until they crossed the Scotswood Bridge. Neither had much to say.

Cooper parked on the street in front of a well-presented house with a long drive and a loft conversion. She and Whyte approached the front door. While Whyte pounded on the door to announce their arrival, Cooper hung back slightly, surveying the windows for signs of movement. No answer.

"Try again," Cooper told him. They needed to speak to Cliff Longacre after learning about his bad blood with Captain Jude. Speaking of blood, now his footprint had been discovered on the bridge, tracking him down had become a priority.

Cooper hugged her arms around her chest. The thin, chiffon blouse in a shade of jade green felt warm enough in the chaos of her kitchen this morning, but not out here. It was inadequate in the November air, and she could feel her arms and hands beginning to shake.

A nosy neighbour wearing impossibly long eyelashes poked her head out. "If you're looking for that strapping lad, he's already left for work. Saw him head off about six-thirty."

Cooper swore under her breath. *What work?* Electron wasn't going anywhere yet, not with SOCOs still working on the scene.

She handed the neighbour her card, "Call me if he comes home."

Whyte opened her car door for her, walked around the car and got in the passenger side. "Want me to call that corporate prick? Hargreaves, was it?"

Cooper nodded, executing a lightning-fast three-point turn.

AT THE DOCKS, CRANES loomed overhead, and workers bustled about. Cooper flashed her badge at the security barrier. "Looking for Sean Hargreaves. VāyuVolt Renewables."

The portly man in the booth squinted and jerked his thumb towards the quay. "He'll be by Zephyr. Big green ship. Can't miss it. Park on the right, and I'll escort you over."

Cooper and Whyte almost sprinted down the pier, dodging crates and coils of rope. Their escort struggled to keep up. Ahead, the boat's engines thrummed to life, disturbing the surface of the water. Zephyr was no Electron. She was smaller, older, a duller shade of green, and there was no helipad. They came to a halt when a posh bloke in a suit blocked their path: Sean Hargreaves.

"Detective Cooper," he said officiously. "Good to see you again. I trust my colleagues have been cooperating." He turned to Whyte, extending a hand. "Sean Hargreaves. VāyuVolt Renewables. Good to meet you..."

He paused for Whyte to introduce himself.

"We've met before," he said. "DS Whyte. We need to speak with Cliff Longacre immediately. He's now a person of interest."

The offered handshake went unanswered.

Hargreaves smiled thinly. "While I appreciate your dedication, after all, Captain Jude McDermott was an exemplary member of our team here at—"

"I've read his HR files," Cooper said, cutting him off.

Hargreaves faltered for a second before picking up where he left off. "While I appreciate your dedication, DCI Cooper, we have critical maintenance to perform. Those turbines, though state-of-the-art, won't service themselves, and we need our bosun onboard. Delaying Zephyr's departure would mean reduced renewable capacity for tens of thousands. The UK is a leading force in renewables, and we wouldn't want the grid to take its power from coal and gas when we have a beautiful twenty to twenty-five knots of winds forecast for the next week. Would we?"

The wind didn't feel beautiful to Cooper. It felt Arctic. The run along the quay had helped, but her body heat quickly waned.

Hargreaves spread his hands in a conciliatory gesture that set Cooper on edge. "Zephyr leaves in five. You can arrest our bosun if you feel you must. Or, you and your partner may come aboard and speak to him in the comfort of one of our meeting rooms. Your choice, Detective."

Cooper glanced at Whyte, his face unreadable. She ground her teeth. For all his platitudes, Hargreaves was concerned about one thing only: the bottom line. Profit came before solving a brutal murder.

"I'm not her partner," Whyte corrected him curtly. "She's a detective chief inspector. A damn good one. I'm just a DS."

She cleared her throat to suppress a smile. Whyte wasn't *just a DS*. There was no such thing as *just a DS*, but she appreciated him setting the corporate mouthpiece straight. And the compliment, she enjoyed that too.

"Fine," Cooper snapped. "Add us to the manifest." It wasn't like she could let Cliff Longacre sail off over the horizon without speaking to him. "I'll be interviewing Mr Longacre the second we've left the dock."

She stormed up the ramp, Whyte on her heels, and a sense of foreboding in her gut. She was headed back to sea. Just bloody perfect.

ZEPHYR LURCHED BENEATH COOPER'S feet as it cast off. Smaller and far less steady than the hi-tech Electron, she gripped a rail for stability as the ship navigated out of the Tyne into the swell of the North Sea.

Whyte stood beside her on the deck, unruffled as always, but she caught him sneaking a concerned glance her way.

"You look like an ice cube, boss." He tugged at the cuff of the stylish woollen jumper he wore. "You can borrow this."

Before she could politely decline, Cliff Longacre strode towards them, a blond Adonis in a tight polo shirt. Square jaw, chiselled muscles, eyes bluer than the November sky. Your typical action hero type. Cooper imagined he'd set many hearts aflutter in his day. Might've worked on her when she was young and stupid, back when she'd gone crazy for bad boys like Tina's dad. Live and learn. These days, she preferred a man with more brains than brawn.

"Hello again," Cliff greeted, his expression stern. "Heard you wanted to speak to me. I'm happy to chat as soon as I've finished my departure procedures. Got a ship to run at the moment. In the meantime, enjoy the view."

He gestured at the receding shore and wind-swept beaches. Behind them, the iconic Tyne piers stretched into the sea, the ends of each furnished with lighthouses, the southern one damaged from a fierce storm.

Cooper crossed her arms, rubbing her triceps. "Fine. But I expect your full cooperation, Mr Longacre. Don't keep us waiting too long."

Cliff nodded and sauntered away, leaving Cooper and Whyte to admire the scenery. Despite the circumstances, the salt breeze was invigorating. Gulls wheeled overhead, rowdy and free. If only her mind could be so unburdened.

"We should head indoors," Whyte said after a few minutes, "get you out of the cold."

She didn't argue, allowing Whyte to hold open a series of heavy doors as they made their way to the mess and helped themselves to bottled water. It wasn't much warmer inside, so Cooper walked laps of the room while Whyte sat at a table.

"How'd you want to play it?" he asked.

"Try to catch him in a lie. We'll ask if he was on the bridge with India, Gray and the medic after they discovered the attack. If he says no, we'll ask why his footprint was there."

Finally, the man himself strode into the mess, his crisp polo marked with a brown grease stain. "Follow me," he said, leading them through metallic corridors to a small meeting room. He flicked the lights on, brightening the place with fluorescent bulbs. Of all the times Cooper had sat in interview suites, she'd always led the way, been the one to turn the lights on and close the door behind a suspect. This felt off-kilter. She didn't like it.

Cliff waited for Cooper and Whyte to squeeze in next to each other on the opposite side of the table, their shoulders touching, before taking his seat.

"Right. What can I do for you?"

Cooper leaned forward, elbows on the laminate tabletop, locking her gaze with his baby blues. "Tell me where you were on Friday the twenty-seventh of October."

"The day Jude was killed?"

Cooper noted he didn't use the term Captain. "Yes."

"I was on Electron."

"I know that, Mr Longacre; I was there too. Let's be more specific."

Cliff took a deep breath, his chest swelling. "I was off watch. I was in bed when we hit the turbine. Almost shit myself."

"And Kay can attest to that?" Cooper asked.

He paused, seemingly shocked that Cooper knew his wife's name and that she was also part of Electron's crew.

"Actually, no. Kay's alarm went off at four-thirty. She had to begin prepping the galley for breakfast. Once she was ready, I walked her to the galley, nipped to the bogs then went back to sleep. When the impact occurred, I jumped up, got dressed and went to see what the hell was going on."

"You went to the bridge?"

"Of course."

That was easy. "To be clear. You were on the bridge with India, Grey and Georgie while they worked to save Hal's life."

"No." He shook his head. "No. I wasn't *on* the bridge. I went *to* the bridge. Went to see what was happening but India stopped me. Pretty much screamed at me not to step foot in there. She sent me straight off to assess the damage from the impact."

"And you weren't on the bridge earlier that day?"

"No. Like I said, I was in bed."

"What size shoe do you wear, Cliff?"

"Fourteen."

Whyte sat up, biro balanced between his fingers. "Apparently, you're the only one of the crew to wear fourteens."

"I wouldn't know."

"I would," Cooper said. "I checked." She waited quietly for a few moments before asking. "So, tell me, if you weren't on the bridge that day, why was a size fourteen footprint found by our forensics team right in the middle of the crime scene?"

Cliff remained calm with relaxed shoulders and a straight spine. "Because I'm in there all the time. I wasn't in there on Friday, but I would have been the day before. And the day before that."

Cooper shared a look with Whyte, giving him permission to ask the critical question.

"We don't mean any old footprint," Whyte said, sliding a crime scene photograph across the table, tapping the middle of the image to draw Cliff's attention to the area circled in red. "We mean a bloody footprint."

"That's impossible."

"You were on the bridge either during or after the attack," Whyte pressed.

"No. I wasn't. You can ask India."

"We will," Whyte said. "We'll be asking her why she lied. Why she didn't mention you being there."

"She didn't lie. And neither did I. India's a professional; she did the right thing, not allowing anyone else in there."

"We'll see," Whyte said.

Cooper took over. "What was your opinion of Captain Jude McDermott."

Cliff's face twisted in distaste.

"Don't worry about speaking ill of the dead with us," she told him. "We know your wife called him Captain Judas. That's quite the nickname."

"It's an apt one," Cliff said. "And don't worry, I'm not going to give you the same *he was a good leader, firm but fair* bullshit everyone else has. I thought Jude McDermott was a slimy little pervert, a coward and a cheat."

"You admit having a grudge against him?"

A bark of deep, mirthless laughter. "Oh aye, I had a grudge all right. Same as I had against Hal, the smarmy, geeky wee shit. Pair of 'em, thick as thieves."

Cooper's pulse quickened. Now they were getting somewhere. "Enough of a grudge to want them dead?"

"Shit, I could've cheerfully throttled them both."

CHAPTER 22

THE LOUNGE ON ZEPHYR WASN'T AS fancy as the one on Electron; that much was undeniable. Still, it served its purpose. The low chairs reminded Dr Emily Hartley of her university days. The ones in the dorms had also sported fraying fabric and foam that had lost its bounce. Her knees protested as she sank into the seat. Plopping her bag on her lap, she let out the involuntary groan that always accompanied sitting down.

Alongside Hartley, the group consisted of Dr Priya Kapoor, a faculty member on sabbatical from Bangalore, and three PhD students: Michael, Ben, and Nikki. They sat in a circle, laptops perched on their knees, poring over data from the last expedition. Despite being cut short, Electron's voyage had yielded plenty of information to analyse. The small round table between them was cluttered with papers, tablets, and mugs of coffee in various stages of consumption.

Priya's fingers flew across her keyboard, compiling water quality reports. "pH levels are within the predicted range, but there's an unexpected spike in nitrogen content near the easternmost turbines."

Michael grunted, scratching his beard. "Might explain the drop in seal sightings in that quadrant."

Hartley nodded. "Pull up the underwater footage from that area. Let's see if we can spot any anomalies."

While Nikki found the required files, Michael cleared the middle of the table. The cuffs of his hoodie were pulled over his hands, but Hartley still spotted a white bandage wrapped tightly around his fingers. She caught his eye. "What happened?"

"Ah, nothing to write home about," he said, moving his mug of coffee to the floor.

"You should see the medic."

"It's nowt."

Nikki placed the tablet in the centre of the table, and all five of them leaned in as she pressed *play*.

"Visibility's good," she said, tucking her sleek black bob behind her ear and pushing her glasses up her nose.

"It's excellent," Hartley agreed, examining what the cameras had picked up on OGE24. She could clearly make out the yellow transition piece of the turbine and base below it.

"There's an increase in coral growth already," Michael said.

A flash of movement. A dark shape, just out of focus.

Nikki rewound, ready for them to watch again.

"What is that?" Priya squinted, leaning closer. "Too big for a seal."

Ben snorted. "Maybe it's the wind farm monster." Still in his twenties, Ben was the most juvenile of the group – in both years and attitude. "It lies in wait of unsuspecting SOVs."

Ben grabbed Nikki's chair, shaking it violently. "Help! The monster's coming for Zephyr," he joked dramatically.

Nikki slapped his hand away from her chair.

Hartley shot him a withering look. "Cut it out. And it's not a monster; it's a minke whale."

Priya's round face spread into a wide grin. "They've come back to the site? That's fantastic."

Hartley leant back in her seat. Some lower back support wouldn't go a miss. "Unfortunately, we'll sail through the site in this big, noisy thing. Hopefully, the noise and vibrations don't disturb the marine mammals."

"We'll find out when we analyse the next lot of data, I suppose," said Michael, fussing with his hoodie.

"Sooner we get back on Electron, the better," Ben added. "The Wi-Fi sucks on here, and have you seen the cabins? We have to share! I haven't slept in a bunk bed since I was eight. As for the showers—"

Priya's serene expression hardened. "Someone died, Ben. I don't think the police care if you have to share a room. They'll keep Electron as long as they need."

Hartley coughed. For a group of academics, it was impossible to keep them on task. She should have brought undergrads along instead. For a solid ten minutes, she managed to keep them focused on water quality until the second officer entered the lounge. Ben's wandering eyes ceased focusing on the figures on the spreadsheet and started focusing on India's svelt figure instead.

She strode past them to the far side of the lounge, her back ramrod straight, eyes fixed on a porthole.

Ben's gaze followed her, a sly grin spreading across his boyish face. "Do you think they were shagging?"

"Who?" Hartley rubbed her temples.

"Her and the captain."

Nikki rolled her eyes. Priya and Hartley frowned. Ben leaned forward, voice dropping to a conspiratorial whisper. "They were definitely shagging."

Michael pointed to his laptop. "I think we can agree nutrient levels are stable... But, while we're on the subject, I always thought the captain looked at her like she was his daughter."

"That's what makes it so gross," Ben chuckled.

"Phosphate levels are within normal ranges," Hartley said, raising her voice slightly. They were supposed to be professionals.

It was no good. Ben was still distracted. "I know she's like in her forties, but you would, wouldn't you?" he asked Michael, nudging the bigger man's ribs.

"Without a doubt." Michael at least had the decency to return to the topic they were commissioned for, addressing Hartley. "Silicate levels seem to be supporting a healthy diatom population."

"Which is beneficial for the local food web—"

Nikki cut in, her northern accent tinged with disbelief. "In what fictional reality would a woman like India Morgan give either of you dweebs the time of day? Besides, if she and the captain were together, wouldn't she be more upset? She's all business as usual."

Ben scoffed, eyes still on the second officer, who was spending her break reading an industry magazine. "That's because she was only doing it so she could sleep her way…"

Hartley's stomach churned. Idiots. Surrounded by idiots. Some of the brightest minds and they had the attention span of sand eels. She cleared her throat. "If we could focus on the research," she said sharply. "We still haven't gone over the data from the tracking devices."

The door swung open again. It was the medic.

Michael tucked his hands under his legs. "I have the tracking data, and it's really quite interesting."

Georgie crossed the lounge and joined India, who looked highly annoyed at her reading time being interrupted. Hartley could relate to that.

"WANTING HARM TO COME to someone and actually killing 'em and two very different things."

Cliff Longacre fixed Cooper with a stare. She knew what he was saying was true. God, she'd wanted terrible things to happen to people over the years. She'd even gone as far as hinting to a crime boss that she'd like someone's legs broken. But there was a giant leap from wishing someone ill to actually injuring them. It was a bigger leap still to murder.

Nevertheless, Cooper believed the science. Atkinson had found Cliff's bloody footprint slap bang in the middle of the crime scene. He'd been standing next to their stab-wound-riddled bodies. Atkinson was an expert in forensic podiatry. There was no way he was mistaken. Yes, she was biased, but if Atkinson said it was Cliff Longacre's footprint, it was Cliff Longacre's footprint.

"So, why exactly would you want to throttle Jude and Hal?"

Cliff took his time answering, working his jaw for a while and casting stern glances around the claustrophobic room. It was then Cooper felt how isolated she and Whyte were. Sure there were plenty of crew about, but in the tiny meeting room, wedged between the table and the wall, with great big Cliff blocking the exit – if he kicked off, would she and Whyte be able to control him? Cooper wasn't so sure.

"I wasn't always a deckhand," Cliff said eventually. "I was part of the nav. team. Second officer, like India is now. Hal and I were both up for the position of first mate. Look how that turned out." He let out a dry chuckle. "Hal's in the hospital. I inspect lines for chafe."

"Bosun's a good job," Cooper said.

"Aye. It is. Had to work my arse off to get it. Not what I wanted to be though."

"So what happened?"

She knew what had happened. She'd read their HR statements, but getting it from the horse's mouth was always the best.

"I'd suspected Jude was having it off with this lass, Mandi, for a while. Flirty glances. Shit like that. They had their own little in jokes and always stood or sat weirdly close together."

Cooper shifted an inch to her left.

"Then, one night, I was on watch and had nipped back to my quarters to get a phone charger when I saw Mandi coming out of Jude's cabin. It was three in the morning. Only one reason for her to be there at that time." He raised his brows, giving a pointed look at them both. "I knew calling him out was a risk, that the timing was terrible with the first mate position opening up, but I couldn't stand back and do nothing. He was married. He was having an affair with one of his subordinates. A junior crew member. It had *hashtag me too* written all over it. It wasn't good for the company and it wasn't good for Mandi. So, despite my gut telling me not to, that it would be professional suicide, I said something."

He cracked his knuckles, a tension rippling down his forearms.

"Told him to pack it in. That it was unprofessional and an abuse of power. The next day, I'm about to board a crew transfer vessel when I'm frog-marched out of the port and told to stay home until some bullshit so-called investigation is over. Apparently, I'd been bullying the poor, wee captain. All I was guilty of was not getting to HR before he did. What a piss take."

He chewed the inside of his mouth. "Five days later, while I'm still reeling from what happened, I hear word has got out that I'm an alcoholic. *Recovering* alcoholic. Six hundred and twelve days sober. The only one onboard who knew was Hal Simpson. He'd seen me coming out of an AA meeting in town. He must have told someone. Spread it about like *I Can't Believe It's Not Butter*. Little shit. I should've wrung his skinny little neck."

"So Hal, got the job?" asked Cooper, though she already knew the answer.

"Proper shan if you ask me, but no surprise really. No one wants a bullying alcoholic second in command."

Cliff closed his eyes and slowed his breathing. "But it wasn't like I was sat at home sticking pins in voodoo dolls. I moved on. Or I tried to. As you might have noticed, I'm still a bit pissed off about the whole thing." He let out an empty laugh. "Aye, but still, bosun's well-paid. Me and the missus have been saving. We're going to pull the little one out of school and take a career break. Go travelling. Spend a year in South America. Can't bloody wait."

Closing his notepad, Whyte said, "That sounds great, but I wouldn't go leaving the country just yet."

The bosun's eyes flashed.

"And please remove your boots," Whyte added, handing him a clear bag.

"Why?"

"Because they're evidence."

"No, they're not," Cliff said cooly. "These are brand new. Fresh on today."

Whyte bristled. "And where are your old ones?"

"No idea," he answered, and something in his tone made Cooper believe him.

She pushed her chair back, glancing under the table at a pair of unscuffed workboots. The same standard issue, brown leather boots she'd seen everyone else on Electron wearing, from India to the medic to the galley chefs. Everyone except Cliff Longacre, who had greeted them on the helipad wearing trainers as white as his bleached teeth.

CHAPTER 23

Northumbria Police Department.

URGENT ALERT: Theft of Poisonous Plants.

November 1st.

To: All Health Care Providers and Emergency Departments.

Overview: This is an urgent notification regarding the theft of highly poisonous plants. The stolen plants include deadly nightshade (*Atropa belladonna*) and castor bean plant (*Ricinus communis*). Both plants contain potent toxins that pose a severe risk to public health. Immediate awareness and preparedness are required.

Details of the Stolen Plants:
1. **Deadly Nightshade (*Atropa belladonna*)**

   ○ **Toxin:** Atropine, scopolamine, and hyoscyamine.

   ○ **Symptoms of Poisoning:**

     • Dilated pupils, sensitivity to light, blurred vision.

     • Tachycardia (rapid heartbeat), convulsions.

     • Loss of balance and coordination, staggering.

     • Rash.

     • Dry mouth and throat, slurred speech.

     • Urinary retention, constipation.

     • Severe headache, confusion, hallucinations, delirium.

2. **Castor Bean Plant (*Ricinus communis*)**

   ○ **Toxin:** Ricin.

   ○ **Symptoms of Poisoning:**

     • Severe abdominal pain nausea and vomiting, diarrhoea.

- Dehydration, decreased urination, hematuria (blood in urine).

- Hallucinations.

- Seizures.

- Organ failure (liver, kidney, and pancreas).

Action Required:
  1. **Increase Vigilance:**

  ○ Be on high alert for patients presenting symptoms consistent with poisoning from these plants.

  ○ Consider these symptoms, particularly if there is no other obvious cause.

  2. **Immediate Treatment Protocols:**

  ○ **Deadly Nightshade:**

    - Administer **atropine** as an antidote.

    - Provide supportive care, including intravenous fluids, activated charcoal if ingested recently, and continuous cardiac monitoring.

  ○ **Castor Bean (Ricinus poisoning):**

- There is no specific antidote for ricin.

- Provide supportive care, including IV fluids, electrolytes, pain management, and monitoring for organ failure.

3. Reporting and Documentation:

○ Report any suspected cases of poisoning to local health authorities and the National Poisons Information Service (NPIS) immediately.

○ Document all cases with detailed patient histories and potential exposure information.

Public Health Notification:
Northumbria Police are coordinating with local health departments to issue public health alerts. These will include information on recognising symptoms of poisoning and instructions for seeking medical attention promptly.

Contact Information:
- Emergency: 999

- Non-Emergency: 111

- **National Poisons Information Service**

  ○ Website: https://www.npis.org

Additional Notes:
- Please ensure all healthcare staff are briefed on this situation and are prepared to handle potential cases of poisoning.

- Maintain an adequate stock of atropine and supportive care materials.

- Disseminate this information sheet to all relevant departments and personnel.

Thank you for your immediate attention and cooperation.

Sincerely,

DS Paula Keaton
Northumbria Police CID

Keaton pressed send and logged out of the shared computer. With the help of a consultant at the Royal Victoria Infirmary, she'd alerted every hospital and healthcare provider in the Northeast, warning them about the thefts of the poisonous plants. One, deadly nightshade, and the other, whose seeds could be turned into ricin.

"Right," she said, reluctantly getting to her feet. "You ready?" She waved a photocopy of the bookstore receipt that the gardener had found in the garden.

Martin heaved himself upright, letting out a moan. "Thought you didn't think it was relevant?"

"I don't," said Keaton. She tightened her ponytail and drained the dregs of a can of diet soda. "But it's our only clue at the moment." She looked Martin up and down, taking in his facial expression. It was a look she knew well. Clenched teeth and forced bravado – the mask of someone trying to pretend they weren't in pain. "You doing your exercises?"

"Of course."

"How often?"

Martin shrugged. "I dunno. A few times a week."

"A few times a week? You're meant to do them a few times a day, you daft bugger." She playfully slapped the back of his head, messing up his hair. "Hold still, I'll smooth it back down. Look, I've done enough rehab to know it's worth listening to the physios. They do actually know what they're talking about." She shadow-boxed the air, showing how much her damaged shoulder had come on since dislocating it while tackling a serial killer.

"But—"

"But it's boring. I get it. But you know what else is boring? Hobbling around on those things for months longer than necessary." She eyeballed the crutches. "I know you and Saff probably have some kinky patient-nurse thing going on—"

"I wish."

"But I want you fighting fit. You're my backup. Do your bloody exercises, okay? Don't make me draw up a star chart for you."

He laughed as they edged towards the exit. "What do I get if I collect all the stars?"

Keaton held the door as he ambled through. "No more lectures."

"Deal."

CLIFF LONGACRE HAD MOTIVE. Plenty of motive. He also lacked a credible alibi and couldn't explain why his bloody footprint was beside Jude's body or why he'd put on trainers that morning instead of his work boots.

"I was in a hurry. The boat had just hit a turbine. I grabbed the nearest clothes at hand."

Cooper paced one of Zephyr's many corridors, looking for some privacy. In the end, she stepped out onto the deck, shocked to see how choppy the sea was. White foam formed on the crests of the waves, which hit the green hull with a ferocity she hadn't noticed on Electron. Ahead, the bow rose and fell in short, sharp slams, the noise of which echoed throughout the vessel. She held her phone above her head until a bar of signal appeared. It lasted long enough for Atkinson to answer her call, then promptly dropped out. Sighing, she searched out India, who had just returned to the bridge from a break. She was her usual bucketful of sunshine, welcoming Cooper with nothing more than a nod and a look of annoyance.

After obtaining the Wi-Fi code, Cooper had no choice but to clarify India's version of events.

"Are you absolutely sure no one other than yourself, Graham Bell and Georgie Peters entered the bridge on Electron?"

"One hundred per cent." She pressed a button twice, and the vessel responded, turning slightly to port. "Not until the forensic team arrived."

She looked thinner and more tired since Cooper had seen her last, but like before, she was in her element amongst the control panels and charts.

If India was telling the truth, Cliff would have to have been in the room during or shortly after the murder occurred but must have left before India and Gray arrived.

"Thank you," Cooper said, wafting the Wi-Fi code.

When India didn't reply, Cooper left. Redialling Atkinson's work number.

"Hey, handsome." It sounded forced. She rolled her eyes at herself. "Where are you?"

"Still on Electron. You?"

"You know that other VāyuVolt vessel that left the Tyne about two or three hours ago?"

"Yeah..."

"I'm on it."

He laughed. "Chasing bad guys?"

"Chasing bad guys," she repeated.

"You're not alone, are you?"

His protective instincts had caused problems previously. Cooper had learned to accept them as love, and Atkinson had, in fairness, toned them down over their time together.

"Not alone," she confirmed. "Listen, this isn't a social call," she said, changing the subject. "I need your brilliant brain to play detective for me."

"Go on."

"Cliff Longacre is wearing brand-new boots. When I met him on Electron, he was wearing trainers. When we all disembarked, the crew left everything but what they were wearing on board. There's no way he smuggled those boots past us."

"So they're either washed up on a Dutch beach or somewhere on Electron?"

"Exactly. I don't care if you need to tear Electron apart; I want those boots. And if you can find a trail of footprints leading to Longacre's quarters, then even better."

CHAPTER 24

MARTIN GASPED AS HE stepped over the threshold. "It's like something out of Harry Potter."

He gaped as the warm, inviting ambience of Barter Books enveloped him. The high-vaulted ceilings, arched windows and exposed brickwork of the old railway station gave the place a spacious, airy feel. Still, there was a cosiness created by rows and rows of wooden bookshelves and reading nooks.

"You've never been here before?" Keaton asked, picking up a cookery book and flicking through the pages before putting it back on the shelf.

"Never."

"Bring Saff. She'll love it."

He loved it. And he wasn't even much of a reader. Tall bookcases laden with an eclectic mix of second-hand books stretched throughout the vast space. Their coloured spines, some with gold lettering, hinted at a world of stories. More than anyone could read in a lifetime.

A miniature train chugged along a track, winding its way through the store, a nod to the building's former life. In the crime fiction section, a woman with long, thick curls was thrilled to find a PJ Tracy thriller. At the till, an elderly man bartered a price for a selection of history books, hence the bookshop's name.

But they hadn't come here to browse. Once the gentleman with the history books shuffled away, Keaton stepped forward, presenting the receipt to the sales assistant.

"This is for our buffet," he told them, pointing to the old waiting rooms converted into a café.

Inside, the aroma of coffee mingled with the scent of old books. It was enough to make Martin want to buy a stack of yellowing novels, but in truth, he wouldn't know where to start. Was he a sci-fi sort of man? Espionage? He had no idea. The last book he'd read was a John Grisham that his dad had loaned him on holiday one year.

A woman had her nose buried in a different John Grisham, not even glancing up as she tucked into a hot beef sandwich, gravy dripping down the side. Martin felt his stomach rumble; even the poached eggs at the next table looked tempting.

He received a sharp elbow in his ribs. "Stop drooling and take this to the counter. Get us some bait while you're at it."

Five minutes later, Martin joined Keaton at a table, having ordered two bacon butties. He balanced his crutches against the wall and carefully pulled his chair out, trying not to disturb the greyhound sleeping beneath it. "Grub will be five to ten minutes."

He placed a scrap of paper on the table and slid it over to Keaton. "Judy Knox," he said, reading the name written on the paper. "That's the name on the credit card used in the transaction on our receipt. She ordered two of those lovely hot beef sandwiches, one tea and one cappuccino."

"Judy Knox," Keaton repeated. "I'll call it in. By the time we've eaten, we should have her details."

WHYTE REMOVED HIS WOOLLEN jumper and handed it to Cooper.

"I'm fine."

"Don't be a hero. It's November, we're halfway across the North Sea, and the heating here is rubbish. Take it. Please."

She couldn't argue with his logic. The heating on Zephyr was more like air conditioning. She pulled it over her blouse and felt the instant hit of Whyte's residual body heat. It was like wearing a hug. It smelled of him, too.

"What do you think of Cliff's story?" she asked, arranging the jumper so the cuffs of her blouse poked out the ends of the sleeves and tucking the waistband into her trousers. She had no mirror, but she thought it looked okay.

"That he hated Jude and Hal, but not enough to kill them?" Whyte sat on the edge of the table in the small meeting room. Cliff had gone back to work. The door was open, and they lowered their voices whenever someone walked by. "If I was in his shoes, I'd be pretty damn mad."

"And speaking of shoes..."

Whyte smiled at her. "Cliff claims he was all alone and sound asleep. He woke up and slipped on some lovely, clean trainers. Claims he has no clue where his boots are or why his bloody footprint is next to the murder victim. I say we let him finish his shift and arrest him once we return to port. We search his house, check his devices, see who he's been in contact with or texted since this all happened."

"I agree." Cooper opened a packet of crisps she'd got from the mess and offered them to Whyte.

He took one. "No getting crumbs on my jumper," he said with a wry smile. "Kidding. You should see how I eat in the flat. I'm a right pig."

"I don't believe that," said Cooper, taking two crisps and dropping a crumb on her chest with comical timing. She wiped it away.

"No, I am. Not as bad as Olly. Watching him eat is like watching a toddler. But I'm not far off. Seriously, I can't eat pasta without getting sauce on myself. *Proper clarty*, as my dad would say."

"What's it like living with him?" she asked, getting drawn into a personal conversation with him for the first time in God knows how long. "Living with Justin, sometimes it's hard to separate work and home, especially if we're working on the same case. Hard to switch off, you know?"

Whyte nodded. "I practically live with Saff as well. She's there most nights. It's nice, though. They're both tidy, and for a while, we had a no-work-talk-in-the-flat rule. Had to put a quid in a jar. Once it reached fifty quid, we went to the Lonsdale and spent it on lager and chips."

She was glad the three of them had each other. She knew little about Saffron Boyd since she moved up from Yorkshire, but she'd seen her blossom under Whyte's support. Martin too. He always seemed like such a lost puppy following Keaton around, hoping for a pat on the head. Boyd and Whyte were good for him, especially after that mad, drugged-up gangster slashed his Achilles tendon. Things like that were hard to get over.

Cooper ate another crisp. "I've been thinking about Jude and Mandi's affair."

"That Cliff wasn't the only one with motive?"

"Exactly. Do you think it's worth looking into Jude's wife? See if this Mandi had a boyfriend or husband?"

He shrugged. "I spoke with the officer who gave Mrs McDermott the news. She was distraught by all accounts. I don't think she knew about Jude's affair, and if she doesn't..."

"Then we shouldn't add to her pain. You're right."

Cooper's phone vibrated in her pocket. It was Atkinson.

"Your ears must be burning," she said. "Tell me you found the boots."

"Not yet. Working on it, though. No sign of them in Cliff Longacre's room. No sign of anything untoward in there. Certainly no blood."

"Hmm," she said, disappointed.

"To be honest, there's not much in the way of blood outside the bridge. I've managed to trace some of Gray and Georgie's foot and fingerprints as they've moved to the medical bay, but other than that, everything is contained to the bridge."

"Damn," said Whyte, obviously able to hear.

"Is that Elliot?"

"Yeah, Whyte's here."

"Is Daljit with you? Paula?"

"No, it's just us."

"Right." A pause. "You know Tina's match starts at seven? What time will you be back?"

"Good question," she said to Atkinson down the phone. Then to Whyte, "Can you go check?"

It took hours to get to Odin's Gale and back, but Cooper hoped the turnaround would be quick. As Whyte left, she asked optimistically, "What do you fancy for dinner? I know it's midweek, but we could get fish and chips after the match."

"Tina's off fish at the moment, remember? You will be there for the centre pass, won't you? Tina's really excited about starting as shooter tonight."

She loved how Atkinson treated Tina as if she were his biological daughter and how he supported her hobbies and studies. He even knew all the netball jargon. However, she didn't love his tone of voice – the accusatory lilt implying she was failing as a mother. If she worked part-time and Atkinson full-time, no one would bat an eyelid if he missed a netball game or Danny's first steps.

"Hang on. Whyte's back," she said, covering the phone with her hand. "What time are we due back?"

He looked sheepish. That feeling of foreboding settled in Cooper's stomach once more.

"Eight," he said.

"That's not so bad." She'd miss most of the game but might catch the end if she was first off the boat. Whyte could handle Cliff's arrest, especially if they had backup waiting at the port.

He shook his head. "Eight tomorrow morning."

Cooper put the phone back to her ear, but Atkinson had already hung up.

CHAPTER 25

MUTED CONVERSATIONS AND THE clinking of cutlery followed Georgie Peters as he walked through the mess hall. His morning on Zephyr had been quiet, with only an injured knee and extreme period pain requiring his attention. Georgie joined the queue for hot food, his tray clattering as the cook slapped down a steaming bowl of beef stew. The aroma hit him, rich and hearty with a hint of thyme. Much better than dusty field rations in the desert.

The fridge door hissed as he helped himself to a bottle of water before grabbing a small bowl of lettuce, red onion, and juicy tomatoes from the salad bar, more out of habit than appetite.

As he passed a table of technicians, a snippet of gossip caught his ear.

"Mebees India found out about Mandi, went mad with jealousy and killed Jude?"

It was Lars. He was Dutch and reminded Georgie of a miniature Cliff Longacre – a blond, muscled, pretty boy.

Big Jim scoffed. "India and Jude weren't like that. They were like an old married couple. They loved to bicker and wind each other up, but they weren't romantic. Nee way."

Georgie's jaw clenched at the light-hearted joking and finger-pointing.

Lars looked up, grinning. "Hey, Doc! Join us?"

He shook his head. "Thanks, lads. I'll pass. Got some thinking to do."

He settled at a corner table, grateful for the solitude. Outside the porthole, massive turbine blades circled above the choppy sea.

The stew warmed him from the inside, but his mind drifted to colder places. Sand-filled boots. The metallic tang of blood. Screams that never quite faded. He'd told that skinny Cooper woman that he'd expected to see people die at some point in this role. Deaths were rare on wind farms, but energy giants forked out for full-time medics for a reason. When accidents happen at height or at sea, it's best to have someone there who can treat a broken bone, stop massive blood loss or shove a dislocation back into its socket. But what happened to Hal and the captain... Georgie hadn't expected that. He was shocked at how much the blood caught him off guard. He couldn't quite believe someone on board could be a murderer. Still, at least here, no one was carrying an AK-47.

Georgie's spoon scraped the empty bowl. He stared at the turbines, their relentless motion hypnotic, and soon his mind drifted, as he thought it would, to the night before the murder. He needed to go over the events in his mind. Did he remember it all correctly?

He'd been up late in the medical bay, reviewing the latest edition of a medical journal, when he received news an old army buddy who now lived in Sydney had suffered three strokes in quick succession. He phoned him immediately, and they chatted as if no time had passed since they had last seen each other. It was midnight on Electron, ten a.m. down under.

By the time Georgie hung up, it was four in the morning. He tidied his desk and began the walk back to his cabin on the accommodation deck. The corridor was empty until he turned a corner and saw a figure ahead. Gray Bell.

"Gray," Georgie called, his voice gravelly with fatigue. "You alright, mate?"

Gray turned, his face pure exhaustion. "Can't sleep, Doc."

Georgie's medical instincts kicked in. "Anything bothering you?"

Gray shrugged. "Just... can't seem to shut my brain off, you know?"

He did know. He knew that feeling all too well. "Listen, get yourself to the mess and get a cup of chamomile. If it doesn't do the trick, come by tomorrow. We'll sort you out, yeah?"

"Sure, Doc. Thanks." Gray's shoulders slumped as he shuffled away.

Georgie watched him go, guilt clawing at him. Gray looked troubled. More than troubled really.

He should've pressed harder, stayed longer. But the siren call of his bed had been too strong, and who was he to pry into another man's demons when he could barely keep his own at bay?

Someone on the next table dropped a fork. The sound of it hitting the floor was enough to snap Georgie back to the present. He surveyed the room, wondering if he could spot a killer just by looking at them. He'd treated enough soldiers to know they all had the same look in their eyes. Lars? Big Jim? Gossiping about the second officer to deflect their own guilt? No. He didn't think so.

Gray entered the mess, making a beeline for the coffee machine. His eyes were glassy, unfocused. The telltale look of someone medicated to the gills. The fluorescent lights highlighted the shiny cut on his forehead. Georgie's stomach clenched. He'd been the one to stitch the lad up. The needlework was neat and precise, but it would still scar. Gray would wear a permanent reminder of that night on Electron for the rest of his life, see it every time he looked in a mirror.

But as Gray left, triple espresso in hand, Georgie questioned if Gray's late-night wanderings had been more than simple insomnia. And if so, what would he do about it?

CHAPTER 26

ADMIRING HER FRENCH MANICURE, Dianne Knox balanced the phone against her shoulder. The magnolia reception area was bathed in harsh fluorescent light, reflecting off the new satin paint job. Outside, the sky was a dull grey, hinting at rain.

"We only have emergency appointments. Is it an emergency?" Dianne inquired, her voice carrying a practised professional tone.

Apparently, French manicures were out of fashion. Her daughter said white-tipped nails categorised one as an older Gen X-er or a Boomer. Well, what was wrong with that? Dianne wondered. Some things were simply timeless classics. A little black dress. Red lipstick. Some things never went out of style, regardless of what the youth thought.

The caller was in a foul mood. "If it was an emergency, I'd have gone to A&E. I just want to see my GP."

"Dr Choi has no availability. You'll have to call back at eight tomorrow morning."

She pushed back her cuticles while listening to him growl in his raspy voice.

"I start work at seven. How am I supposed to call then?"

"I don't make the rules, Mr Legg. You could always try the walk-in centre."

He let out a series of expletives and hung up. How proletarian. No sense of decorum. He didn't even thank Dianne for her time.

Dianne prided herself on her role at the doctor's office. She was the gatekeeper, the first line of defence against time-wasters and hypochondriacs. Although, glancing around the waiting room, she could see a few had slipped by her. The young man in the Adidas tracksuit didn't look sick, and the woman with the pixie cut was definitely faking her abdominal pain. They were probably after sick notes, the pair of them.

The automatic doors glided apart, emitting a soft swooshing noise. A smartly dressed man in a dark blue suit and white shirt entered. He used grey, NHS-issued crutches as he hobbled into the surgery, the ends of which clicked against the tiled entranceway before softening as he stepped onto the carpeted area. Finally, a genuine patient.

He approached the desk. That irritated Dianne. Why can't they just type their details into the screen like the sign told them to?

"Just pop your date of birth into the touch screen, sir," she said, pointing at the machine.

He had dark hair and a youthful face. He ignored her hint, propping his crutches against the counter and reaching inside his jacket to produce some form of ID."

"DC Oliver Martin. I'm looking for Mrs Dianne Knox."

DIANNE KNOX DIDN'T SEEM especially pleased about Martin turning up at her place of work. She spoke in angry whispers while casting annoyed glances at the others in the waiting room. Her face was made up with expensive cosmetics, her expression pinched while he tried to appease her.

"I'm just following up on something. Trying to rule the evidence out if anything."

"Evidence? It's not evidence. It's a till receipt for goodness sake."

"Can you confirm it's *your* till receipt?"

She looked very put out, shifting her weight to the other foot and sucking her cheeks in.

"Yes. I can confirm I had lunch at the café in Barter Books. That's not a crime, is it?"

"Not at all," said Martin, suppressing a laugh. "And where did you go afterwards? How did you spend your day?"

"What does that have to do with you? What is this about?"

Raising his voice ever so slightly, Martin replied, "It's about a suspicious death." He watched her reaction closely, noting the way her eyes widened just a fraction.

Dianne looked around the waiting room again before hissing, "For crying out loud," and lifting a panel in the counter to shuffle Martin inside the reception office.

"The public aren't usually allowed back here. But I suppose you're not really the public."

She said *public* as if it were a dirty word. As if she considered the people waiting for their GP appointments as a different species, one beneath her.

"I visited Alnwick Gardens."

"Alone?"

"No. Why would I order two meals and two drinks if I was dining alone?" She stopped short of rolling her eyes, but she clearly thought it was a stupid question. She had the same expression as one of his old primary school teachers whenever he didn't understand something. "I was with my husband, Jeremy. It was his day off, so we had a nice day out in Northumberland. Not that that should concern you. He's the owner of Folklore, you see. He's an extremely busy man, and won't be impressed when I tell him about this later."

"FOLKLORE?" ASKED KEATON FROM the driver's seat while Martin filled her in on his conversation with Dianne Knox. It sounded familiar, but she couldn't place it. "Is that the swanky boutique in Ponteland?

The one where all the stuck-up WAGs and kept women shop?"

"The one where Cheryl Cole was spotted last week? Heard you need a mortgage to buy a handbag. No idea. It might be. Either way, Dianne confirmed the till receipt was hers and that she'd visited the gardens that day. She showed me the bank transaction for the tickets."

Keaton checked her mirrors before shifting gears and changing lanes. "The receipt is a no-go – as we suspected. They were just tourists and day trippers like everyone else."

"Agreed. The name Colin Finch meant nothing to her." Martin switched on the radio. An old Bananarama track was playing.

"Turn that over," she said with a mock groan.

"DI Singh would like it."

"Singh's not here," said Keaton, jabbing the touch screen until BBC Radio Newcastle came on. The presenter speculated about how the Fenwick department store might decorate its windows this Christmas.

"So, grasshopper," Keaton continued, "What's our next avenue?"

"I say we follow up with Colin Finch's disgruntled nephew."

DIANNE KNOX'S ANNOYANCE HAD yet to cease simmering since she watched that young DC Malcom, Mark, or whatever his name was, limp out of reception. She picked up his business card, tapping it against the desk. Martin. That was it: DC Oliver Martin. A prickling sensation, like eyes boring into her back, caused Dianne to glance up. She caught the young man in the Adidas tracksuit staring at her. His gaze was unsettling, too intense for her liking. How much had he heard? Narrowing her eyes, she quickly checked his name on the system: Jason Watts. Noted. He might find it harder to secure an appointment the next time he called.

Satisfied with her petty act of retribution, Dianne tried to concentrate on her work. She needed to file the morning's paperwork and ensure all the patient records were updated. But as she settled back into her chair, she jabbed the keyboard a little too hard in her frustration. A sharp pain shot through her index finger, and she winced, seeing the split in her nail. A crack in the perfectly polished French tip and a metaphorical crack in her usually poised demeanour.

CHAPTER 27

THE VIEW FROM THE portlight was captivating, but Zephyr's gentle rocking did nothing to calm Cooper's nerves. She watched the sky darkening, causing the sea to dull with it. Short, choppy waves rippled west towards the shore. Towards home. Of course, they were too far out to see the shore, but she thought of home nonetheless, and it wasn't a comforting thought given her last conversation with Atkinson.

Her phone started to chirp. It was Keaton – a welcome distraction. They spoke for a few minutes while Keaton updated her. They were trying to locate Daniel Finch, Colin Finch's nephew, but had no luck at his parents' house and were gathering some local intel to try to work out where he might be.

When she hung up, she noticed Whyte had joined her, his serious features etched with... she didn't know. Anxiety, maybe.

"Got a minute?" he asked, his voice low.

She froze, thinking, *here it comes*. "Bit busy. Thought I'd speak with India and go over her statement again. Make sure she's one hundred per cent sure about who was and wasn't on the bridge. Can it wait?"

"It's... personal. Important." He shifted his weight, looking intently out the portlight.

Her stomach dropped. She'd seen the looks, caught the lingering glances. But she'd hoped...

"Look, whatever it is—" she started.

"Please." The raw emotion in his voice caught her off guard. "I need to talk to you."

It wasn't like she could run away. She was trapped on the bloody boat with him until morning.

"Okay," Cooper said, steeling herself. "What is it?"

Whyte took a deep breath. "It's about my father."

She blinked. "Your dad?"

He nodded, his face tightening. "Remember I told you about his dementia? It's been rough."

Relief flooded through Cooper, followed quickly by shame. She'd been so wrapped up in her own paranoia that she'd forgotten about Whyte's personal struggles. *It's not all about you, Erica.*

"How's he doing?" she asked softly.

He ran a hand through his dark hair. "Some days are better than others. I still take him to church every Sunday and then out for lunch afterwards. He likes the routine, you know?"

Cooper nodded, picturing Whyte patiently guiding his father through the familiar motions, sitting in the same pew in church, the same table at the pub.

"Sometimes he's grand," Whyte continued. "Cracking jokes, telling stories about the old days. But other times..." He trailed off, his eyes distant.

"He gets confused?" she prompted gently.

"And agitated. Doesn't know where he is, who I am." Whyte's voice cracked slightly. "It's like watching him slip away, bit by bit."

Cooper's heart ached for him. She wanted to reach out, offer some comfort, but she held back.

He took a shaky breath. "But that's not why I wanted to talk. Dad's been diagnosed with cancer."

The words hit Cooper like a physical blow. Her scars seemed to twinge at the mere mention of the word. "Oh, Whyte. I'm so sorry."

He nodded, swallowing hard. "It's pancreatic. That's... that's actually why I wanted to talk to you. I thought, well, with your experience... You can tell me to mind my own business. I understand if you don't want to talk about it."

Cooper felt a wave of remorse wash over her. All Whyte wanted was some insight into what his father might face. Some reassurance.

"Of course," she said quickly. "Anything I can do to help."

They waited while a group of technicians hurried by on their way to the mess for dinner, their conversation peppered with words like starving and famished.

"I'm so hungry, I'd eat a buttered brick," exclaimed one technician, which was misheard, causing belly laughs from the others.

Cooper breathed deeply, her mind jumping back to her own treatment. "If he needs radiotherapy and chemo, it'll be tough," she said, her voice soft but steady. "The fatigue can be overwhelming. Some days, just getting out of bed feels like climbing Everest."

He finally looked at her, drinking in every word.

"There might be nausea, hair loss," she continued.

"He doesn't have any," he half-joked.

"Not just up here," Cooper said, running her hand over her buzzcut. "His eyebrows, his eyelashes. All of it. But it's important to know everyone's experience is different. How I felt might not be the same for your dad."

Whyte nodded, his jaw clenched tight. Cooper could see the worry etched into every line of his face.

"The most important thing," she said, leaning forward slightly, "is to be there for him. To help him through the bad days and celebrate the good ones."

A memory flashed through Cooper's mind – Tina bringing her tea in bed, making her laugh when everything felt hopeless. She couldn't remember what Tina had said to make her laugh now, but she remembered the feeling of laughing so hard her sides hurt.

"I don't know what I would've done without Tina," Cooper admitted. "Having someone there made all the difference. I still feel bad she had to take that on when she was so young. I mean, if anyone should have been holding my hair back while I spewed, it should have been Fuller."

The nurse had warned her at the time about how a shocking number of men leave their wives or girlfriends after a cancer diagnosis. *Poor women*, she thought. *Neil would never do that.*

"You and Fuller?" Whyte raised a thick brow. "He was punching well above his weight."

She smiled. He was right. Cooper just didn't know it at the time.

Then Whyte's expression hardened again; his eyes glistened with unshed tears. "I'm scared, Coop," he confessed, his usual emotionless facade crumbling. "I don't know what to do."

"Be a good son. That's what you do. You keep his routine, take him to his appointments, speak with his doctors, keep his fridge stocked. That sort of thing."

"I can do that," he said wearily.

"And you do it all with a smile."

They stood silently for a moment, the faint hum of the boat's systems providing a backdrop to their thoughts.

Without thinking, Cooper wrapped her arms around Whyte. He stiffened for a moment, then melted into the embrace.

CHAPTER 28

THE HEAT OF THEIR bodies mingled together as they stood there, lost in the moment. Cooper could feel the rise and fall of Whyte's chest against hers, their heartbeats almost in sync.

Cooper's palm traced down Whyte's spine in a soothing gesture. She felt a shiver run through him. The tension and pain of the past few days drifted away, replaced by a sense of connection and understanding.

As Cooper pulled back slightly to look into Whyte's eyes, she saw a mix of gratitude, sadness, and wanting. Before she could second-guess herself, their faces inched closer, her lips parting.

The kiss was brief, no more than two seconds, but long enough for their tongues to meet in a fleeting, charged touch that left them both breathless. It was intense, a spark of electricity passing between them as they yearned for more.

It was a kiss fifteen years in the making. One they would have shared as new recruits had Whyte not made a mistake and Cooper not held it against him for over a decade.

Just as quickly, they broke the embrace, cheeks flushing, neither knowing what to say. The reality of the moment slapped them both, and they started apologising at once.

"I'm so sorry—"

"No, it was my fault—"

Whyte chuckled awkwardly. Cooper looked at the sea through the portlight to sea, feeling sick to her stomach.

But before she could untangle her feelings further, raised, angry voices echoed from the mess. The sudden intrusion shattered Cooper's thoughts, bringing her back to Odin's Gale, the SOV, the murder.

The two detectives exchanged a look, the unspoken understanding that they were there to work and whatever was happening required their attention.

Inside the mess, tables of technicians in black polo shirts and the ship's crew in their white polos, all stared at the only table of people not in uniform. Five of them, all in jeans and jumpers, were gesturing at a laptop on their table. Two of them stood, pointing angrily at the screen.

"That's the research team," Whyte told her. "From the university."

"The same ones from Electron?"

"Looks to be. We ran background checks on them all. Nothing came up."

197

They approached. The laptop was playing the six o'clock news. Words scrolled across the bottom while a balding man addressed the camera from the sandy expanse of Bamburgh Beach. The laptop screen flickered, casting a blue glow across the scientists' faces. Cooper's eyes narrowed as she watched the news correspondent's face, tight with manufactured concern.

"Shocking data... catastrophic bird deaths... linked to offshore wind farms."

"That's bullshit," one of the scientists shouted.

"What's going on?" Cooper asked, her voice authoritative. They quietened, turning to look at her.

Whyte made a quick introduction. "This is Dr Hartley, the lead marine biologist."

Hartley, in a knitted green sweater, with her long, grey hair tied in a plait, held her hands up in frustration.

"They've completely misrepresented our findings, that's what. This is outrageous!" She stood. "Sorry, I need to phone these fools. Get this nonsense straightened out."

As Hartley left, another of the group spoke up. "Hi. I'm Ben," he said with a shy wave. "Somehow, they've got hold of our data—"

"Someone leaked it," said another in an Indian accent.

"We don't know that," Ben continued. "We could have been hacked. Anyway, they've got hold of our data, and it's the top story nationally. We're pissed off because they've messed with the figures. They're quoting total bird deaths. With avian influenza ripping through the country, we've been sending specimens to the lab for diagnosis, trying to establish what percentage are killed that way and what percentage we can accurately attribute to Odin's Gale."

"Michael," a scientist in a black hoodie said, introducing himself. "Look, we're not pro or anti-wind farms. We're pro-science. We just want the truth. Are wind farms killing birds?"

"And are they?" Cooper asked, genuinely interested.

He shoved his hands into the pocket of his hoodie. "Yes. But not in the numbers you might think. A drop in the ocean – pardon the pun – compared to how many die because of cars, or from flying into windows, or because of cats. Do you know how many birds die because of domestic cats?"

She shrugged, thinking of her conversation with Luna Sinclair. "I'm guessing a lot."

"Fifty-five million a year."

Cooper let out a low whistle.

"And that's just the UK. But you don't see anyone lobbying to ban cats, do you?"

Whyte snorted. "My downstairs neighbour's cat's a right menace. Wouldn't mind—"

Cooper shot him a sideways look.

"But I digress. The reason we're really pissed is because what we've actually found is that offshore turbines create artificial reefs. Plants grow on the bases, which encourages more fish. The waters here are teeming with fish, providing food for the seals and, you guessed it, the seabirds. We've tagged the seals. They go from turbine to turbine feeding. Then, whoosh, they're straight off to the next wind farm. It's actually fascinating."

It was.

"But that's not the headline they go with, is it?" Ben said, slapping his hand on the table. "No. The damn doom-mongers just want to distort our findings. That little weasel..." He jabbed his finger towards the correspondent. "...Probably took a backhander from big oil."

"Wait! Shut up for a second." Michael paused the news, rewinding ten seconds. He played it again. "Two hundred and three?" He opened a new tab and scrolled through a spreadsheet. "Whoever leaked our data didn't even give them our latest figures. They're quoting stats from two weeks ago."

He spun the laptop around, pointing at a date stamp. "Look here. This table is from two weeks ago. It's completely outdated."

Cooper wondered, as much to take her mind off the man standing next to her as anything else, why someone would leak the data from the marine life study. And why release old data? Was it intentional misdirection or sloppy work? Would oil and gas giants really stoop so low as to hack the information, manipulate it and send it to the major news outlets? Probably, she concluded, but it was not her concern right now.

HOURS LATER, AFTER DARK, Cooper found herself in a small cabin that had been made up for her. The room was sparse but comfortable, with bunk beds, a desk, a chair, and a television. It was similar to Luna Sinclair's quarters on Electron but not as modern.

As she settled into the bottom bunk, Cooper struggled to relax. The gentle rocking of the ship felt like an incessant reminder of where she was: two hundred nautical miles from home.

She pulled out her phone, thumb hovering over Tina's name. Sighing, she typed a message asking how the game had gone.

Kicked ass. 45 - 10.

Cooper showered Tina with compliments. As she waited for a response, her thoughts drifted to Atkinson. She fired off another text.

Miss you.

Minutes ticked by. No reply.

Cooper stared at the silent phone as she lay there in the dark, a knot of guilt and absolute panic forming in her stomach.

Cooper berated herself, her thoughts spiralling. What had she been thinking? Would Whyte tell anyone? Would rumours start spreading through the department? She tumbled through the implications – this wasn't just a slip of passion; it was a breach of professional conduct. She had spent years building a reputation, and now, with one impulsive moment, she risked a reputation of a completely different kind.

Her heart pounded at the thought of Atkinson finding out. How could she begin to explain this to him? She imagined his hurt and betrayal, the disappointment in his eyes. The thought of him knowing the truth filled her with dread, and she catastrophised about him leaving, or worse, leaving and wanting to take Danny with him. The fear of Atkinson's reaction clawed at her, but she was equally frightened of what it meant for her own sense of self. She had to make things right.

The quiet in her room felt oppressive, broken only by muffled movements from the next cabin where Whyte had settled in.

She fought the urge to knock on his door, to share her growing unease and ask what his intentions were, if he planned on telling anyone. Instead, she lay back on the narrow bunk, mind whirling with unanswered questions and, worse, the lingering warmth of their earlier kiss.

She closed her eyes, preying a deep sleep would soon engulf her, but a tentative knock on the cabin door made her flinch in the darkness. She sat up, eyes wide open.

CHAPTER 29

HEART POUNDING, COOPER SQUINTED at the cabin door. She wasn't ready for this conversation. Didn't know if she trusted herself. Another rap, more insistent this time.

She swung her legs off the bunk, bare feet hitting cold lino. She wrapped the bedsheets around her bare frame and cracked the door open, peering into the dimly lit corridor. It wasn't Whyte who stared back at her; it was Georgie Peters, his weathered face creased with deep lines.

"DCI Cooper," he said, just above a whisper. "Sorry to wake you. I need a word."

She blinked, mind still foggy. "What's wrong?"

Georgie glanced down the hall. "I lied to you," he said.

"Excuse me?"

"Not a lie exactly," he said, swallowing. "A lie of omission. I didn't tell you something I should have."

She studied him, noting the tension in his posture, the way his hands didn't fidget or twitch at all. As if he'd been trained never to show nerves. "About Jude's murder?"

He nodded. "I should've told you sooner. I need to get it off my chest."

Cooper was very aware of the thin sheet covering her. "Give me a minute to dress," Cooper said. "I'll meet you in the medical bay."

He gave a curt nod and strode away, his footsteps echoing in the quiet ship.

Cooper shut the door, leaning against it. What had the medic left out? Why tell her now, in the dead of night?

She pulled on her trousers and blouse, hesitating at the woollen jumper folded on the desk. It was cold, but she left it where it was.

THE LIGHTING IN THE medical bay was harsh and bright, causing Cooper to squint as she entered. Georgie stood by a metal cabinet, his back to her, shoulders hunched.

"So, Georgie," Cooper said, "what couldn't wait till morning?"

He turned. He looked exhausted. "The night before the captain and first mate were attacked, I was up late. Really late. I was on the phone with an old friend who lives in Australia now. He had some bad news regarding his health and I thought he could do with some cheering up."

Cooper nodded, not understanding where this was going. "And?"

"I'd had less than three hours of sleep when the impact woke me." Georgie's voice cracked. He cleared his throat. "If I'd had more sleep, if I'd been more alert when it all happened, maybe..." There was a haunted look in his eyes. Remnants of old battles. "Maybe things would have been different. Jude might still be alive."

"Do you really believe that?"

He paced the room before sitting behind his desk, shoulders rounded. He pointed to the chair opposite, the way he had when they'd first met on Electron. "No," he admitted. "Jude was gone long before I got there. After that amount of blood loss, there was nothing to be done."

"Then why torture yourself?" Cooper pressed, sensing there was more.

He rested his elbows on the desk, leaned forward and lowered his voice. "Because I wasn't the only one up late that night."

Interesting. "Go on."

"I saw Gray when I was walking back to my cabin. He was just wandering the corridors like he was in a daze. It was four in the morning. He looked... troubled."

Whyte had studied the shift patterns of everyone on board. Gray was off watch. He was due to start work with India at eight. He should have been in bed.

"Thank you for telling me," Cooper said. "Did he say anything?"

"Only that he couldn't sleep. I know being up past your bedtime isn't incriminating, and Gray, well, he's the sensitive sort. I don't think he'd have it in him. But..."

"You thought I should know? You did the right thing." Cooper was very interested to see what Gray Bell had told DI Singh when they talked. Was someone else lying by omission?

Seemingly relieved to clear his conscience, Georgie stood, pulling his shoulder blades together. "There's one other thing." He paused, then opened a cabinet. "Bandages are missing. Codeine too."

Cooper caught the implication. "Someone's treating their own injuries? Self-medicating?"

Georgie nodded grimly. "Someone who didn't want to come to me."

Chapter 30

Cooper left Zephyr as soon as the boarding ramp hit the quayside. It wasn't quite daylight, but the sky had softened from inky black to porpoise grey. Cooper's parting words to Whyte were brief and businesslike.

"Something's come up, and I'm needed on Electron. Can you arrest Cliff Longacre, collect prints and DNA, and have his phone sent to digital forensics? Interview him again, see if his story changes at all."

He nodded, his jaw clenched, eyes fixed on her, but when he opened his mouth to speak, Cooper added, "I think everything else should wait. For now." Her voice was as tight as her chest.

Her footsteps echoed on the quay as she left one ship in favour of another. Her handbag felt heavy on her thin shoulders, weighed down by Whyte's jumper, neatly folded at the bottom, under her planner, phone, and purse.

Before leaving Zephyr, Cooper had obtained Singh's notes from his chat with Graham Bell: the third officer hadn't mentioned wandering the ship at four in the morning. It was approaching five when she woke him and asked for an interview. Cooper had hoped to catch him in a lie, but Gray offered the information freely. When asked why he failed to mention it last time, he talked of shock, stress and confusion.

Fair enough, Cooper thought. If she changed her mind, she'd bring him in for further questioning, but for now, she wanted to know what the forensic team had for her.

Electron loomed before her as she walked along the wharf. The ship was a hulking metal beast of Granny Smith green, its topsides sparkling with early morning dew.

The kiss. The guilt. The case. Cooper felt a pang in her gut. She pushed it down, focusing on the task at hand, striding towards the ship where the familiar lean figure of Sean Hargreaves intercepted her. He wore a brown suit and pristine shirt.

"Welcome back ashore, DCI Cooper."

Cooper figured he knew fine well that Zephyr would be out at sea all night and suspected he'd withheld that information on purpose.

Her eyes narrowed. "Mr Hargreaves."

"When can VāyuVolt expect Electron back in service?" he asked, his tone pressing.

"When the investigation's complete."

Hargreaves scowled. "We have deadlines to meet. Surely—"

"Surely you understand a murder investigation takes precedence over profits." Cooper cut him off, her hard stare boring into him. "Your first mate is still in Intensive Care."

Hargreaves opened his mouth to argue, but Cooper brushed past him, pausing at the gangway and taking a deep breath. Solve the murder, she told herself. Take care of everything else later.

"Well, well, look what the cat dragged in," a voice called out.

Cooper's heart skipped a beat. Atkinson. Tall and handsome despite the white forensic onesie.

She turned to face him, forcing a neutral expression. "Hey, you."

"Dirty stop out," he said with a wink.

Cooper's cheeks burned.

He gave her an apologetic smile. "Sorry I didn't text you back. Danny was sick after we got home from the game, and once I'd bathed him and read him a story, I was out for the count."

She swallowed hard, fighting back the sudden urge to cry. "Don't worry about it. So, what's the latest?"

"Oh, you're going to love this. Follow me."

They fell into step, heading through Electron's passageways to the bridge.

The nerve centre of Electron remained in organised chaos. The SOCOs had peppered the high-tech room with their usual tiny stickers and miniature flags, identifying every possible forensic clue.

"The storage on here is something else," he said. "There are lockers and drawers everywhere. Under every console, built into the chairs, everywhere."

Atkinson rested a gloved hand against a wall. "But feast your eyes on this little surprise."

He pressed the wall firmly. There was a soft click, then a panel, almost indistinguishable from its surroundings, swung open.

"A hidden compartment," Cooper gasped.

"Exactly. This one houses a safe. I got the code from India Morgan. Nothing of interest in there as far as we're concerned, but next door..." He pressed another panel and it opened to reveal circuit boards, servers and hard drives.

She stepped closer, taking in the intricate mess of technology before her.

"Almost all of this wall houses the gadgetry behind Electron. They're crammed with wires and cooling fans. All except this one where..." His eyes practically sparkled. "...where there's a small space behind the graphics processing unit. It's about thirty-five centimetres cubed. Big enough to hide—"

"A pair of boots?"

"Take a look," he said, handing her a small torch. "Thought you'd like to see them in situ."

Without a word, Cooper peered into the dark space, angling the torch to cut through the shadows in the hidden compartment. Her breath caught as the beam revealed brown leather streaked with crimson. "Holy shit."

"You told me to tear the boat apart looking for them. No wonder we couldn't find a trace of them in Cliff Longacre's room or anywhere else. The boots never left the bridge."

Cooper echoed the words under her breath. "The boots never left the bridge."

Her eyes scanned around the room, trying to place herself within the crime as it happened.

"Longacre waits until the captain is alone, murders him, but is disturbed by the first mate, who he subsequently attacks and leaves for dead. He doesn't want to leave a trail of breadcrumbs, so he removes and stashes his boots, and what? Tip-toes out of here in his socks?"

Atkinson shrugged. "Potentially."

As she surveyed the room, Cooper couldn't shake the feeling that they were missing something crucial. "I don't suppose anything else was hiding in there?"

"Like the murder weapon or the balaclava? I'm afraid not."

She pursed her lips, thinking. "Hal described the weapon as a kitchen knife."

"Doesn't Longacre's wife work in the galley?"

He was right. "She does indeed. Have you—?"

"Any knife with even a remotely sharp blade is bagged and in the lab. We can't test them all for microscopic traces of DNA, though. The budget would never allow it. But I do have photographs of them all. If Hal can narrow it down, we could test a few of them."

"Good idea."

She'd take the photos to the hospital as soon as she left Electron. She'd ask Whyte to do it, but she wasn't ready to talk to him yet. Not until she'd got a grip on her nerves.

"I know what you're thinking."

Cooper froze, realising she'd been staring out the huge window facing upriver towards Newcastle. *God, I hope not.*

"You're thinking, *what if someone else was wearing Cliff Longacre's boots when they attacked those two men?*"

A red herring. The thought had crossed her mind. But if that was the case, the killer could be anyone with size fourteen feet or smaller, which was, unfortunately, every single other person who had been aboard that day. In other words, they were back to square one. Unless...

"Whyte should have Longacre's prints and swab samples within the hour," she said, her voice tight.

They already had a bloody footprint; if they could match his fingerprints, blood or saliva to the scene, they'd have a solid case, especially if they found it on the panel housing the electronics. The investigation might be floundering, but it wasn't flotsam. Not yet.

CHAPTER 31

A NERVOUS ENERGY SIMMERED throughout the conference room. DI Singh regarded the cramped space packed wall-to-wall with DCs and PCs. Strip lighting accentuated the bags under the eyes of those present. Some very experienced veterans. Most young pups. Some were female. Most were male. A handful of sergeants were sitting in on the action, ready to enjoy the show. Singh's crisp stone-coloured three-piece suit stood out amidst the black uniforms. A half-eaten jalebi, abandoned on a napkin, taunted him from the podium. He'd finish it later.

He'd considered handling this quietly, giving everyone a friendly warning, but being typecast as a soft touch would not do. He knew he had a reputation for manners, but his politeness should never be mistaken for weakness.

Singh's gaze flickered onto DCs Martin and Boyd. The young man squirmed, averting his eyes.

Singh recalled their earlier conversation, the way Martin's voice quivered as he confessed, exported the chat and emailed a copy to him. He'd told Martin he'd done the right thing in phoning him, tried to reassure him that his whistleblowing would stay between them, yet Martin sat with his hands tucked under his thighs so no one could see them shake.

Singh stood and smoothed his suit jacket as a hush fell over the room. He turned to a whiteboard.

Boys will be boys.

In impeccable handwriting, the words glared in red ink. Confused murmurs rippled through the crowd.

"Who has heard this saying?" Singh's voice cut through the chatter.

A smattering of nods. DC Martin's head dipped slightly, his eyes downcast. He wasn't the only one. Singh's fingers twitched, resisting the urge to adjust his tie. He scanned the room, noting the subtle shifts in posture, the averted gazes, the clenched jaws.

"I do not subscribe to this philosophy," he continued, projecting his voice, speaking to those in the back row as much as the front. "In fact, as the father of two girls, I believe boys will be..."

The marker squeaked as he crossed out the final word, replacing it with five more. He read the new phrase slowly and confidently, stabbing the board with the marker as he enunciated each word one at a time.

"Boys. Will. Be. Held. Accountable. For. Their. Actions."

The room fell silent.

Singh caught a few of the younger DCs' expressions, their faces drained of colour. Splendid, Singh thought. Let them sweat.

Near the back of the room, Keaton looked amused, impressed even.

He took a deep breath, his nostrils flaring slightly, taking power from the purposeful pause.

"If you have no idea what I'm talking about, then good for you," he said, his voice slow and controlled. "I hope you being here to witness this will serve as a deterrent." The tension in the room ratcheted up a notch. "However, if you are one of the children involved in this disgraceful WhatsApp group..."

He held up a file containing pages and pages of A4 paper. "The Not-So-PC-PCs, you are about to be held accountable for your actions. Some of you will be put on the naughty step, some of you will be grounded, and some of you are about to be kicked out of home."

A sharp intake of breath from somewhere in the back as the metaphor sank in.

In the crowd, a whisper of, "Who grassed?"

Singh's gaze swept the room, searching for any telltale reactions.

"Time to reflect on your behaviour," he said, locking eyes with some of the audience. Martin looked ready to bolt, but he held his nerve. "Later today, the Independent Office for Police Conduct will begin sifting through this drivel, but I've taken the liberty of highlighting a few of my favourites. Let's start with Bensham being referred to as *Benshamistan* and a domestic abuse victim being labelled a *pikey* before her breasts were rated – and I quote – a solid six out of ten."

Singh's usually soft voice was edged with steel as he continued. "A gross misconduct panel will discipline several of you for failing to report or challenge these messages. The rest of you, the ones who wrote messages deemed inappropriate, offensive, or that breach police standards of professional behaviour, you *will* be fired, you *will* be thrown to the press."

The threat hung in the air, heavy and palpable. He let the silence stretch, watching as the seriousness of his words settled on the room. Faces shifted from anger to resignation.

"Behaviour of this kind undermines public confidence. It undermines *my* confidence in all of you."

And judging by the looks on some of their fellow PC and DCs' faces, he knew they felt the same. Some were disgusted at what they'd heard, and others barely recognised colleagues they thought they knew.

"Now," he said finally, "anyone not in my department, get out of here."

The room remained still for a heartbeat before the shuffling began, a speedy exodus of those with guilty consciences. He watched them file out until only a few remained.

"Bloody hell," said Keaton, laughing. "Remind me not to get on your bad side. Have to say, calling them children and telling them they were on the naughty step was a nice touch."

Singh picked up what remained of his jalebi, savoured it, then asked, "Who's the daddy?"

CHAPTER 32

"YOU'RE THE DADDY," KEATON CONFIRMED. "Can I smell cardamom?"

Singh brandished a Tupperware box from under the desk. As he peeled the lid away, the sweet scent of citrus and saffron wafted over the now almost empty room. Without the hordes of worried faces, the space seemed vacuous and oversized for their meeting of four.

"Jalebi?" Singh's eyes twinkled as he offered the coiled orange spiral treats to the others. "Made them fresh last night."

Keaton leaned forward, eyeing the pastries. "Bit early for dessert, isn't it?"

"Nonsense," Singh chuckled. "It's never too early for jalebi."

Keaton let out a pleasurable groan. "So good. April used to make something similar." Then, after a long pause. "Yes, I mentioned the ex. No need for the awkward silence, guys."

Boyd took a tentative bite; her eyes widened. "Oh wow, that's incredible."

Martin shook his head. "I'm not hungry."

"Come on," Singh said, trying to reassure him with a smile and a shake of the Tupperware. "You need the sugar. It's done now. You'll get a slap on the wrist for not reporting it—"

"But he did report it," Boyd interrupted.

Martin gave her a pitiful look. "I'd prefer it this way. If I'm the only one not to receive any disciplinary action..." He didn't need to finish the sentence. If the others knew he was the one to dob them in, he could be shunned or bullied. "If I called for backup and none came... I guess I'm not as strong as you."

"You are. And I understand," she told him, squeezing his hand. "No one outside this room needs to know."

"Agreed," Singh added. "Now, let's put this morning's nastiness behind us and get down to business." He opened a notepad and arranged his pens and highlighters. "Let's begin with the Electron case."

Keaton and Boyd chewed quickly, the former dribbling syrup down her chin.

"News from DCI Cooper," Singh continued. "The forensic team found the mysterious size fourteen boots hidden on the bridge. They're on their way to the lab for testing. The bosun, Cliff Longacre, has been arrested. DS Elliot Whyte's processing him now. I'll be joining him to interview Cliff shortly."

Martin's face was still a sickly shade of white. "And the knife?"

"No sign of it. Cooper's headed to the hospital. She's going to see if Hal Simpson can identify it from the ones found on Electron. From there, the lab may run DNA analysis."

Keaton snorted. "That knife's probably at the bottom of the North Sea."

Singh nodded grimly. "Perhaps. Perhaps not. I've got Dr Swanson's report here." He handed out copies to the three others. "The murder weapon is confirmed as a small, single-sided blade. Very small in the scale of the knife attacks we usually see. This wasn't a single wound to the jugular or femoral artery. This was—"

"Death by a thousand cuts?"

Singh nodded at Boyd. "Indeed. Or three hundred and thirty-one cuts, to be precise."

Silence fell over the room as they digested the information. A small blade. Easy to conceal. Easy to dispose of.

Singh shuffled some papers, his brow creasing. "Now, the Poison Garden case. Any luck with Daniel Finch?"

Keaton shook her head, frustration obvious in her voice. "Nothing yet. We visited his parents' place, but they haven't seen him in a few weeks. Apparently, that's not out of character."

Martin chimed in, "And we're still waiting on Dr Swanson for Colin's autopsy. At this point, we don't know if we're actually dealing with a murder. We're a bit stuck."

"And you've informed the authorities about the stolen plants?" Singh asked.

Keaton verified they had. "Every hospital and GP in the region should have received the alert by now."

"Right. Perhaps it's time to shift gears. That kipper fraud complaint from Craster last week – it's not a priority, but it might be worth looking into while you wait."

Keaton perked up, looking grateful for any action. "Fancy a trip up the coast?" she asked Martin, slapping him on the shoulder as she got to her feet.

Martin sighed, but there was a hint of a smile. "I suppose someone has to keep you out of trouble."

THE AIR WAS THICK with the scent of brine when Keaton stepped out of the car in Craster. Martin followed, looking less than thrilled about the brisk coastal wind.

"All right," Keaton said, surveying the village. "Let's find our angry fish wife."

The village, nestled on the rugged coastline, was a picture of rustic charm. Stone cottages with weathered roofs huddled together, the occasional chimney puffing gently like an old man smoking a pipe. The crescent-shaped harbour held a handful of fishing boats that bobbed lazily on the water, their reflections rippling.

In the distance, the imposing ruins of Dunstanburgh Castle watched over the village, its jagged silhouette standing out against the sky.

Keaton and Martin didn't have to look far.

A woman in skinny jeans with weather-beaten skin was smoking on her doorstep, gesticulating wildly at her nervous-looking neighbour.

"Daring to pass off that cheap rubbish as Craster kippers. Calling himself the Kipper King?"

Her voice carried over the caws of seagulls and the crashing of waves against the breakwater.

"That's got to be our smoker's wife," Keaton muttered. "What was her name again?"

Martin consulted his notes. "Maggie Ryle."

"—Kipper King indeed. The only thing royal about his product is how royally bad it is."

"Mrs Ryle?" Keaton asked, interrupting her rant. "DS Keaton and DC Martin. We're here about the complaint you filed. Wondered if you'd like to make a statement."

"Gladly." Maggie handed her cigarette to her neighbour and led the detectives indoors into her humble but immaculately tidy home. Maggie Ryle was clearly the sort of woman who couldn't abide dusty dado rails or fingerprints on her kitchen cupboards.

"Tea? Coffee? I can whip up some kippers on toast if you like."

Keaton didn't know how well kippers and jalebi would mix in her stomach, so she politely refused. "We're good, thank you. I understand there was an altercation over the weekend?"

Maggie sighed, resting her back against the kitchen counter. "It was Saturday, and yes, things got a little heated. My husband and I run one of the smokehouses. He's a third-generation smoker. We've been featured in Living North, been on the local news, and Kensington Palace even placed an order once. I don't mean to brag; I'm just trying to get across that we're an established business, and people know us."

"You're a local institution," added Martin.

"Exactly." Maggie filled the kettle. "If you're not having a cuppa, I still need one." She flicked the switch and added a tea bag to a mug. "But having a well-established brand doesn't mean we're raking it in. Margins are tight and rents are high. Plus, the bloody energy companies are taking the piss with their price hikes. Anyway, the weekends are our biggest trading days. We can't afford to have a weekend off because that's when you get folk coming up from Newcastle or down from Scotland for the day. Or further afield. I'm hearing more and more London accents these days. But on Saturday, no one was coming into the smokehouse. Not one soul. So I went out to see if the world had ended or something, and guess what?"

Keaton didn't get a chance to guess.

"Some little toe rag had set up a stall right by the harbour. Big sign behind the stall calling himself the Kipper King. Wearing a crown and everything. As if! Now, because of where he's set up, anyone following the coastal path from the castle will bump into him before coming to the smokehouses. So I call some of the lads on the boats, but none of them have heard of him. No one's got any new buyers. So I have a gander at his produce, and I swear to our almighty, he's buying cheap frozen fish from one of those wholesalers, smoking them in his kitchen and trying to pass them off as the genuine article. He's robbing honest folk blind, and I told him so."

The kettle boiled and Maggie brewed her tea.

"How did he take that?"

"Oh, he huffed and puffed. I told him he was sullying the name of Craster and taking money away from local fishermen and smokers. He might have called me a silly little woman and pushed me, and I might have smacked him across the jaw."

For a moment, Keaton really hoped she'd hit him round the face with a wet fish, but she suspected she'd done it the old-fashioned way. "Excuse me? You slapped him? Punched him?"

"Punched him. Yes, I know I'm incriminating myself, but he did start it, and there were witnesses. Am I in trouble?"

Maggie added milk to her tea, not looking especially worried about falling foul of the law.

"For now, no," Keaton told her. "We'll try to find this so-called Kipper King and get a statement. But if he did push you first, I think you'll be fine."

She shrugged, nonplussed.

Martin, who'd been writing down the events as Maggie recalled them, asked her to sign and date the statement, and then they left Maggie to enjoy her tea. As they walked back along the street to the harbour, they passed a few stalls setting up to sell jewellery, local crafts, ice cream and souvenirs.

"Fancy an ice cream?" Keaton asked Martin, who trailed behind on his crutches. His face was still downturned and sullen.

"It's November."

"Oh, come on." She hated seeing him like this. "If it's never too early for jalebi, it's never too cold for ice cream. My treat. When we were little, Riley and I would always buy either the weirdest flavour ice cream we could find or the weirdest combination if our Dad was in one of his rare good moods and we were allowed two scoops."

After settling on the two-scoop combo of coconut and activated charcoal – one snow white and the other jet black – Keaton and Martin disagreed on which they liked better, with Keaton preferring the slightly smoky undertone of the charcoal.

As she finished her unconventional dessert, Keaton's eyes widened. "Well, I'll be damned. Look who's back."

The Kipper King had returned with his stall, setting up shop as if nothing had happened. With a plastic crown perched on his head, he hailed passing hikers, offering three for two on his smoked fish.

"You'd think he'd have learned his lesson after getting decked at the weekend," Martin said, approaching the stall and flashing his ID. "Sir, are these authentic Craster kippers?"

The Kipper King was a larger-than-life figure with a burly build, barrel chest and forearms like

Popeye. His face was round, pale, and smooth as if he had spent his days indoors applying moisturiser rather than in fishing boats and smokehouses.

The Kipper King stammered, straightening his crown. "Well, they're... inspired by—"

A voice from the other side of the harbour cut them off. "They're garbage is what they are!" Maggie yelled, wagging a finger as she marched towards them, fury written on her face.

Keaton winced. "Looks like we're just in time for round two."

"You've got some nerve." Maggie walked right up to the man; she looked so small in comparison but didn't flinch, looking him dead in the eyes. "You're a fraudster and a—"

"Hey, darling, everyone's entitled to earn a living."

"Don't *darling* me," Maggie snarled, giving him the hackiest of hacky looks. "These are cheap knockoffs."

Keaton held up a hand. "We'll sort this out, Mrs Ryle. For now, why don't we all take a breather?"

But in a flash, she was on the Kipper King, her fist connecting with his nose. Blood sprayed as he staggered backwards in shock.

"Bloody hell," Keaton muttered, rushing forward. She grabbed Maggie's arm, restraining her. "That's assault, Mrs Ryle. You're looking at charges this time."

The Kipper King, holding his bleeding nose, waved a hand. "No, no charges. I'll go. Just... keep that mad woman away from me. She's a right lunatic! I don't need this kind of trouble."

The Kipper King started to pack his things away while Maggie continued her rant, taunting him, accusing him of only refusing to press charges because he knew he was a fraud.

Keaton sighed, only releasing Maggie once the Kipper King was safely in his van and driving away. She'd still have to caution the woman. She might have got away with Saturday's punch, but today's? Unprovoked and right in front of two officers? No. Maggie Ryle would be arrested for assault. Still, Keaton was impressed. She thought her old rugby mates were tough; the herring girls were apparently on another level.

Chapter 33

Hal's slumber was interrupted by the rhythmic beep of the heart monitor hooked up to the man in the next bed. Not that he'd slept well. Aside from the induced sleep on his first night here, he'd been plagued by nightmares, waking in pain, dripping in sweat. He blinked, adjusting to the harsh strip lighting on the ward's ceiling. Six days. Six long days since he was stretchered onto the deck of Electron, loaded into a helicopter, and airlifted to the RVI hospital.

He may have only just awoken, but it wasn't morning. It was early evening, and a curvaceous nurse with kind eyes was fussing over his dinner. She cut his chicken into bite-sized morsels so he wouldn't struggle with his knife and fork.

"You're one lucky lad, Mr. Simpson." She shook her head, tutting.

He'd been told that over and over since he got here. Been told how he was lucky to be alive, that if he'd lost any more blood or if the wound on his leg had been an inch to the right.

Lucky. They kept saying that word, but it felt like a joke. He didn't feel lucky. He felt sore and scared. His body ached from the wounds, but his mind was worse. Trapped. Every time he closed his eyes, he could still feel the knife, see the blood.

"Now, are you sure you're all right with your spoon? I don't mind staying and helping you eat."

Hal winced as he picked up his spoon in his bandaged hand. "I'll manage," he told her. To be honest, he wanted to be left alone.

As she bustled away, Hal spooned chicken and vegetables into his mouth, the taste barely registering. The pain meds were kicking in, wrapping his body in cotton wool and his mind in a comforting fog.

Sleep. He needed more sleep. But Hal's hopes of drifting straight off after dinner were dashed. Apparently, the detective with the short hair was on her way to see him. The last thing he wanted to do was go over the gory details again.

His gaze drifted to his left hand, heavily bandaged. Layers of gauze covered deep gashes across his palm and fingers. The memory of the blade slicing his skin was still raw, sending waves of panic through him.

COOPER PAUSED AT THE foot of Hal Simpson's bed, taking in every detail. He looked better than the last time she'd seen him. His skin had regained some colour, though his eyes were still rimmed with exhaustion. The fear was still there, lurking behind his eyes, and his glasses needed cleaning, his curly brown hair greasy and unwashed.

His space in the ward was less sparse than before. Someone must have brought him his belongings from Electron. A mobile phone was plugged in, charging. A duffle bag of clothing was open at the foot of his bed, and his glasses case and some chocolates were on the bedside cabinet.

"How're you feeling today, Hal?" Cooper asked while a nurse checked his vitals and removed a dinner plate littered with leftover chicken and vegetables.

"Exhausted," Hal croaked.

"There's been a development in the case. I wanted to let you know we've arrested Cliff Longacre."

She expected relief, shock, maybe even satisfaction. Instead, Hal's face crumpled.

"Sorry. Sorry. It's just a lot to take in. Cliff? Really? I mean, I knew it was one of the bigger blokes onboard, but— Cliff? I never thought..."

He grimaced, looking at a wound on his arm, tears welling in his eyes. "Sorry. I've been really missing Jude today. I can't believe I'll never work with him again. It just doesn't seem real that he's gone."

Cooper's throat tightened. "It's going to take a long time for you to process it all, Hal. Have you been offered any counselling?"

He nodded. "Yes. But I can't. Not yet."

Moving closer to his bed, Cooper pulled a tablet out of her bag. "Hal, I need to show you something." She opened a digital file, and tens of image thumbnails appeared on the screen. "These are knives our forensic department took from Electron. I know it's hard, but do any of them look familiar?"

Hal squinted at the screen, fatigue evident on his face.

Each knife was photographed against a white background with a ruler beside it for scale. He scrolled slowly, brows low in concentration. Eventually, his finger hovered over one image.

"That one," he said, looking up to meet Cooper's gaze. He pointed to a small knife with a black handle. "I'm not a hundred per cent. But it looked a bit like that one."

Cooper's pulse quickened. A lead. Finally. Hal identified a knife from the kitchen where Kay Longacre worked. A potential link. She tapped out a quick message to the lab, fingers flying over her phone's screen.

> Evidence #KE-87. Priority analysis. Luminol. Hemastix. Amido. Everything.

She hit send, a smile twitching the corner of her lips. The knife had appeared clean, but appearances could be deceiving. The lab had tricks up its sleeve, ways of coaxing secrets from the most unassuming objects.

"Thank you, Hal," Cooper said, pocketing her phone and storing the tablet back in its case. "You've been a huge help."

He nodded weakly, looking lost and fragile. Cooper left Hal to recover, wondering if the young man would ever step foot on Electron again or if that day had taken more from him than just his blood.

CID WAS EMPTY WHEN Martin and Keaton returned to type up their reports. Martin rubbed his eyes, exhaustion settling in from his head down to his injured leg.

That's when he spotted it. A Tupperware box perched on a nearby desk. Singh must have left the rest of his jalebi stash. He wouldn't mind Martin helping himself to one. He'd turned them down this morning, but now his belly rumbled.

Leaving his crutches by his desk, he limped over cautiously. On closer inspection, it was a different box. His initial disappointment turned to curiosity when he read the yellow Post-it note stuck to the lid: *Dropped off at reception.*

Under the yellow note, a piece of card, no more than two inches long, decorated with roses, read: *For DS Paula Keaton and DC Oliver Martin. Thank you for all your help.*

"What've we got here?" Keaton asked, appearing at his side.

"Biscuits."

Gorgeous, golden-brown, mouthwatering biscuits.

"Mystery thank you biscuits," he specified, grabbing one. "Someone's trying to fatten us up."

"After the ice cream and jalebi, we might as well roll ourselves to crime scenes."

Keaton took one for herself, and together, they chewed, swallowed and nodded in agreement. Very tasty indeed.

Martin sat on the desk and wiggled his foot. "Any guesses on our secret admirer?"

Keaton shrugged, taking another. "Maybe Cooper's gone soft on us? No, it can't be that. Must be the home invasion in North Gosforth. They just gave him three years. The couple who owned the house were bakers, weren't they?"

"Mmm." Martin pointed at her. "That'll be it." But something nagged at him. On the same day Singh referred the WhatsApp group to the IOPC, a gift happened to appear on his desk. Had the others worked it out already? Were the biscuits packed full of laxatives? He pushed the thought aside, savouring the sweetness. Sometimes, a biscuit was just a biscuit.

AN HOUR LATER, MARTIN squinted at the report in his hand. The words blurred, refusing to come into focus. He blinked hard, rubbing his eyes.

His head throbbed, a dull ache building in his temples. Martin dropped the report, his fingers trembling as he pressed his palms hard against his forehead, as if he could somehow push the ache away.

"You all right?" Keaton's voice seemed to echo unnaturally loud.

He tried to respond, but his tongue felt thick, uncooperative. The room tilted sideways.

"I... I don't..." he slurred.

Terror seized his chest. What the hell was happening? Something was wrong. Very wrong. He tried to stand, but his legs buckled beneath him.

The last thing Martin saw was Keaton's face, eyes wide with alarm, as the floor rushed up to meet him.

Then, darkness.

CHAPTER 34

PUSHING HER TROLLEY THROUGH the aisles of the big Morrisons in Tynemouth, Cooper glanced at her shopping list, mentally ticking off the items she needed. Around her, countless others did the same thing. Commuters on their way home from work, stocking up for the weekend. Families with children in tow grabbing what they needed before Judo class or Scouts.

Her hand hovered over the avocados, feeling their smooth, waxy skin before selecting two that gave ever so slightly under pressure. She added them to the mixed salad leaves and the bag of apples. Next came free-range eggs, a few bottles of craft ale, a loaf of wholemeal bread for Atkinson, and sliced white for Tina. Try as she might to leave her work persona at CID and don the coat of mother and girlfriend, her mind still returned to the case – and to Whyte, whose jumper remained in her bag.

Hal had potentially identified the knife, giving her a much-needed confidence boost. But questions still swirled in her mind. Did Kay Longacre know Cliff had taken the knife from the galley? Perhaps she provided the weapon herself after he'd walked her to the galley that morning. Did she egg him on? Encourage him? Maybe Cliff had slipped into the kitchen with her and stolen it without her knowledge. Either way, Kay would be grilled just like her husband.

She crossed her fingers and prayed to the god of forensic science that the lab would find the evidence they needed.

Chicken breast, dried herbs, tins of chopped tomatoes. She paused in the pasta aisle, trying to remember if Tina preferred penne or farfalle, the ones shaped like little bow ties. She grabbed the penne. Olive oil, Greek yoghurt, and semi-skimmed milk.

List complete, she headed for the checkout, absentmindedly arranging the items on the conveyor belt. Fishing her phone out of her pocket in preparation to pay, something caught her eye. Their joint account balance was lower than expected. Much lower. They were down two thousand pounds.

Cooper's heart thumped as she stared at the screen, worry creeping into her thoughts. Fraudsters? Had someone hacked their account? Cloned their cards? She quickly navigated to the transactions section of the app, her hands trembling slightly.

The latest transaction stared back at her: a transfer of one grand to R. Atkinson and another to E. Atkinson. Rowan and Ellis – The twins. Relief mixed with frustration as the reality sank in. The boys' mother had asked Atkinson to help them out. He'd initially refused, but he must have changed his mind and sent them the money.

She exhaled deeply, her initial panic subsiding but giving way to irritation. It wasn't the money that bothered her – it was the lack of communication. This was their joint account, after all.

The cashier's voice broke through her thoughts. "Are you paying with your phone, pet?"

Cooper nodded blankly, swiping to complete the transaction. "Yeah. Sorry. Miles away."

"You and me both, pet."

The card reader beeped in approval, and she moved her bags to the trolley. As she drove home to Latimer Terrace, Cooper tried to suppress the anger, but it bubbled up to the surface regardless.

Back home, six crows lined the front wall, their dark forms silhouetted against the light from the living room window. Tina's habit of feeding them had turned them into permanent residents. As Cooper neared the door, one dove at her, forcing her to dart indoors just in time.

She slammed the grocery bags onto the kitchen counter.

Atkinson looked up from his laptop, surprise flashing across his face.

"Erica, you're home early—"

"Two thousand pounds? Were you planning on telling me?"

His expression shifted from surprise to guilt. "Ah. I was going to—"

"When?" Cooper's voice rose. "After you emptied our account? You said you weren't going to bail them out again."

Atkinson sighed, running a hand through his hair. "They called last night, desperate. They need money for food and rent."

"They need money for beer."

He looked like he wanted to snap at her for interrupting but held it back. "They were desperate—"

"And you couldn't wait to discuss it with me first?"

"I would have if you'd been home," He shot back. "But you were out all night on Zephyr."

Kissing your subordinate. Like Captain Jude and Mandi.

"You can't use that against me. I was working a case. It wasn't like I planned it. I couldn't exactly get airlifted back."

Cooper angrily grabbed items from her grocery bags, arranging them on the counter.

"They needed help, Erica. What was I supposed to do?"

"Discuss it with me!" Her palm hit the counter. "We're supposed to be partners."

Justin's face hardened. "Partners? You're barely here."

238

Her chest tightened, remembering Whyte's lips against hers. Was she actually angry at Atkinson, or just furious at herself?

"Sorry. That was unfair. But you weren't here, and their rent was due."

"That's not the point," she said, forcing her voice to stay level. "You can't just use our joint funds without consulting me."

"Our joint funds?" He removed his glasses, rubbing his eyes. "That's what this is about. You're mad I used our joint funds instead of my personal savings because you contribute more to them because you work full time."

Cooper flinched. She hadn't meant it like that.

"That's low." His voice was quiet, hostile. "Just because my financial contribution to this family isn't as big as yours doesn't mean my contribution overall is any less. I'm the one feeding Danny in the middle of the night, changing his nappies, ferrying him between here and Julie's."

"I know," Cooper tried to say.

"I'm the one stalling my career so you can thrive in yours."

"I know, and I'm grateful."

"I was the one courtside cheering Tina on last night. If I weren't here, she wouldn't have even been able to get to the match. And what if this were the other way around? If I was working full-time and you wanted money to spend on Tina, I wouldn't hesitate to say yes."

"Don't bring me into this."

Cooper and Atkinson froze. Tina was standing in the kitchen doorway like a teenage goth ninja with her baby brother cradled in her arms.

"If you want to give me two grand, I won't say no. But I'm bargaining on a full scholarship to Harvard or Yale. Failing that, I still have all the Bitcoin I mined. I'll be fine. No need to argue."

Cooper felt heat rise to her cheeks. "Hey T. It's fine, sweetie. We're not arguing. Just a little disagreement."

"Didn't sound little."

Atkinson forced a smile. "Nothing to worry about."

Tina looked inside the shopping bag and wrinkled her nose. "Urgh. Penne. You know I hate penne."

Cooper couldn't take it anymore. The walls felt like they were closing in. "I need some air," she muttered, grabbing her jacket.

She stormed out, the door slamming with a crack that reverberated through the quiet street. A second later, she heard Danny's wail.

Useless. You can't even close a door properly. Can't buy the right sort of pasta.

She was halfway down the path when a dark shape swooped towards her.

Pain exploded across her scalp. Sharp talons raked her skin.

"What the—"

Bloody crows.

Cooper swatted at the bird, feeling warm blood trickle down her forehead. The bird cawed noisily, circling for another attack. Before she could react, its sharp beak sliced across the top of her head. Cooper yelped in pain, swatting at the bird as it flew off. Clutching her head, she hurried into her car, blood trickling down her scalp while dark thoughts circled her mind.

Can't be a good mother.
Can't balance work and home.
Can't hold a relationship together.
Can't solve the case.

CHAPTER 35

METALLICA BLARED, THE HEAVY bass grumbling through the car as Cooper pushed into fifth gear, edging the car closer to the speed limit. She shouldn't drive this fast, this recklessly. She was a grown woman with two children and a respectable job. She was no boy racer. Yet she still accelerated, gripping the steering wheel until her knuckles bleached white. The engine's roar grew louder.

Her phone buzzed. She ignored it.

She had to breathe. She needed to get her shit together before going home.

Eighty miles per hour. Her phone lit up again. Cooper knew she shouldn't take her eyes off the road. Still, she glanced at the screen regardless. She expected to see Atkinson's name, but the missed calls, all five of them, were from Saffron Boyd.

"Damn it, Saff," Cooper muttered, slowing to seventy-five and turning off her favourite song, the one she always returned to when her mood was low. The sudden silence felt crushing.

"Saff. I'm off for the evening. I'm sure whatever it is, DI Singh can handle it."

A pause.

"Saff?"

"It's Oliver. He's in an ambulance on his way to hospital. Paula too."

Cooper's breath caught. She slammed the brakes, the seatbelt digging into her collarbone. The car lurched and skidded as she indicated and pulled into the next lay-by to a barrage of irate car horns. "What?"

She pictured Keaton – broad, strong and fearless – sprinting onto Newcastle Race Course, putting her own life in danger to pursue a desperate serial killer. She pictured Martin – young, empathetic, shy – holding his nerve while a drugged-up menace known as the Dragon threatened him with a machete. She felt sick, wondering what harm had come to them. The taste of bile and worry crept up her throat.

"What happened? Who hurt them?"

She pictured gangs, violent thugs and dealers, her mind conjuring a thousand worst-case scenarios.

"I don't know," said Boyd, her voice quivering. "They were at HQ. They both collapsed. That's all I know. I'm sorry."

"I'm on my way."

"They won't be allowed visitors," Boyd told her. "Not yet. I— I just thought you'd want to know."

Cooper sank into her seat, a hand pressed against her chest. Keaton was practically invincible. What could cause her to collapse? Exhaustion? No. That woman was never exhausted; besides, exhaustion was neither contagious nor worthy of an ambulance. Carbon monoxide?

Cooper thanked Boyd and tossed the phone aside. Back into gear. Mirror. There was a break in the traffic. Signal. She flicked the indicator. Manoeuvre. Tyres squealed as she pulled back into the main road. She'd do a one-eighty at the next roundabout and head home. She felt childish and selfish. Her argument with Atkinson seemed so stupid now – juvenile even. Two thousand pounds was nothing compared to the love, family and good health. It seemed like pennies after the phone call she'd just had. Some things were just more important.

EVERY POTHOLE JARRED KEATON'S body. The gurney rattled beneath her, the siren's wail drilling into her skull. The cramped ambulance felt claustrophobic, filled with too much equipment and not enough air. It smelled of antiseptic and the paramedic's perfume. Bright lights caused her to squint. The paramedic beside her was a young woman with a determined expression, her movements deliberate and gentle as she checked Keaton's pulse and oxygen.

"Stay with us, Paula. Keep your eyes open."

Keaton tried to nod, but her head felt as if it weighed a ton. Her heart was erratic; her mouth parched. She remembered being in CID, her heart racing out of control. She had felt confused, unable to concentrate. Her vision had blurred, and everything looked like it was behind frosted glass. Then she saw Martin collapse, his body crumpling to the floor. Panic had surged through her, giving her a momentary burst of clarity. She stumbled and caught herself on the edge of a desk. Just before she lost control, she managed to call for help. She fumbled for her phone, fingers clumsy. The keypad swirled before her eyes as she struggled to find the nine-key.

"Paula. Look at me."

Keaton's eyelids fluttered. The ambulance doors flew open, and she was wheeled out, the November chill slapping her face. Where the hell was Martin? Her tongue felt swollen as she tried to call out to him, her voice barely a whisper. Where was he? What if he was worse off than her? What if he...

Faces of doctors and nurses came in and out of focus, their voices seemingly detached from their bodies. "What did you take?"

She clutched the Tupperware to her chest. Evidence.

A blurry figure leaned over her. "Can you hear me?"

Keaton nodded, wincing at the movement.

"What did you take?"

They kept asking the same question, their faces filled with concern and urgency like they thought she and Martin had overdosed on something.

"No drugs," she croaked, her voice barely audible. She tapped the box. "Poisoned."

The Tupperware vanished from her grip, their faces tense as they spoke in hushed tones, wondering if they could get it tested.

Keaton's consciousness wavered, but she gathered all her strength to whisper. "Nightshade. Nightshade and ricin."

A sharp intake of breath. Hurried footsteps.

Through half-lidded eyes, Keaton caught the doctor's expression. Worry inscribed so deep it sent a chill down her spine.

"Try to stay awake, Paula. Look at me."

She heard nurses rattle off bullet points from the urgent alert. Keaton knew them by heart. But then, she'd written the bloody thing.

Hospitals, blood, injuries – Keaton had faced it all before without flinching. But now, seeing the alarm in the doctors' eyes, she knew this was different.

Shit, Keaton thought. *Is this it?*

"Paula?"

As her world started to dim, Keaton's thoughts turned to her younger brother, Riley. She hoped he'd be okay, that whatever happened to her, he'd be safe and wouldn't return to their father's. He'd be better on the streets than with that violent bully.

"Paula, wake up."

She tried to hold onto the image of his face, but the darkness was unyielding. Her last conscious thought was of Riley's future.

CHAPTER 36

COOPER'S FINGERS TRAILED DOWN Atkinson's spine, sighing as he kissed her neck. For a heavenly moment, her world fell away. No murders. No suspects. Just them.

Afterwards, they lay tangled in the sheets, Cooper's head on Atkinson's chest. His fingers idly stroked her arm. The silence was comfortable, intimate. The bedroom felt like a sanctuary, its deep blue walls and white trim creating a calming aura. A large mirror on the chimney breast where an old Metallica poster once hung reflected the gentle flicker of candlelight.

She remembered their argument earlier. It seemed so petty and insignificant. Money troubles, schedule conflicts – none of it mattered in the grand scheme of things. What mattered was this: the solid warmth of Atkinson's body against hers. The steady thump of his heart beneath her ear. The gentle rise and fall of his chest as he breathed.

She lifted her head, drinking in the sight of him. Kind, wise eyes that seemed smaller without his glasses. Salt and pepper hair, more silver at his temples. Distinguished. His slender but athletic torso.

"I love you," Cooper said softly. "You know that, right?"

Atkinson's lips curved in a tender smile. "I know. I love you too."

Cooper nestled closer, overcome with love, tiredness and guilt.

"You're incredible with Danny and Tina," she murmured. "I don't tell you that enough."

"They make it easy," Atkinson replied. "Danny's wonderful. He grows and changes every single day. And Tina, well, we seem to get each other in our own nerdy way."

Cooper's throat tightened. She didn't deserve this. Didn't deserve him. But she was selfish enough to hold on with both hands. "It's Friday tomorrow," she said, feeling the need to make an effort. "What do you want to do at the weekend? It's a certain someone's birthday. What do you fancy? Gallery? Cinema?"

"Hmm," Atkinson mused, his voice reverberating through his bare chest into her ear. "How about a quiet night in? Just us and the kids. Maybe watch a film?"

"Sounds perfect," Cooper murmured, snuggling closer. The soft fabric of the duvet comforted her, the warm cocoon distracting her from her worry for Keaton and Martin.

"And..." Atkinson glanced at an old clock ticking on the mantlepiece, inherited from Cooper's grandmother. He squinted in the dim light. "It's after midnight. So, technically, it's Friday now, not tomorrow." He paused. "Will you be home for dinner?" he asked, a hint of hope in his voice.

Cooper hesitated, her body tensed. "I'll do my best, but... I can't promise. I want to, but I can't. I might end up letting you down again."

A hint of hurt crossed Atkinson's face, but it disappeared as quickly as it appeared. "Fair enough. You're in the middle of a murder investigation. I know what it's like, even if I don't act like it sometimes."

"I really will try," Cooper insisted, guilt gnawing at her. "Is Mum coming over? What should we have for tea?"

Atkinson pulled her close and stroked her lower back. "Yes, and how about that lasagne you love? I'll pick up the ingredients tomorrow."

A Tina-friendly recipe. He really was wonderful, and it wasn't long before she drifted off in his sweet embrace, feeling warm, loved and secure. But Cooper's sleep was restless. In her dreams, she worried about Keaton and Martin, her imagination summoning images of funerals, caskets and headstones, haunting her with memories of Tennessee and whose death she would never get over. But then the dream morphed to naked, sweat-soaked bodies, wet sheets and wild sex.

She jolted awake at two a.m., heart racing. Beside her, Atkinson slept peacefully. Cooper stared at the ceiling, willing sleep to return, but her mind was plagued with the unwelcome dream of a man with dark hair and an intense stare.

DCI ERICA COOPER WASN'T the only one to dream of Elliot Whyte that night.

In the sterile intensive care unit, Paula Keaton's head pounded. She looked at Martin, snoring softly in the next bed. Reassured that he must be all right if he was sleeping so soundly, Keaton rubbed her brow, trying to piece together the nonsense her subconscious had devised in its poison-induced delirium. It was more hallucination than dream.

Whyte was there, prancing in a fluffy pink tutu, juggling rubber ducks. Singh was there too, singing opera while the rubber ducks quacked in harmony. Then Whyte dropped the ducks, and they scattered on the floor, opening their beaks and spewing rainbow-coloured bubbles. Riley asked her to dance, and while Singh continued to sing, they pirouetted through a landscape filled with talking tea cups and characters from old TV adverts: The Judderman, Mr Soft and the Smash Martians.

"You're awake. How are you feeling, Paula?" The doctor's voice was low, mindful of Martin. She checked her chart, flipping through the notes before returning it to the docket at the end of the bed.

"Like I played three games of rugby back to back, then took a load of acid."

The doctor smiled. "Vivid dreams?"

"Like Alice in Weirdoland."

"That'll be the belladonna – the nightshade. Belladonna interferes with the neurotransmitter acetylcholine, leading to – how should I put this? Leading to altered mental states. Thirsty?"

Keaton shook her head. *Altered mental states?* In other words, she was off her rocker.

The back of Keaton's hand was bruised where a needle pierced her skin. A tube connected it to an IV bag hanging from a stand beside her bed. The ward was quiet save for the humming of monitors and the soft steps of nurses making their rounds. The lights were dimmed overnight, but Keaton could still make out her pale blue bedding and the geometric pattern on the hospital gown she was wearing. She couldn't remember putting it on and briefly wondered where her clothes were and who had undressed her.

"Is my colleague okay?" she asked, nodding towards Martin. Her neck ached in response to the slight movement. She really did feel like she'd been crushed under a scrum in her Saracens days.

"He reacted badly, but he's on the mend. We've given you both atropine to counteract the belladonna. It works by blocking the muscarinic acetylcholine receptors, impeding the toxic alkaloids.

Keaton gave a *mmm hmm* as if this was a perfectly normal conversation to be having.

"We don't think there was in any ricin in the biscuits, but if there was, it was in microscopic amounts. You're both on IV fluids and electrolytes and have been given fifty grams of activated charcoal to help absorb any remaining toxins in your gastrointestinal tract."

"I've had more than that," Keaton said groggily, still smiling at her bizarre dream. She tried to push herself to a seated position, remembering the odd combination of a smoky flavour, creamy texture, and ice-cold temperature.

The doctor glanced up from the heart rate monitor. "Pardon?"

"We—" She pointed at Martin. "—had charcoal ice cream yesterday. It was nice – bloody weird – but nice. There's something off about eating jet-black food, though. Like that squid ink pasta. It tastes good; it just doesn't look like it should be edible."

The doctor's mouth hung open slightly, and she tilted her head as if something suddenly made more sense.

"Well, that explains why neither of you have organ failure. You're both doing very well, all things considered. Nightshade is one thing, ricin – if there was any – is another. Very nasty business and had you been older, frailer, or in bad health, you wouldn't be here. But you're both young and healthy and had charcoal in your system. It must have bound to the toxins, reducing how much was absorbed into your gastrointestinal tract."

Keaton, eyes cast down, looked at her stomach. The way she was sitting and the fold of the nightgown made her paunch look rounder than it was. She missed her six-pack.

"The new DI has a sweet tooth. I think he's becoming a bad influence. All I do is eat lately." It wasn't Singh; it was being single, feeling lonely, not sticking to set meal times. "I used to be a professional athlete. I used to be able to put away three thousand calories a day and not put on an ounce."

"We're going to keep you in a while so we can monitor your organs and nervous system, but for the record, you're in great shape." The doctor quickly cleared her throat. "Besides, that sweet tooth probably saved your life."

CHAPTER 37

HE LEANED OVER THE microscope, ignoring the faint aroma of coffee from a forgotten cup on his desk. Besides the coffee, Hong Evanstad's workstation in the forensic laboratory was immaculate and organised, just how his mentor Justin Atkinson would like it.

The lab had the clinical glow of a room dominated by stainless steel surfaces and artificial lighting. Hong's gloved hands moved nimbly, adjusting the slide and making precise notes on his findings. The sample under the lens confirmed that the boots found behind circuitry on Electron's bridge belonged to Cliff Longacre. The DNA extracted from dried blood on the laces matched Jude McDermott. He switched slides to examine nano-sized fragments of dried red liquid found in Longacre's quarters. He knew instantly it wasn't blood. An energy drink, perhaps, ink more likely, but definitely not blood. Every tiny fragment of evidence held the potential to unlock the truth behind the case, but this was not it. Not the news the police were hoping for.

Hong tidied the slides back into their wallets, removed his gloves, and washed his hands before entering his password into the lab computer. Several cases needed his attention, and the urgency of each weighed heavily on him, but his was not a job that could be rushed. Any deviation from best practice could contaminate evidence or leave the prosecution open to doubt in the courtroom. He opened the notes he'd been sent from a murder in Fenham – a man had killed his wife and children before walking towards the A1 and throwing himself off a motorway bridge. The photos were horrific, and yet, not the worst Hong had seen. They weren't even the worst he'd seen that week.

A red dot encircling a white number one appeared over his email icon. Hong clicked, liking to keep his inbox clear. It was Police Scotland and labelled *Urgent*. Interesting. Very interesting.

COOPER HAD A TERRIBLE night's sleep, but she wasn't the only one. All through HQ, feet dragged, mouths yawned. The style was one of rumpled shirts and loosened ties. Standards were slipping, she thought, until she spotted DI Singh in his pressed royal blue suit, deep in conversation with Whyte.

"Morning, Daljit. Elliot," Cooper greeted, her voice steady but her gaze firmly fixed on Singh. "Any news from the hospital?"

Singh handed her a steaming cup of tea. Cooper sniffed it.

"Coconut?"

"And mango. A little bit of the tropics on this terribly British day," he said, gesturing to a window filled with grey skies and drizzle. "DS Keaton and DC Martin are both stable. DC Boyd is with them now. I thought it was best she took the day off."

"Of course," Cooper said, nodding. She stepped back, sipping the tea, using the cup like a mask to hide her face. "And you?" she asked Whyte, knowing he lived with Martin and must be shaken. "You okay?"

He took a beat before answering. "Fine," was all he said.

If Singh could sense the tension, he at least did Cooper the courtesy of acting as if he couldn't. "Unfortunately, our time with Mr Longacre hasn't moved us any further forward. His story remains the same."

"Lawyer?"

"Yes. Kieran Glenn from Glenn, Phillips, and Noble."

Recognizing the firm, Cooper nodded. "Good choice. Is Longacre still in the cells?"

"He is, though our twenty-four hours are up. I got an extension to thirty-six in the hope our friends in forensics would have the results from the knives we had tested, but so far..."

"Wishful thinking, Daljit. Do you have the transcript from the interview?"

"I've already emailed it to you." Singh pressed his fingertips together like he often did before bidding anyone farewell. "Now, if you'll excuse me, I have a meeting with the IOPC starting in ten minutes."

As Singh walked away, humming to himself, Cooper turned to Whyte, the words hovering on the tip of her tongue.

"Listen, I—"

Her phone buzzed insistently, Hong's name flashing on the screen.

She looked at him apologetically.

"Answer it," he said, though his tone suggested it wasn't an order, nor was he granting her permission. He knew better than that. His tone simply intimated that he understood, that the case was what mattered.

THE DOOR TO THE lab was heavy. Cooper shook the excess water from her umbrella and stored it by the entrance. Inside, the air was chilly, even colder than outdoors. Cooper wiped her feet and was met by Hong Evanstad, his lab coat open, revealing a jumper the colour of Rioja. He led her to a lift, which they rode to the second floor before approaching Hong's workstation.

"Talk to me, Hong," she said, cutting straight to the chase. "What do you have for me?"

He straightened, rubbing his neck. "In terms of evidence that Cliff Longacre was on the bridge at the time of the murder? Nothing. Nada. Zip."

Cooper's jaw clenched.

"The boots are his. No doubt about it," he continued. "We already knew he was the only one to be issued size fourteens, and his DNA's all over the inside of the boots. He must have worn them without socks a few times," he added, wrinkling his nose. "He was a shedder."

"Shedder?"

"He sheds his skin."

Cooper stared at him. "Like a snake?"

"Not in one go. But some people have naturally dry skin that flakes constantly. Like dandruff but over one's entire body."

Cooper had the sudden urge to moisturize.

"I like shedders," he continued. "They make my job easier. But, aside from that, I've got nothing to tie Cliff Longacre to the scene. We've tested every inch of his quarters, examined his clothes from the day, the white trainers he wore when he met you. Nothing."

Cooper sighed and slumped into the chair by Hong's workstation. "So while his shoes were there, the rest of him probably wasn't?"

"Precisely." Hong grinned, then gave an annoying little chuckle.

"What?"

Hong reached across her and clicked *ctrl* and *P*. The printer by his desk whirred to life. When it was finished, he handed her the report from Police Scotland.

"This is from three years ago," she said.

"Read," Hong said in the same matter-of-fact tone Whyte had just used.

Police Report: Vandalism at Ravenwood Logging Camp, Scotland.

Incident: Destruction of property.

Location: Ravenwood Logging Camp, Inverness-shire, Scotland.

Reported by: Site supervisor, Mr. Fin McIntyre.

Incident Overview:
Workers arriving at Ravenwood Logging Camp on the morning of the fifth of October discovered significant vandalism to logging equipment and several trees. This act of sabotage has caused approximately £500,000 in damages and led to considerable operational delays. As a result, the camp has been temporarily shut down, affecting the employment of over 100 workers and causing substantial financial implications for the company.

Description of Incident:
An unknown male was captured by security cameras on the outskirts of the camp. The suspect is approximately 5'10" with a slender

---

build. He was observed wearing a camouflage jacket, dark trousers, and carrying a backpack. Notably, the individual was seen holding tools typically used in tree spiking, including a hammer and long metal spikes.

Tree Spiking:
Tree spiking involves driving long metal spikes into trees, often deeply into the trunk. This act is intended to deter logging by causing potential harm to loggers and damaging sawmill equipment when the spiked trees are processed. Such actions pose serious risks to workers' safety and can lead to significant equipment damage.

Evidence of Injury and Blood Analysis:
During the vandalism, the suspect appears to have injured themselves. Blood was found near a tree with several spikes, suggesting the individual might have accidentally struck their own hand while hammering a spike. Samples of this blood were collected for DNA analysis. However, as of this report, no match has been found in existing databases.

Investigation Status:
The suspect remains unidentified. The camp has been thoroughly examined by a forensic team for additional evidence. The incident is being investigated as an act of eco-terrorism, with local authorities collaborating with national environmental

crime divisions. Additional efforts are being made to identify the suspect through extended DNA analysis and a review of environmental activist groups known to use such tactics.

Ramifications:
The vandalism has led to significant financial losses, estimated at £500,000, not only due to the cost of repairs but also from the operational delays and loss of timber. The temporary closure of the camp has put over 100 workers out of employment, impacting their livelihoods and the local economy. The company is also facing increased insurance premiums and potential contractual penalties due to delays in fulfilling logging commitments.

Cooper skimmed the report, her face stoic while adrenaline started to course through her. She recalled their hunch that an eco-activism group had infiltrated VāyuVolt Renewables. Her thoughts turned to Violet Sinclair, the young, idealistic woman who died two years ago when the small, ill-suited, and unsafe vessel she was on was struck by North Star. They'd ruled out Luna Sinclair, Violet's sister, who worked aboard Electron. She may have been a robust, sturdy woman, but could she overpower two men? Cooper didn't think so. Besides, while she might have a motive to want to harm the two men who'd been at the helm during her sister's death, the description given by their only witness didn't match Luna. Not at all.

"What am I looking at here, Hong?" Cooper asked, her voice low and intense.

Hong took a deep breath. "One of the samples from the crime scene flagged this report. It matches the unknown male eco-terrorist."

Cooper had a feeling her world was about to spin on its axis. Her next question was nothing more than a single word. "Who?"

His reply hit her like a punch to the gut.

"Mr Hal Simpson."

CHAPTER 38

THE PIECE OF PAPER vibrated in Cooper's hands. She set it down, pushing her hands into her pockets to stop them from shaking. She clenched her jaw so tight she felt her temples throb. She felt like the walls of the sterile lab were closing in. Everything felt upside down. Could it be that everything she thought she knew about the case was all a charade?

Hal Simpson was a mild-mannered first mate and victim of a brutal stabbing attack that saw one man die. At least that was the impression she'd been living under because she now knew Hal Simpson to be an eco-warrior with a rap sheet worth half a million quid.

She began pacing, aware of Hong watching her. Her heels clicked against the linoleum as her diffused shadow followed her around the room. She thought of Hal lying in the hospital bed, tubes and wires snaking from his battered body. God, she'd felt so bad for him. Pitied him.

"He got on top of me. Stabbed me here and here. Then— Then I gave up. Played dead like a fucking coward."

She'd believed him. *Idiot.*

"His wounds," she said aloud. "The cuts were real. The blood was real. She could see them clearly in her mind, but Hong opened a file and displayed a selection on his computer. When she'd viewed them for the first time, she pictured Hal cowering on the floor of the bridge, lying in the foetal position on his right side, holding his arm over his head to protect himself. Now she saw something different. Now she saw the truth.

"Self-inflicted," she said. "They're all on his left because the knife was in his right."

Hong shook his head. "How can a person do that to themselves?"

"Because a few carefully placed knife wounds and some blood loss are better than a life sentence."

Jude's body was peppered with frantic and chaotic wounds from all directions. Hal's wounds were more uniform. Parallel lines carved his left ribs, yet nothing had pierced deeper, and there was no damage to his lungs. The cuts on his arm were all delivered from the same angle. And his damn leg. Cooper rubbed her eyes. The cut to his leg that had miraculously missed the femoral artery. There was nothing miraculous about it.

It was all an act. A carefully staged show where Hal was the storyteller and she was the poor dupe.

Cooper burst out of the lab, her sanity reeling. As she stalked down the corridor, dialling Whyte's number, Atkinson's words echoed in her head.

"Whyte," he answered.

"The boots never left the bridge."

Silence. Then, "I know."

"No." She stopped dead in her tracks, waiting for the lift, her breath ragged. "The boots never left the bridge because the killer never left the bridge."

Ding.

She stepped inside, jabbing her finger against the ground floor button, willing her signal not to cut out.

"Hal Simpson."

"What? Are you sure?"

"No," she said honestly. "But his DNA just flagged up an unsolved eco-terrorism charge, and his wounds..."

"All on his non-dominant side."

"Exactly." The lift doors opened. Cooper broke into a run, making a beeline for her car and fumbling her keys. "India and Gray didn't discover two victims that day; they discovered the victim lying next to his killer."

"Bastard."

"You're telling me."

She slammed the car door and gunned the engine, tyres squealing as she peeled out of her parking space. She clenched the steering wheel, weaving through traffic.

"Grab your coat and meet me outside HQ in five. We need to get to the RVI."

INSIDE THAT VERY HOSPITAL, DS PAULA Keaton sat upright in her bed, sipping water, her broad shoulders hunched slightly. The bed was firm and uncomfortable, draped in stiff sheets that felt scratchy against her skin. At least they smelled nice. The scent of laundry detergent was powerful enough to cover the feint odour of disinfectant but not tough enough to cloak the underlying stench of sickness. The hum of machines monitoring vital signs buzzed faintly in the background, and the constant sound of footfall in the corridors clip-clopped over every conversation.

She leaned towards DC Oliver Martin. DC Saffron Boyd hovered nearby, fussing over Martin's pillows.

"Who'd want to poison us?" Martin wondered aloud, his usually styled hair mussed from lying in bed.

Boyd's hands stilled on the pillow. "I don't know, but I'm glad they failed."

"Statistically, you're the most likely culprit," he said, winking.

Boyd didn't look amused.

"I hate to say it," Martin said to Keaton, "but April used to make some wicked biscuits."

Keaton let out a bark of laughter, wincing slightly at the movement. "Statistics are one thing, but I can promise you my ex did not scale the walls of Alnwick Gardens to off me. Besides, April was the one who cheated on me. If one of us was going to poison the other, it'd be me poisoning her."

Martin scoffed. "You're not the poisoning sort. I see you more as a *hit them in the head till they go cold* kind of girl."

Keaton's eyes twinkled as she turned to Boyd. "He's such a charmer. Really knows how to give a lass a compliment." Then to Martin. "You know I'm a big softie really."

"Your secret's safe with me," Martin replied, tracing a cross over his chest.

Keaton stretched, her wide *latissimus dorsi* filling the hospital gown. "Speaking of secrets, I think the doctor fancies me. Said I was in great shape."

Martin's eyebrows shot up. "You going to get her number?"

Keaton shook her head, waving off the suggestion. "Hard pass. I'm not ready to see anyone yet. Besides, there are rules. Doctors can't date patients. It's unethical. Like a teacher dating a student."

"Or a therapist and client," added Martin.

"True," Boyd chimed in, her eyes downcast, recalling a bad memory. "Like a DCI trying to seduce a subordinate."

COOPER PRESSED HER FOOT firmly on the accelerator, eyes darting between the slick, wet Coast Road and the rearview mirror, vigilant for any obstacles.

"Fucking hell!" she cursed, slamming on the brakes as a taxi cut her off.

She drove west towards Newcastle, the suburban scape blurring past them, the concrete of Tyneside dull in the autumnal light. The chill of early November had settled in, and the last leaves fluttered down from the trees, carpeting the streets brown. Cooper's breath fogged the inside of the windscreen, and she switched on the demister with a quick, irritated motion.

Whyte sat silently beside her, glancing at the left wing mirror. Was he thinking about the case or about the other night?

"I'm going to report myself to Professional Standards," she blurted out, changing lanes.

Whyte turned to her, disbelief carved across his face. "You're what? Don't be ridiculous."

"What happened between us... it was wrong, and I'm sorry. Like Captain Jude McDermott and his relationship with Mandi, I'm in a position of power over you. It's inappropriate."

Cooper's jaw tightened as she rode the amber wave past Corner House and the Cradlewell, merging onto the Central Motorway. "You were vulnerable that night, Elliot. You'd been talking about your father's diagnosis. It wasn't right of me."

"Vulnerable?" Whyte rolled his eyes, leaning back in his seat. "I'm a grown man, Coop. I will live."

The city revealed itself ahead, the grey November sky threatening more rain. Cooper's voice rose over the hum of the engine. "If it were the other way around—"

"But it's not," Whyte interrupted, his tone firm. "I won't have you wrecking everything you have over a kiss. If you report it, I will deny it."

The Royal Victoria Infirmary was just a few minutes away now. She swerved onto the exit ramp, the buildings of Newcastle closing in around them. They passed the bustling Haymarket, where students and professionals mingled as they crossed the streets, the towering presence of St. James' Park football stadium looming to their right.

"It was just a tough week," Whyte said. "We have a good team at CID. I don't want that to change, and the department has enough to worry about with this WhatsApp business. I missed Amy, and you missed Justin. That's all. It's not like it'll happen again."

"Right," said Cooper as she pulled into the RVI's main entrance.

"Right," echoed Whyte.

A gust of wind sent leaves swirling across the car park. Cooper found a parking spot near the emergency department and killed the engine, the sudden silence awkward. She turned and stared at him, any argument she had dissipating.

CHAPTER 39

A MOUSY-HAIRED NURSE WITH prominent teeth greeted Cooper as she approached Intensive Care.

Cooper flashed her ID. "We need to see Hal Simpson," she stated with a tone that left no room for delay.

The nurse gave a nod of recognition, her face spreading into a toothy smile and a look of fondness.

"Of course. This way, please." She briskly led them down a narrow corridor, dodging gurneys and wheelchairs. "Lovely young man," she said. "Ever so polite. Horrible what happened to him. Just horrible."

Somewhere, a baby bawled loudly. As they walked on, the occasional abstract painting or noticeboard punctuated the pale, sickly hue of the hospital's walls. Cooper stumbled, tripping over the foot of a man hunched in a plastic seat. He didn't look up from the bucket he cradled in his lap. The peak of his baseball cap tilted down to the bucket, shielding Cooper from seeing its contents.

Ahead, a dishevelled young man, frustrated and bewildered, was deep in conversation with an overflowing bin. He gesticulated wildly as he spoke.

"You see, it's all going downhill, mate," he began, pointing a finger at the bin as if it were a fellow conspirator. "The country's going to pot. Dumbed down, I tell you. Can't even have a proper debate anymore."

He paused, seemingly waiting for the bin's silent agreement before continuing.

"Used to be, you'd have intellectuals on the telly. People with some sense, some knowledge. Now? Reality stars and influencers with fake tits and glow-in-the-dark teeth. It's all about who can shout the loudest, not who makes the most sense."

The bin, of course, remained unresponsive, its metal frame reflecting the overhead lights.

"And don't get me started on education. Kids these days... barely know their history. Can't do basic math without a calculator. We're raising a generation of idiots, I tell you." He shook his head, eyes glinting with the fervour of his rant. He couldn't have been a day older than twenty-two.

Another pause, as if he expected the bin to offer some form of condolence.

"Back in my day, we respected knowledge. We valued intellect."

Cooper glanced over her shoulder at Whyte, who walked two paces behind her. He looked half sympathetic, half ready to laugh. "Poor bastard," he said. "But to be fair, that bin made more sense than most politicians."

Classic police humour. Whyte knew the heartache of watching someone's mind slip away and yet could still find humour in the darkness. He had to. They all did. It was the only way to cope at times.

When they reached Hal's room, Cooper's pulse quickened with all the questions she had for the first mate. Where was the weapon? Was the idea always to frame Longacre? How long had he been planning this? And what hurt more – stabbing himself in the ribs or knowing he didn't get away with it?

This was it. The moment of truth.

The nurse pushed open the door and pulled back the curtain surrounding Hal's bed. "Hal, you have visitors, pet."

Cooper stepped forward. The sheets were pulled over Hal's head, reminding Cooper of countless corpses she'd seen in the morgue. But it wasn't just the sheet that reminded her of death; it was the stillness. The rise and fall of breath was missing.

"Hal?" Cooper whispered, stepping closer. She reached out, yanking back the sheets to reveal nothing more than a pile of pillows strategically placed to mimic a sleeping body.

Her stomach dropped, a cold wave washing over her. "He's not here."

The nurse, clearly flustered, stammered, "Maybe he just nipped to the loo..."

Cooper's eyes darted around the cubicle, quickly taking in the scene. Most of Hal's personal possessions were missing. His phone charger, his wallet, and the small duffel bag from the foot of his bed were all gone.

Cooper spun to face the nurse. "He's done a runner. When was the last time you saw him? Really saw him – not just a shape under the sheets?"

The nurse blinked rapidly, her face paling. "I... I brought him a cup of tea after you left yesterday evening. It was about half six."

Whyte cursed under his breath, moving to the doorway and scanning the corridor for any sign of Hal.

"I need hospital security," Cooper called after him. "I want them manning every door, looking for Hal Simpson. Now!"

KEATON PLAYED WITH A loose thread on her blanket, mindlessly scrolling through Instagram.

"What are you thinking?" Martin asked.

The biscuits had seemed like a harmless gift – a kind gesture from a grateful citizen or a well-meaning colleague. But they were clearly designed to silence her and Martin for good.

"We must have got closer to identifying the thief than we realised. That's why whoever did it tried to take us out."

"But how?" Boyd asked, closing her copy of Marie Claire. "You didn't even have any real suspects. No offence."

"None taken." Keaton shrugged. "Daniel Finch – the night watchman's nephew – was our only lead, and we hadn't even found the bugger yet. We don't even know if he knew we were looking for him."

Martin rubbed his stubble-covered chin. "I need a shave. Whoever did this knew we were the ones investigating the theft and Colin Finch's death. Those biscuits were addressed to us both. Full names and ranks. Whoever it was had our contact details. Maybe they work at the garden, and that's how they got in? It must be someone we've spoken to."

"They were hand-delivered to the station," Keaton said, tugging at the thread. "No postal stickers. Who dropped them off?"

"Courier service," Boyd said. "DI Singh called me earlier."

Keaton's phone buzzed, pulling her from her thoughts. She glanced at the screen and raised her brows.

"It's the gardens," she said, answering. "DS Paula Keaton here."

Martin and Boyd leaned in, straining to hear. Nosy parkers.

Keaton listened, nodding as the caller spoke. "You're certain? All right, thank you very much." She hung up, her gaze meeting Martin's.

"Well?" he prodded.

"That was their head of finance. He's gone through their transactions and the Knoxes bought two tickets for the gardens, just like Dianne Knox told you. But the time on the log was just after noon."

Martin's brow furrowed. "Hold on," he said, sitting up straighter. "That doesn't make any sense. If they were at the gardens at twelve but went to the café at two..."

"How did the café receipt end up in the garden?" Keaton finished.

Boyd fanned herself with the magazine. "They must have gone back. Are they multi-entrance tickets? The ones where you can come and go as often as you like during the day?"

Keaton's eyes narrowed. "No idea. But why lie about it?" She looked at Martin. "She definitely told you they went to Barter Books *after* the gardens?"

"Hundred per cent." Martin tipped his head back, staring up at the ceiling tiles as he thought. "Maybe Dianne Knox was just confused? It happens. She is getting on a bit."

"Hardly. She's in her fifties," Keaton said with an eye roll. "Saff, I take back what I said about him being a charmer. Anyway, what do we actually know about the Knoxes?"

In the corridor, two security officers ran past.

The three detectives craned their necks, their instincts making them curious to know what the rush was but not curious enough to get out of bed to find out.

Martin's face scrunched in concentration. "Dianne works at the doctor's surgery, and she mentioned that her husband Jeremy owns that swanky shop in Ponteland. Folklore, right?"

Boyd ceased fanning herself. "That's not Folklore. That's – oh, what do they call it? FOMO. Yes, it stands for fear of missing out."

FOMO? YOLO? It was only a matter of time before someone opened a comedy club called LOL or a curiosity shop called WTF.

"Folklore's that restaurant in town. Not far from here, actually." Boyd pointed over her shoulder towards the window and Queen Victoria Road beyond. "Think it's on Leazes Lane."

Martin's eyes widened. "The vegan one?"

Boyd tucked a strand of blonde hair behind her ear. "No. I don't think it's vegan."

Keaton's mind started connecting dots. "So Jeremy Knox isn't a shop owner. He's a chef."

Her eyes met Martin's, a spark of realisation passing between them.

"Why would a chef want to poison us?" he asked.

"Why would a chef want ricin in the first place?"

COOPER SPRINTED DOWN THE hospital corridor, heart beginning to pound. Uniformed officers from the city centre flooded into the ward.

"Fan out!" she barked. "Check every supply closet, every bathroom, the cafeteria. Hell, check the damn roof if you have to!" She had a vision of Hal leaving the way he'd come in – by chopper. It was ridiculous. But then so was stabbing yourself half to death to make yourself look like a victim.

Her eyes darted from door to door, adrenaline coursing through her. He could be anywhere.

"Think, Cooper," she muttered to herself. "Where would you go if you were him?"

Hal was clever. Clever enough to elude Police Scotland. Clever enough to crew a ship of Electron's size. Too clever to make a run for it without a plan.

"Whyte!" she called out, spotting him up ahead. "Security footage."

"Already on it." He pressed his phone to his ear before dashing off.

Hal was injured, weak from blood loss. He couldn't have gotten far. Unless...

"Damn it," she hissed, realisation dawning. "He had help."

AN HOUR LATER, THE search had produced a big fat zero. Cooper strode towards the security office, her jaw clenched tight. She pushed open the door to find Whyte hunched over a bank of monitors, his dark eyes illuminated by their bluish glow.

"Anything?" she demanded, leaning in close.

Whyte shook his head, frustration obvious. "Nothing concrete. It's like he vanished into thin air."

Cooper scanned the screens. "He didn't vanish. We're just not seeing it yet."

A security guard shifted nervously beside them. "We've rewound the footage from this morning. No sign of your suspect leaving the building."

"Then we go back further," Cooper snapped. "He's injured. Someone had to have helped him. Look for orderlies, nurses, anyone acting suspicious."

They scrutinised the footage. He wouldn't head home, he was too smart for that. To family or friends? She hastily messaged HQ to have someone compile a list of associates.

"There!" Whyte exclaimed an hour later, pointing at a grainy image. "That man. Does his gait look off to you?"

Cooper squinted. The figure on screen moved with the odd, shuffling walk of someone with limited mobility in one leg, his face hidden by a cap.

She watched him leave through the main entrance. The security guard switched to an external camera showing black and white night vision.

"There he is," Whyte said, pointing a finger at the man in the hat.

He stopped briefly to rub his leg before hobbling left, fishing something from his pocket – glasses. He unfolded the arms and placed them on his face, removed the hat and shook out his curls.

"That's him." Cooper straightened, her voice tight. "Timestamp?" she asked the guard.

"Seven fifty-three last night."

Whyte swore under his breath. "He's got a hell of a head start."

Cooper grabbed her phone. "But we've got his direction. Let's move!"

The hunt was on. She dialled HQ, demanding access to city centre cameras, patrols, the works. She wanted his face with every news outlet in the city within the next thirty minutes.

"Excuse me, ma'am." One of the uniformed officers who'd helped with the search stepped into the room, his eyes keen. "I found something. By the suspect's bed."

CHAPTER 40

WHILE WHYTE LIAISED WITH the operators of the city's CCTV cameras, Cooper ran back to Intensive Care, her footsteps echoing in the hallway as she followed the officer back to Hal's room.

"Here we are," the officer said, gesturing inside.

Cooper's eyes swept the room again, lingering on the empty bed and the scattered remnants of Hal's presence. A dog-eared paperback on the nightstand. A half-empty box of chocolates.

"What did you find?" Cooper asked, her voice sharp.

The officer pointed to the floor. "Under the bed, by the table. Might've fallen out of a card or the chocolate box."

Cooper crouched down, wincing as her knees cracked. Was she already at the age when joints started making noises? When did that happen?

A strip of photo booth pictures lay face-up on the linoleum. Hal's grinning face stared back at her, his arms wrapped around a woman perched on his lap. The woman's head was thrown back in laughter, her blonde hair captured mid-flick, fanning behind her like the wing of a bird in flight. Her eyes were almost closed, a stripe of bright blue eyeshadow covering her lids, which crinkled with joy.

Cooper's stomach clenched. The woman was almost unrecognisable. Almost. Her loose blonde hair had been tied back when they'd met, her face bare, without make-up.

"Shit," she muttered under her breath, staring at the woman's familiar jewellery. She pocketed the photo and then phoned another woman.

IN THE ADJACENT WARD, Keaton paced back and forth, her ponytail swinging as she dragged the IV drip around on its wheeled stand. One wheel squeaked, another refused to turn.

"All right team, why would a chef nick poisonous plants? Theories."

Martin spoke up first, sniggering. "Aside from wanting to off his annoying wife?"

Boyd's head swivelled. "Oliver!"

"You never met her," he said, laughing. "But seriously, maybe... culinary experimentation? Like using dangerous ingredients to push boundaries? People love fugu, don't they, even though they know there's a chance they could get poisoned? Or he could be trying to combine random ingredients like how you mix the bark of one plant with the leaves from a totally different one to get ayahuasca."

"Aya-what?" Boyd asked.

"Ayahuasca. They brew it into a tea, and it makes you hallucinate like crazy. It's supposed to connect you to the spirit world or something. Whyte knew someone who went to Brazil to try it. Said he spewed for like an hour then imagined his skin was covered in tiny microscopic aliens that were trying to build a nest out of his body hair."

Boyd raised an eyebrow. "And people drink this willingly?"

"Yeah, for the *experience*." Martin made air quotes with his fingers. "I'd rather have a boozy weekend in Prague, but that's just me."

"When your leg heals, I'll book the flights," Boyd said. She stood and moved to his bedside, wrapping a hand around his ankle to stroke his injured Achilles. "But we're not just drinking Staropramen all day. I want to see the Old Town, the Charles Bridge, the Jewish Quarter. But you might be onto something with the drug idea. Don't Silicon Valley execs microdose with various substances? Maybe this chef wants to work with tiny amounts of poison to increase creativity, or perhaps they have aphrodisiacal effects."

Keaton smirked. "Kinky. But none of this justifies someone stealing the plants or trying to poison us. If their intentions were above board, why go to those lengths? What else?"

"Extortion," Martin added quickly. "Poison people, then offer the antidote for a price."

Keaton paused. "I like it. Though there's no antidote for ricin, remember? Let's find out if anyone's atropine supplies have gone walkies recently."

"What about a personal vendetta?" Boyd offered. "A grudge against a critic?"

"Now you're talking. Get on Google. See if that Parker Bowles lad, Jay Rayner or Grace Whatsherface have given him a scathing review. Who does the restaurant reviews for the Chronicle?"

"Eddie Eats," Martin said. "But I think he's just into his pub grub and Sunday lunches."

"Worth checking out his recent reviews just in case." Then Keaton went quiet, a memory replaying in her head. She was sitting in this same sterile hospital waiting for Hal to wake up from surgery while Cooper, Whyte and Singh went on their chopper adventure.

Martin said something; Keaton wasn't listening. Something clicked.

"Give me your phone," she said, palm open, gesturing at Martin.

He obliged, unlocking it. Her fingers flew across his phone screen, pulling up Saffron & Sage's website and scrolling down to find the links for its social media pages.

"What you looking for?" he asked.

Keaton told him about April's business, how it had always been her dream to have her own restaurant in the city.

"That's April's place?" Martin asked. "But you said it failed its health inspection and that—"

"I know what I said. I was being petty. Don't look at me like that. Anyway, another chef was on her social media... Fuck me." Keaton scanned the screen.

"What is it?" Martin struggled in his bed between his damaged leg and the IV in the back of his hand.

"There were comments here. Angry ones. Another chef accused April of nicking his recipes. I definitely saw them. I swear. But they're gone now. Deleted."

Boyd looked concerned. "Folklore?"

"I— I don't know." She searched her brain, sifting through the memory. She couldn't say for certain. She could remember the tone of the messages, remember the knot in her stomach at seeing April looking so happy in the photographs. Happy without her.

"He's covering his tracks?"

Keaton nodded. "Looks that way." She scrolled back through the website, this time pausing at the contact information. Her thumb hovered over the phone number.

"You all right?" Martin asked.

Keaton forced a smile. "Peachy." She hit dial, her palms sweating.

Three rings. Four.

"Saffron and Sage." The voice was young, female, clear and professional.

Keaton swallowed hard. "I need to speak with April."

A pause. "She's in the middle of service—"

"Tell her it's Paula."

There was an agonising wait while Keaton listened to the sounds of the restaurant: background chatter, cutlery scraping crockery, and some terrible acoustic version of a '90s hit."

"Paula? Has something happened? Is Riley okay?"

"Riley's fine," Keaton said firmly, pushing down the ache in her chest. "I need you to listen to me. You need to stop serving. Now. Close the restaurant."

April scoffed. "Are you mad? We're fully booked."

"April, please. It's important—"

The line went dead, and for a moment, Keaton just stared at the phone.

CHAPTER 41

COOPER WATCHED THE SECOND hand on the clock tick while waiting for India Morgan to answer her call. It went to voicemail. Cooper tried again. Finally, the second officer and acting captain answered, her voice cracking through the speaker, sounding distant.

"India Morgan speaking."

"India, it's DCI Cooper here."

"Hello, Erica."

"Where are you?" Cooper demanded, her voice taut.

"Fifty-five degrees, forty-five minutes north. One degree, forty-six minutes east."

"You could have just said Odin's Gale."

"Well, that wouldn't be very precise, Detective. Odin's Gale is bigger than—"

"Bigger than Greater London. Yeah, I've heard that before."

Cooper pinched her nose, trying to stifle the irritation bubbling beneath the surface. India got under her skin. She was cold, driven. But what annoyed her the most was how much they were alike, except for the fact India appeared to have her shit together, and Cooper was a hot mess. Admiration twisted with jealousy as she asked, "Are you on Electron? Zephyr?"

"Electron. She's been released back to VāyuVolt Renewables, and I'm very pleased to be back at the helm. It's not the same, of course. I'm not sure it ever will be. I miss Hal terribly. Jude too. What's this about?"

Cooper hesitated, weighing her words carefully. India was blonde, but not the blonde she was interested in. Not the one tied to Hal and to everything that was unravelling.

"Luna Sinclair. Is she on board?"

"She is. Doing repairs on OGC17 as we speak. Is there something I should know?"

Cooper looked at the clock, seeing the seconds tick by from the last confirmed sighting of Hal Simpson. She explained how Hal and Luna were in a relationship, how Hal was now missing, and her best chance of finding him was via Luna. "I'll explain more when I see you. For now, don't let on. Please keep an eye on her."

"Of course. But what do you mean *when you see me*?—"

Cooper ended the call; she was already dialling a second number.

"Nixon," the superintendent's gravelly voice answered.

"I want a chopper."

"And I want to hire Scarlet Johannson as my new secretary but the budget isn't going to stretch to either of those things.

Cooper gritted her teeth, describing how Hal Simpson was now their prime suspect for the murder of Captain Jude and that he was wanted in Scotland on charges of eco-terrorism. "Luna Sinclair is on Electron. She is in a relationship with Hal and is the sister of Violet, the girl who died in the collision. Right now, she's our only lead."

Silence hung in the air. Cooper held her breath.

"Fine," Nixon relented, promising to have a helicopter on the roof of the RVI in fifteen minutes."

Cooper put her phone back in her pocket and headed for the stairs.

WHILE KEATON REPEATEDLY HIT the redial button for Saffron & Sage, Martin called Singh. His phone was pressed tight to his ear, his dark hair spiky from continuously running his fingers through it.

"Yes, sir. We believe Jeremy Knox, the head chef and owner of Folklore, is the one who stole the poisonous plants. His wife lied to me about when they visited the garden," he said, his voice low and urgent. "He has a problem with another chef in Newcastle—"

A flurry of movement caught his eye. Boyd was grabbing her coat and heading for the door.

"Where are you going?" Martin asked, covering the mouthpiece.

"Saffron and Sage," Boyd replied, fastening the buttons on a beige-coloured coat. "It's just a few streets away. I can get there first."

Martin's stomach clenched. "Wait—"

But she was gone, the door to the ward swooshing closed behind her.

"Sorry, sir," Martin said into the phone, distracted. "Can you repeat that?"

He barely registered Singh's voice on the other end. Boyd was fragile, haunted by her past. All Martin could think about was her racing to save lives, potentially endangering her own.

BOYD'S LUNGS BURNED AS she sprinted down the street, her conservative heels clicking on uneven concrete paving slabs. The sky was darkening, thick clouds cloaking the city with the threat of more rain. She skidded to a stop in front of Saffron & Sage, took a deep breath, and pushed through the rich orange and soft green door.

The cheerful tinkle of the bell was jarringly out of place. All eyes in the crowded restaurant turned to her. Boyd felt her cheeks flush, hating the attention.

"Everyone, stop eating!" she shouted, her voice trembling slightly. "Please, this is important."

Forks clattered onto plates. She heard someone mutter, "Nutter."

"Is anyone feeling unwell?" Boyd asked, scanning the room, fumbling for her ID. "Any blurred vision? Heart palpitations?"

The restaurant was full of diners seated at reclaimed wooden tables. Pots of herbs adorned the windowsills and hung from the ceiling, filling the space with an earthy aroma. Mismatched chairs added a shabby chic vibe. The atmosphere was one of confusion.

"What's going on?" someone demanded.

"Exactly what I'd like to know."

Boyd turned to face the angry voice coming from the kitchen. She was the most glamorous chef Boyd had ever seen. Her chef whites were cinched in at the waist to accentuate an hourglass figure. She removed her hat to reveal hair styled into neat, rockabilly victory rolls. Her face, though furious, sported a thick flash of fabulous black eyeliner.

"You must be April."

"What the hell is going on here?" she demanded, glaring at Boyd.

Boyd straightened her spine, meeting April's fiery gaze. "I'm DC Saffron Boyd. I work with DS Paula Keaton. I'm afraid she's in hospital. Someone poisoned her."

April opened her mouth but seemed lost for words. A look of worry and confusion coating her face.

Moving closer to the chef, Boyd lowered her voice so even the closest tables couldn't hear. "Our main suspect is someone you might know. Jeremy Knox."

April's face changed to disbelief. "Jeremy? That pathetic saddo from Folklore?"

Boyd gave a curt nod. "That *saddo* put two people in the hospital and may have killed another. We know he accused you of—"

"I didn't *steal* any recipe," April hissed, annoyance showing. She placed a hand on her hip, pouting her Cupid's bow lips.

"It doesn't matter if you did or didn't," Boyd said calmly, though she could feel all the eyes in the place burning into her. "Knox believes you did, and now you and your customers are in terrible danger."

CHAPTER 42

THE WIND WHIPPED ACROSS the rooftop, biting through Cooper's thin jacket. She shivered, wrapping her arms around herself. She could feel the tension in her legs and shoulders, but worst was how the cold grabbed the back of her neck. Some days, she missed having hair that could double as a scarf.

Whyte sidled up beside her. "Cold?"

"What gave it away?" she muttered through chattering teeth.

He stifled a chuckle and gave her a roguish smile. "Want to borrow my jumper?"

Cooper shot him a warning look. His other jumper was currrently shoved halfway down her laundry basket. "I'll pass."

"A hug?"

She knew what it would be like to feel his body heat seeping into her frozen limbs. She pushed the thought away. "Stop it. That's not funny."

"One day it will be."

"That day is not today."

The distant thrum of rotors broke through the sounds of city traffic. The police helicopter appeared on the horizon, a black speck growing larger by the second.

"Here we go," Whyte said. "Hope we see seals again. That was cool."

Cooper's stomach turned over. Flying wasn't usually a problem – not on an Airbus with beer or a G&T in hand – but these rickety death traps were a different matter. She steeled herself as the helicopter touched down, blades buzzing, kicking up a vortex of debris.

Whyte offered her a hand. She grabbed the rail instead, clambering into the cramped cabin. As they lifted off, Cooper grabbed the edge of her seat, but to her surprise, the anxiety that gripped her during their previous flight was muted.

Maybe she was finally getting used to it, she thought. Or maybe she was just too preoccupied with the case to care.

THE KITCHEN OF SAFFRON & SAGE was considerably bigger than the helicopter's cramped confines, but Boyd still found it claustrophobic. It was packed with front-of-house, cooks and catering gadgets. A sink overflowed with chopping boards and crockery. Service had been paused while sous chefs and kitchen porters exchanged glances, waiting for fresh orders.

Boyd gathered the workers around her, the smell of pine dish soap mingling with oregano and garlic. She rested her hands on the clean, metal top of the preparation station, savouring the cool feeling against her sweaty palms.

"April, you said you've known all the staff here since you opened. You trust them."

"That's right."

"But have you taken on any new suppliers recently?"

April shook her head. "No, we have our preferred butcher, fishmonger, greengrocer..."

Boyd looked around, making it clear she was talking to everyone now. "Has anyone been hanging around that you don't recognise? Anyone acting suspiciously? A delivery driver you've never seen before?"

Around the kitchen, everyone shrugged or shook their head.

April frowned, thinking. "Not that I can—"

"Wait," a server interjected. "What about that tea that came this morning?"

Boyd's ears perked up. "Tea?"

"Yeah," April said, realisation dawning. "Some fancy herbal blend. A free sample. There was a note saying if we liked it, we might want to put it on the menu. It was on the doorstep when I opened up."

Another server to Boyd's left started to shake. Her long hair was tied in a braid that hung over her left shoulder. She cradled a mug between her palms, steam rising upwards, obscuring her long plait. "I was on a break," she said, holding the mug away from herself. "It smelled nice. I thought— Oh, God."

Dread crept over Boyd. "How much have you had?"

"Half a cup," she answered, shaking violently now. Her fingers went slack, the mug slipping from her grasp, ceramic shattering across the metal prep station. The dark red liquid crept over the surface, dripping to the floor like blood trickling from a lifeless body.

CHAPTER 43

THE HELICOPTER'S VIBRATIONS THRUMMED through Cooper's body, a constant buzz rattling her bones, reverberating in her chest. She dialled Atkinson's number, glancing at Whyte, who averted his gaze out the window, looking at the choppy sea beneath.

"Hey," she said, her voice barely audible over the chopper's roar. "Listen, I've had to fly back to Odin's Gale. I'm sorry, I—"

"You're not going to be home for dinner?"

Cooper's stomach clenched, a familiar worry climbing up her spine. "I'm sorry. There's been a development—"

"I know. The job comes first."

Cooper closed her eyes, fighting the urge to defend herself. She could feel Whyte's presence, acutely aware of his attempt to ignore her conversation.

"It's not like that," she said softly.

"No, that's not what I meant," Atkinson said. "I mean *I know*. I understand. I get it. And I'm sorry if I've been needy. I didn't appreciate how lonely being a stay-at-home parent can be – and I work two days a week. What I'm trying to say is, do the job you're meant to do, just... be careful out there, okay?"

"I will."

"And Erica?"

"Yeah?"

"I love you."

She couldn't suppress the smile. "You too. I'll call you later."

She ended the call and cleared her throat.

"You good?" Whyte asked, his coffee-black eyes searching her face.

Cooper nodded, not trusting her voice. She turned to look out the window, desperate for a distraction.

"Christ," Cooper muttered. "Look at that."

Below, the sea churned, a rolling mass of grey and white. A tempestuous swell rolled, the surface heaving and sighing like a living, breathing creature. White caps dotted the surface – angry teeth, ready to swallow anything that dared to come too close.

"Weather's taking a turn for the worse."

As if on cue, the helicopter lurched, buffeted by a strong gust. Cooper's hand shot out, looking to grip – anything. She stopped herself, her fingers an inch from the DS's knee. She tucked her hands under her thighs and searched the angry sea for the first glimpse of Odin's Gale and the

SOV Electron. It wouldn't be long, she told herself, hoping that Electron could handle the waves better than the helicopter could handle the wind.

BOYD STOOD IN THE middle of Saffron & Sage, her eyes darting nervously around the restaurant as she addressed the patrons. Moments earlier, she'd sent the distressed server to A&E on foot, accompanied by a bartender. The ambulance would have taken twenty minutes; it was quicker for them to walk.

"I'm sorry, everyone, but we need to close immediately," she announced, her voice quiet but firm. "There's been a potential... incident."

A murmur rippled through the crowd. Despite Boyd's orders that everyone should stop eating, one man shovelled as much bread into his mouth as possible before being asked to leave. He washed it down with a large glass of red.

Boyd swallowed hard, fighting her natural shyness. "We believe someone may have attempted to sabotage the restaurant," she continued. "Please understand this is not the fault of the staff or chefs. And I'm sure they'd appreciate it if you refrain from leaving negative reviews."

April stepped forward, wiping her hands on her fitted chef's whites. "Everything served today is, of course, on the house."

Boyd nodded gratefully at April before turning back to the customers. "We believe the issue is confined. However, if you experience any unusual symptoms, please seek medical attention immediately. If in doubt, go straight to A&E."

As the patrons filed out, some taking their food and drinks with them, Boyd wondered if she'd made the right decision. Should she have sent them all to the hospital just in case? April was confident no one had been served the tea, but what if there'd been cross-contamination? Still, she couldn't fill an already overcrowded accident and emergency with *what-ifs*. She pushed the questions aside, focusing on the task at hand.

Once the last customer left, Boyd chewed a nail, a nervous habit she'd never quite shaken. "Can you tell me anything else about the delivery? Who brought it?"

April frowned. "Not really. It was just there when I opened up this morning. The package was sitting on the doorstep."

"Cameras?"

"No. Sorry."

"Did you see anyone suspicious hanging around? Anything out of the ordinary?"

"Nothing. It was a normal morning, except for that package."

"Okay," Boyd said, wishing she had more information. "I'll take the tea to be analysed and someone will come by to take a formal statement. Please arrange a deep clean before reopening."

"Of course," April said. Her face darkened, her lined eyes searching the floor for a moment. "I need to know. Paula— Is she going to be all right?"

THE HELICOPTER TOUCHED DOWN on the massive deck of Electron with a bone-jarring thud. Cooper gritted her teeth, her hands numb under her thighs. The wind howled, tugging at her clothing as she stepped onto the helipad.

India Morgan strode towards them, her stony face mirroring the grey sky. "Welcome back aboard, Detectives," she shouted over the dying rotor wash. "Any chance you brought my bosun back with you?"

Cooper worked her jaw. "If my theory is correct, Mr Longacre will be a free man by the end of the day."

India escorted Cooper and Whyte off the helipad in the direction of the bridge. "That's good to know. As discussed, I haven't repeated our conversation, nor have I told the technicians of your arrival – though the chopper would be hard to miss. Now, would you care to elaborate on why Hal would discharge himself from the hospital and what his relationship with Luna Sinclair has to do with any of this? Are my crew in danger?"

The bridge was vastly different to when Cooper last saw it. Gone were the little flags and stickers marking evidence. All the blood had been wiped clean. The chaos tidied away. She remembered the first aid kit strewn on the floor from Georgie's attempts to help Jude and Hal. Bandages, gauze, scissors, tweezers, a scalpel, a thermometer and an emergency blanket. All of it caked in blood. She remembered the SOCOs on their metal stepping stones, the flashes of cameras and the blinking screens. It was as if none of it had happened. The bridge was pristine. White with bright green accents to match VāyuVolt's logo and green energy branding.

Cooper hesitated, mulling her words as she looked around the airy, high-tech space. How much should she reveal? The case was far from closed.

"Let's just say new evidence has come to light. Where can we find Luna?"

India nodded, her expression neutral. "She's in the cinema room. Follow me."

CHAPTER 44

COOPER FOLLOWED INDIA TO the small cinema room onboard Electron; her eyes immediately found Luna sitting in the back row. The room was dark, except for the glow of the screen. In plushy seats, a group of wind farm technicians were engrossed in the romantic drama.

India flicked on the lights. Everyone blinked at the sudden brightness.

"Sorry to interrupt... What *are* you watching?"

"The Notebook," said a technician with tattooed arms and a bald head. "And we were just getting to the mushy part. Big Jim's already welling up."

Big Jim wiped his eyes on his shirt collar. He was easily one hundred and twenty kilos. "I'm not crying. I've just got sunscreen in my eyes."

"Yeah, yeah," said the tattooed man. "Funny how you only wear sunscreen on the days we watch the soppy films."

Cooper coughed. "Ahem. You can resume your cinematic experience in just a moment." She locked eyes with Luna Sinclair. "I just need to borrow Luna."

The men *oohed* like school children when someone was called to the headteacher's office.

India turned the lights off and shut the door as they left. In the corridor, Cooper and Whyte faced Luna. "Where's Hal?" Cooper asked.

Luna lowered her brows a fraction, slightly shrugging her shoulders. Subtle movements to convey confusion, nothing over the top. "In the hospital, I'd assume. With his injuries, I doubt they'd let him leave so soon. He'd still be under observation, right?"

She was a good actress, Cooper admitted. "Nice try. Hal left the RVI yesterday evening. You'd think he'd tell you, seeing as you're his girlfriend."

Luna's face paled. "We're just colleagues. I hardly know him. We work in different teams, have totally different roles on board."

Whyte produced the strip of photobooth pictures they'd found by Hal's bed. "Interesting definition of *colleagues*," he said, showing Luna the last and most intimate picture on the strip, the one of the pair kissing.

The irony wasn't lost on Cooper.

Luna tried to look away, but Cooper persisted. "Where's Hal Simpson?"

"I don't know."

"Hal Simpson was second in command of North Star when it hit the boat your sister was on. Your sister died in that collision—"

"Don't you think I know that?" Luna spat.

"What would Violet think? She hated offshore wind farms, and here you are, working at the site where she died and sleeping with the man who could have stopped it."

Luna's composure cracked. "Violet would want us both to be happy!" she blurted out before clamping her mouth shut again, realising her mistake.

Cooper repeated her words back to her. "She'd want you *both* to be happy? Both?"

BLUE LIGHTS FLASHED AS backup arrived at Saffron & Sage. Boyd didn't wait. She jumped in the passenger seat of the first car, and they took off towards Leazes Lane at an alarming pace. The narrow streets of Newcastle's city centre were alive with the bustle of diners, shoppers and students. Buses zipped past a mix of historic and modern buildings. Neon signs advertising shops and eateries glimmered through the overcast day.

"There it is," Boyd called, pointing towards a restaurant on their left. The car pulled up a few doors down, mounting the curb.

The restaurant's exterior was adorned with intricate carvings mimicking Celtic knots and ancient runes. Lanterns, reminiscent of something out of an old legend, cast a warm, flickering light across the weathered stone façade. Boyd opened the heavy wooden door, the dark varnish smooth to the touch. Inside, the theme continued; the walls were lined with rich, dark wood panels, and tapestries depicting mythical creatures hung beside shelves filled with old leather-bound books. The place exuded a sense of mystery as if they had awoken in a Hans Christian Andersen fairy tale.

The hum of conversation in the dining area ceased as patrons took in the three uniformed officers who stood next to Boyd.

A woman pointed at her son, "See, I told you what would happen if you didn't eat your greens."

The officer nearest her, Jones, a man with sandy hair and pale skin, moved closer to her. "Please don't tell your son the police will arrest him if he doesn't do as you ask. We want children to run *to* us if they're in trouble, not run away from us."

Admonished, but understanding, she nodded.

Jones turned to her son. "But you should still eat your greens, lad. You think anyone playing for United is a fussy eater?"

While Jones won over the diners, Boyd discretely told a waiter she needed to speak with the owner. The waiter nodded towards the open kitchen. "He's over there."

He was looking right at her. "Jeremy Knox?" she called.

Knox was of medium height and medium build with white hair and piercing blue eyes. He stood over the pass in the open kitchen, dressed in a stained chef's coat with his sleeves rolled up the elbows. He hurriedly passed a plate to a young waitress. Swallowing hard, his eyes appeared wild and desperate, a sheen of sweat on his brow. He glanced over his shoulder at an emergency exit.

"Don't do it," Boyd warned, her voice calmer than she felt. "There are two officers on the other side of that door."

She approached the pass, smelling grilled pork. Her stomach rumbled. All she'd had that day was a bowl of muesli at home and a chocolate bar from the hospital's vending machine. "We need to have a chat, Jeremy."

Knox's blue eyes fell on the stove to his left, his fingers wrapping around the handle of a cast-iron skillet. In one fluid motion, he grabbed a pan from the stove. The stench of hot oil filled the air.

"Jeremy, don't—"

"STAY BACK!" Knox was beyond reason, brandishing the scalding liquid towards them. He was so close Boyd could hear the sizzle, could see the tiny globules of boiling hell dancing in the pan. "I mean it," he said, wielding the skillet like a weapon. "Stay the hell back, or that pretty little face of yours will never be the same again."

CHAPTER 45

COOPER'S VOICE WAS FIRM on the bridge of Electron as she delivered the words that would change Luna's life forever. "Luna Sinclair, I'm arresting you on suspicion of aiding and abetting Hal Simpson in evading arrest."

Electron's reinforced hull sheltered them from the bitter chill outside, but Luna shivered nonetheless. She tried to look casual, remaining silent, but her hand trembled slightly as she reached for the railing beside her.

"This is a serious offence," Cooper continued, her gaze never wavering from Luna's. "You do not have to say anything, but it may harm your defence if you do not mention when questioned something which you later rely on in court. Anything you do say may be given in evidence."

Electron swayed gently beneath them, the distant, rhythmic bass of the turbines humming through the ship.

"For the time being, you will be detained in the police helicopter until we can transport you to Northumbria Police Headquarters, where you can speak to a solicitor."

Luna looked longingly at the port light, but there was no escape.

Cooper stepped closer, flanked by Whyte. "Unless you wish to co-operate, in which case, we can move to a meeting room. Much more comfortable. So, I'll ask you once more, where is Hal Simpson?"

Luna bit her lip but said nothing.

"Luna, do you understand the charges against you?"

Her strong shoulders slumped, the last residue of defiance fading from her eyes. "Yes... I understand."

"We're going to take your electronic devices now, Luna. Where is your phone?"

"I lost it."

Cooper scanned Luna from head to toe, but Whyte spotted it first. "Left trouser pocket."

Cooper slid her hand into the woman's pocket, feeling the rough threads of her durable work trousers against the back of her hand.

"You can't do that," Luna said.

"I can, and I am." Cooper passed the iPhone to Whyte. "It's got face ID."

He held the screen in front of Luna. She squirmed, turning her head to the side, but the phone unlocked regardless.

Cooper escorted Luna to the chopper while Whyte started scrolling through her messages. By the time she returned, he'd found something in her texts. He showed Cooper a message to a number not saved in Luna's contacts.

"Have you tried calling it?"

"Disconnected."

Cooper leant in to read the message.

55.12989, -1.50832.

"Coordinates," Cooper said.

"For an address in Port of Blyth," he told her.

India Morgan, who'd remained a silent observer at the helm until that point, stepped forward. "Let me see." She took one look at the satellite image on Google Maps and said, "It's a marine supply store. We get most of our electronics from there. The technicians deal with them regularly."

Whyte folded his arms across his chest. He thought momentarily, then asked, "Did she need supplies for this trip out?"

India confirmed she did. "Remote diagnostics are showing that the delta modules are going to blow within the next week. We needed eight delta modules loaded onto OGD32 ready for the specialist electrician arriving on Monday."

Whyte went back to scanning Luna's messages; Cooper nodded as if she knew what a delta module was. "So Luna picked up the modules from Blyth and loaded them onto Electron before leaving the Tyne?" she asked.

"Gray," India called for the third officer, Graham Bell. "Bring up the footage of everyone coming aboard." Then to Cooper, "VāyuVolt installed cameras on the gangway before we set off. After what happened, they thought more surveillance would be a good thing."

Gray found the footage in no time, and Cooper watched as Luna rolled a wheeled pallet up the gangway. A wooden crate 100 × 50 × 50cm was fixed to the pallet with a logo sprayed on the side.

"That's the delta modules," Gray said, pointing at the screen. "Want a printout?"

Cooper was about to answer when Whyte held up the phone. "Found another message to the same disconnected number. Something about a collection tonight."

Cooper frowned. "Tonight?" She took the phone from Whyte, and sure enough, it alluded to something being picked up at around midnight that night. "But, if Luna collected the delta modules last night, what would she be collecting tonight? And why so late?"

"And how would she collect anything from way out here?" Whyte gestured out the large window in front of the helm. All they could see was the circular swishing of white turbine blades cutting through the gunmetal sky.

Cooper scowled at the image of Luna struggling with the crate. It looked heavy, even for a powerhouse like her. She pictured Hal. He wasn't a big man. By his own admission, he was scrawny. She imagined him sitting, wondering how tall he would be and how much room he would take up if he pulled his knees to his chest.

Cooper looked at Whyte, knowing instantly he was thinking the same thing.

She turned to India. "Where is the crate now?"

"OGD32. We loaded it onto the turbine as soon as we got here."

Chapter 46

THE ACRID SCENT OF burning garlic singed Saffron Boyd's nostrils as she stared down the barrel of the hot oil. Heat radiated from the pan, flames flickering menacingly on the burner as sweat trickled down her spine, her blonde hair plastered to her neck. Jeremy Knox's eyes darted madly around the kitchen, the pan of bubbling liquid trembling in his white-knuckled grip.

Boyd's heart hammered. She'd faced down criminals before, but only once like this – when she truly believed her life was at stake.

She froze, remembering the time she was left for dead. She saw Liam Hook's face so vividly in her mind she could practically feel his fists pummelling her to the ground, feel his saliva sliding down her face as he spat on her and kicked her ribs.

"Jeremy," she managed, pushing past the tremor in her voice. "Think about what you're doing. You wouldn't hurt your customers. This restaurant is everything to you."

A muscle twitched in Knox's cheek. For a moment, uncertainty flitted in his expression.

Jones seized his chance. He raised his voice, addressing the stunned diners. "Everyone needs to leave. Now. It's not safe here."

Mumbles rippled through the room.

"Go!" Boyd barked, her fear momentarily evaporating at the thought of innocent people getting hurt.

Chairs scraped against hardwood. Forks clattered onto china. The diners shuffled towards the exit, some clearly wishing to stay and watch the show, to live stream it on Facebook or record it for Youtube.

As the door swung shut behind the last patron, an uneasy silence descended. Boyd and Knox faced each other across the empty restaurant.

Boyd's voice trembled again. "Jeremy Knox, you're under arrest for the murder of Colin Finch and the attempted murders of detectives Paula Keaton and Oliver Martin."

Her words echoed in the deserted restaurant. Only the soft hiss of the stove and Knox's ragged breathing broke the stillness.

He brandished the pan toward her. "I didn't kill him," Knox spluttered. "He fell. Tumbled into a plant and started screaming like a banshee. He looked like he was having a heart attack."

Boyd's heart continued to thunder. She thought of Paula Keaton, wishing she could channel her fearlessness. She took a careful step forward, her eyes never leaving Knox. "The autopsy will confirm that if it's true."

Behind her, Jones snorted. "I'm sure finding an intruder in the dead of night didn't help."

Boyd wanted to flash him a look, tell him that now was not the time, but she couldn't risk looking away from Knox. "That doesn't explain poisoning my colleagues and planning to poison the diners at Saffron and Sage."

Knox flinched. Again, his gaze darted towards the exit.

"And I'm sure April Davis will be consulting a lawyer as we speak," she added.

Knox's reaction was instantaneous. "That woman is a fraud! She steals recipes."

Boyd tensed, ready to move. One wrong word could set him off. "Even if that were true," she said softly. "It's no reason to—"

"She's the talk of the town. That place is fully booked months in advance." The pan in Knox's hand sloshed dangerously. "And it's all stolen. The recipe for the terrine – mine! The foam for the scallops – mine! She stole everything from me. Her place is thriving and mine is on the bones of its arse."

Boyd had never met April until today. She had no idea if Knox's allegations were true, but she knew how much Martin had raved about her food. Could recipes even be stolen? Could you copyright a carbonara or trademark truffle fries? She didn't know.

"Even so," she said, "that doesn't justify trying to poison her customers. You were prepared to kill innocent people, and for what, to have her sent to prison for life? Have her restaurant shut down? Destroying her business isn't going to make yours any more popular."

Boyd's muscles tensed; she knew instantly she'd said the wrong thing. She sensed the uniformed officer beside her shift, ready to intervene.

Too slow.

Knox swung the pan in a deadly arc. Shimmering droplets of oil sailed through the air, glistening like liquid fire as they hurtled toward Boyd and the officers.

Time seemed to crawl. Boyd threw herself to the side just as searing heat licked past her face, close enough to singe the fine hairs on her cheek. Her coat protected most of her body, but oil rained down on the backs of her hands. A scream tore from her throat, raw and guttural, as the scorching liquid showered her skin.

Beside her, Jones convulsed in agony, collapsing to the ground, clutching at his face.

With the clawing smell of burning oil and flesh filling her nostrils, Boyd scrambled to her feet, adrenaline surging.

Knox hurled the pan aside. It clattered against the stainless steel countertop.

Oh God, Boyd thought, watching in horror as Knox grabbed a nearby cleaver.

"Jeremy," she pleaded. "Put that down. We can still work this out."

"There's no way out," he snarled, lunging forward, wielding the blade above his head.

Boyd moved on instinct. Her fingers found the cold metal of a nearby fire extinguisher. She swung it up just in time.

CLANG!

The cleaver struck the extinguisher, the impact jarring Boyd's arms. Knox's eyes widened in surprise.

No time to think. Boyd swung again, putting her whole body into the motion. The extinguisher slammed into Knox's side with a sickening thud.

He stumbled, gasping. But the rage hadn't dimmed. She couldn't let him recover. Dropping the extinguisher, Boyd charged, driving her shoulder into his chest.

They crashed into the prep table. Pots and pans clattered to the floor, the cacophony echoing off the metal surfaces.

Knox grunted in pain, but his hand was already reaching for the fallen knife.

No, Boyd thought desperately. She pounced, grabbing his wrist.

She tried to twist his arm behind his back, but he was too strong for her. The two uniformed officers rushed forward.

"I've got the cuffs," Jones grunted, fumbling with one hand.

The three of them took Knox to the floor, Boyd pressing her knee into his back.

"It's over," she panted, pressing her knee into his back. "Just stop fighting."

Knox thrashed beneath them, his strength fueled by desperation. His face was pressed against the cold tile, his breath coming in ragged gasps.

As the cuffs clicked into place, Boyd exhaled sharply. "It's over," she repeated, this time to herself.

Boyd stood, her legs shaking. The restaurant was in chaos, filled with upturned equipment and smashed crockery. Spilled oil glistened on the floor. The pungent smell of fear and sweat.

"You okay?" the officer asked her, cradling his injured arm.

She nodded, but the panic attack was closing in. The periphery of her vision darkened, and she couldn't breathe. Boyd gripped the edge of the prep station, staring at the blisters forming on the backs of her hands.

Just breathe, she told herself.

In for four, hold for four, out for six.

The kitchen blurred.

In, two, three, four.

Hold, two, three, four.

Then, all that was fuzzy snapped back into focus. She exhaled slowly, knowing it was over. Boyd was okay.

CHAPTER 47

THE NORTH SEA STIRRED angrily. Dark clouds, expectant with rain, loomed overhead. Cooper stood on the deck of Electron, her slim frame buffeted by icy gusts that carried the smell of the impending storm. She eyeballed the turbine in question: OGD32. She was convinced Hal was on there, smuggled in disguised as a crate of delta modules, ready to be collected overnight, under the cloak of darkness. But by whom? His old eco-terrorism pals? Luna and Violet's activist friends?

The pulsing beat of the turbine blades felt like the throb of a migraine. Cooper suppressed a shiver, going through the possibilities. Was Hal alone? Armed?

"Suit up," India ordered, pointing towards the safety gear. "This is no ordinary crew transfer. Ideally, we wouldn't allow non-competent individuals on the turbines during these conditions—"

"And normally, we wouldn't allow civilians to aid in the arrest of a murder suspect," Cooper said.

Earlier, they'd battled it out over the safest way for Cooper and Whyte to apprehend Hal. VāyuVolt didn't want Northumbria Police on the turbine, and Northumbria Police didn't want innocent parties anywhere near someone capable of murder. In the end, they compromised. Cooper and Whyte would be accompanied by two highly qualified technicians: Lars and Jennifer. Ironically, the person with the biggest muscles and their best bet to act as unofficial backup was currently in police custody – Bosun Cliff Longacre.

Jennifer helped Cooper with her PPE. Lars did the same for Whyte. It took a solid fifteen minutes to wrestle the two detectives into their gear, triple-checking every piece of the equipment. Whyte swore as his hair caught in the rubber collar of his dry suit. Not a problem for Cooper, but her hard hat felt tight and alien against her shaved scalp.

"This is worse than riot gear," Whyte said, squirming as Lars circled him, tugging on straps and checking shackles.

"Carabiners secure, harnesses tight," he said. "Yeah, it weighs a tonne. You get used to it, though. You'll resent it less if you remember it's for your safety. Anything can happen out there."

The extra weight was already pressing down on Cooper's thin shoulders. Even when she was nine months pregnant, she'd never felt this heavy or bulky. She glanced down at the steel-capped boots; they felt like lead weights.

"Feel like an astronaut yet?" Jennifer joked as she handed her a pair of gloves. She was the same size as Cooper but carried herself with the confidence of someone who knew her worth wasn't measured by her weight or gender.

Cooper nodded grimly. The gloves were rough and two sizes too big for her, like most of the gear she'd been given.

"Sorry, this doesn't fit quite right," Jennifer said, adjusting Cooper's harness. "It's actually Luna's. To be fair, it doesn't even fit her properly. All this stuff's designed for blokes. They forget a lot of technicians have boobs these days. Don't worry. It'll do its job; it'll just be a bit uncomfortable."

Sure, the kit was awkward, but it was the need for it that made Cooper feel nervous. She chanced a look at the sea, turning away again quickly.

The gangway operator approached, his face stern. "These seas are rough. A two-and-a-half metre swell is at the limit of our operating capacity. It's risky."

Part of Cooper would welcome an excuse not to venture onto the turbine, but she stared him down. "We have to try. He's injured, desperate. We can't leave him overnight."

"Or let him be rescued by God-knows-who," Whyte added.

"Exactly."

The wind howled, sneaking through the layers of Cooper's safety gear to run its icy claws across her chest. She squared her shoulders, faking bravery.

The Ampelmann A-Type gangway extended from Electron, a sleek mechanical arm reaching out towards the turbine. Cooper watched it adjust, offsetting for the massive swells below with fluid precision.

"Impressive," she murmured.

Whyte grunted in agreement.

The operator pressed two buttons on a panel. "Six degrees of freedom," he said proudly, like a boy showing off his new toy. "The gangway will automatically compensate for pitch, roll, heave, yaw, sway, and surge. You'll feel like you're walking on solid ground."

Cooper doubted that very much. For one, the floor was latticework, and she could see straight through it. The first drops of rain began to fall, stinging her face. She blinked, her grip tightening on the railing.

"Ready?" asked Jennifer.

"Yes," Cooper replied. Then to Whyte. "Ready?"

"After you, boss."

As they approached the gangway, Jennifer raised her voice against the wind. "Remember, hold the rail tight. Steady pace, no rushing. The sea might look rough, but I promise the gangway will hold. In Ampelmann, we trust."

"Got it," Cooper replied. She gripped the bannister in her left hand; it came just above her waist and was already slick with rainwater. The high-tech gangway stretched out before her, its metallic surface gleaming. The motion-compensated system was in constant, fluid movement, adjusting to the undulating sea below. It felt both futuristic and precarious at the same time.

Through its floor, Cooper watched the dark, churning sea crashing against the side of Electron, sending mist and spray into the air. Every time a wave hit the hull, the gangway shifted to remain steady. The faint hum of hydraulics and the groaning of metal filled her ears, drowned out only by the wind and the heartbeat of turbine blades.

At the end of the gangway, the turbine towered. An imposing white pillar, taller than Cooper could ever have imagined. A yellow transition piece at its base linked the tower to its foundations below the water. She'd seen them before. From a distance. Stacked up on ships leaving the Tyne. But closer, they seemed enormous.

The rain pelted harder now as the gangway locked securely into the turbine platform with a mechanical hiss. Cooper took a deep breath of salty air and followed Jennifer. The gangway was steady, but it still felt like walking a tightrope above the unrelenting waves below. She felt weighed down, her steps laboured and clumsy. The wind pushed against her every step as if telling her to turn back.

"Stay close," she called over her shoulder to Whyte.

His response was lost in a roar of wind.

God, it was awful. Cooper felt wholly exposed to the elements; her heart pounded, bombarded with adrenaline as she continued forward, each step fighting her instincts.

"You're doing great," Jennifer assured her.

"Almost there," she called back to Whyte, whose wet dark hair was matted down by the rain, water dripping off the ends as he kept his head low against the wind.

Cooper took the final step onto the turbine platform, her gloved fingers aching from grasping the rail so tightly.

Whyte moved up beside her, his face sombre. "Let's go," he said, reaching for the next rail. Together, they climbed a flight of external stairs leading to a metal door with rounded corners. It was covered in bright stickers warning all who entered of the risks.

A hiss behind Cooper made her jump. The gangway had detached from the platform and was retracting back towards Electron. If Cooper felt exposed before, it was nothing to how she felt now, standing on the thin ledge of the turbine, a mere island in the middle of the bloody sea.

She glanced upwards, gasping as the vertigo hit her. At 250m high, she couldn't even crane her head far back enough to see the top of the turbine. *Don't look up. Don't look down*, she told herself. *Just focus on what's in front of you.*

Lars took a key from his belt and unlocked the door. There was a noise of metal sliding against metal as the bolt slid across. He then looked at Cooper and Whyte. "You might find it claustrophobic inside. There are a series of ladders and platforms. If we need to climb, we must do so in pairs, tethered on at all times. No exceptions. Do I make myself clear?"

"Crystal," Whyte answered. "But hopefully, it won't come to that." He pounded his fist against the metal door. "Hal Simpson! Northumbria Police. We know you're in there!"

No response. Not that they could hear over the violent weather.

Cooper clasped the handle, muscles straining as she pressed it down and pushed her weight against the door. A gust of wind nearly tore it from her grasp, threatening to slam it back in her face.

Lars caught it in time. He braced, holding the door as they stumbled inside. The howling storm was abruptly silenced, replaced by an eerie mechanical hum. Motion sensor lighting flickered on. Above, LEDs clicked on one by one, casting sharp beams of cold light into the narrow, vertical shaft.

Claustrophobic was an understatement. The air felt damp and stale, the space closing in around Cooper. She didn't know what was worse – standing out there, fully exposed to the relentless wind and rain, or being sealed in this windowless metal tube, where every breath seemed to echo off the steel walls. It was as if she'd been swallowed whole by the turbine. And somewhere in here, Hal Simpson was hiding.

CHAPTER 48

HER BREATH PUFFED IN the cold, damp air, the internal walls of the tower slick with condensation.

"Christ," Whyte muttered, his breath visible in the chill.

"Stay alert," Cooper whispered, her eyes scanning the cramped space, her steel-capped boots echoing off the round walls as they moved into the centre of the turbine. Beside her lay an empty crate, its lid ajar, the packaging for the delta modules scattered about the floor like discarded sweet wrappers.

A flicker of movement from above caught her eye. She froze, signaling Whyte.

Hal Simpson was huddled in a dark corner on a platform over one hundred feet above her.

He looked half-dead already, shivering violently, his clothes soaked through, clinging to his trembling frame. His arms clutched at his ribs as if holding himself together. Cooper shuddered, not from cold but from the sight of Hal – pathetic yet feral.

Whyte called to him, projecting his voice into the towering void above. "Hal. We know everything. Captain Jude. Luna. Scotland."

He moved to the base of the metal ladder and attached a thick safety tether to a rung with a carabiner clip. Lars, the technician, flanked him and did the same.

In the shadows, Hal backed himself further towards the bottom of the next ladder. Cooper instinctively moved to the ladder, ready to follow the DS. Animals were most dangerous when cornered, and she had no intention of Whyte facing him alone.

That was until Jennifer cupped Cooper's arm. "Only two people at a time on the ladder."

Shit. She wanted to call him back, pull rank and go instead of him. He'd object, of course. She could order him, but as much as Cooper's pride protested, she knew it was the right call to let the two gents go ahead. Hal wasn't a big man, but he was a lethal one; the ferocity at which he must have gone after Captain Jude was evidence of that. He was trapped, desperate and, by the looks of it, still severely injured. If he needed assistance coming down the ladder, Lars and Whyte were better suited. Still, she worried about anyone getting hurt. As much as VāyuVolt didn't want so-called non-competent individuals to risk injury on a turbine, she knew what a PR disaster it would be if Lars or Jennifer were hurt or worse during Hal's capture.

And if something happened to Whyte, she'd never forgive herself.

She reached out, tapping his harness. "Be careful," she urged, her voice quiet.

"I will."

"Promise."

He gave a faint smile as he started to climb. "You're not getting rid of me that easily."

Cooper backed off into the middle of the floor. "It's over, Hal," she called, her voice carrying after Whyte up the tower. "Don't do anything you'd later regret."

Hal grimaced, a mixture of pain and despair. He reached up and gripped the metal rail in his colourless hands. Cooper stilled, ready for anything. With a grunt, Hal pushed himself up. He wavered on his feet, his injured leg barely supporting his weight. Then, like a puppet with cut strings, he crumpled to the floor.

Whyte was at the first platform now. One to go. Cooper felt helpless, standing there, watching. He wasn't as gungho as some she'd worked with. If Keaton had been here, she probably – no, definitely – would have ignored the tethers and scrambled up the ladder as fast as she could. Whyte was more measured. He was the look-before-you-leap sort. Painstakingly, he clipped the first tether as high above him as he could, then released the second tether before climbing a few more rungs. Climb, clip, repeat.

"I didn't mean for it to happen," Hal croaked, barely louder than the muted roar of the storm outside. "Any of it. No one was supposed to die."

The words meant nothing to Cooper; she'd heard them all before in countless confessions. Still, the bare anguish in Hal's voice was unsettling. *Focus*, she told herself. *Don't let empathy cloud your judgment.*

She stepped forward, her boots echoing in the confined space. She stared up at them, feeling dizzy with vertigo. "Hal Simpson," she began. "I'm arresting you for the murder of Captain Jude McDermott." The familiar words rolled off her tongue, regardless of the surreal setting. "You don't have to say anything, but it may harm your defence if you do not mention when questioned something you later rely on in court. Anything you do say may be given in evidence."

Whyte was almost there now. "You need to come with us," he said.

Desperation painted Hal's face. He dove to his left, grasping something from the shadows. It glistened when he raised it in the artificial light. "No!" he shouted desperately.

A wrench. A big one.

"Elliot! Look out!"

Hal released the heavy tool, lobbing it towards the two men on the ladder below him. Whyte pushed himself off the ladder to avoid being hit. Cooper screamed as he fell, watching it as if in slow motion, one sickening millisecond at a time until the tether caught him. He swung, the wrench soaring past him, clipping the very end of the peak of Lars' hard hat.

Cooper covered her mouth with her hand, convinced she'd been about to see Whyte fall to his death. Suddenly, Jennifer tackled her hard, forcing her to stumble to the ground. She crumpled under the weight of the other woman, air forced from her lungs. The wrench slammed into the ground where she'd just been standing. The sharp clang reverberated through the chamber, leaving her ears ringing.

"Sorry, 'bout that," said the technician.

"You saved my life," said Cooper. "Don't apologise."

Above, Whyte was climbing again. He was at the platform, pulling himself through the trapdoor onto the steel structure. He sprang straight into action, pushing Hal against the curved wall, looking around to assess if anything else could be used as a weapon. Hal's resistance crumbled as quickly as it had flared. His body went limp, all fight leaving him in a rush.

Outside, the wind continued to rage, shrieking through every crack and crevice of the turbine. The metallic walls seemed to vibrate with its fury.

Cooper's radio crackled as Whyte messaged her.

"He can barely stand. Think his leg's infected or something. He can't climb down the ladder."

Jennifer was already preparing long coils of rope. "We'll have to lower him down," she said.

She climbed the two ladders swiftly, leaving Cooper alone on the turbine floor like a spare part. She removed her harness, putting it on Hal's cold, limp torso and attached the lines using elaborate knots.

Whyte descended the ladder faster than he'd climbed. With his feet back on the floor, he exhaled like he'd been holding his breath the entire time. He shared a look with Cooper, silently implying the ladder had been far more frightening than it looked.

Above, Jennifer was talking softly to Hal, reassuring him. "Don't worry, mate. We've got you. We've done this before. We'll take it nice and slow, okay?"

Inch by inch, they lowered the detainee down the shaft. Easing the two lines one at a time so one always acted as a brake. At the first platform, Lars re-prepared the lines.

When Hal reached the floor, Cooper moved in, untying the extra lines. She removed her gloves and pressed two fingers to his neck, counting the rapid, thready pulse. His skin was clammy and pale. Shock was a genuine concern.

"Hal, stay with us," she murmured. "We'll get you out of here."

"Cuffs?" Whyte asked.

She shook her head. As she did so, she heard the gangway operator crackling through her radio. "Have you got him? We need to get you out of there."

"Affirmative," she replied.

As if on cue, the turbine shuddered. The rain's intensity doubled, sheets of water hammering against the metal walls. It sounded like a thousand angry fists demanding entry.

Cooper's stomach clenched. This was bad.

The radio crackled again. The gangway operator's voice was urgent this time. "Wind's picking up fast. You need to move. We're at the limit for safe transfer."

Whyte's usually unemotional face flickered with concern.

"No time to waste," Cooper said, her mind trying to devise contingencies. "Can you two manage him?"

Whyte and Lars nodded, already moving to hoist Hal to his feet. "We've got him."

Cooper watched as the two men supported Hal's weight, the injured man's feet dragging slightly.

"All right," Jennifer said, gripping the handle of the turbine door. "On three. One, two—"

She yanked it open, and chaos erupted.

The wind screamed. A sentient, furious thing. It tore at their clothes, threatening to pull the hats from their heads and push them off their feet. The gangway extended before them like a metal hammock swaying in the gale. Of course, it wasn't the gangway that was swaying – it was everything else. Ahead, Electron bobbed like driftwood.

Cooper stepped out first. Almost crying with fear. She partially closed her eyes against the stinging rain. Every step was difficult; the wind pushed and pulled, trying to trip her up.

Don't look down, she reminded herself, gripping the railing. One step. Then another.

Behind her, Whyte's breathing was laboured as he guided Hal across. A muffled curse, then a stumble.

She turned, seeing Hal falter, his legs buckling. But Whyte held firm, his face determined as he steadied the other man.

"Almost there," she shouted over the wind's roar. "Keep moving!"

Just a few more steps. Just a few more—

Finally, her feet hit the solid deck of Electron. Cooper turned, reaching for Whyte's hand to help him bring Hal aboard.

As soon as they were safe, Jennifer shouted to the crew, "We're clear! Retract the gangway!"

The gangway retracted, its quiet mechanical whir drowned out by the storm. Taking a moment to ground herself and regain some calm, Cooper took a shuddering breath and looked around the deck. But instead of steadying her, something she saw piqued her anxiety. Or rather, it was something she couldn't see.

"The helicopter!" she gasped, pointing. It was gone.

A door opened. India Morgan and Georgie Peters beckoned them inside. India gave Hal a withering, disappointed look, shaking her head disdainfully; Georgie stared at Hal with cold detachment, but his fingers twitched as though he longed to act.

India turned to Cooper. "The pilot's taking Luna to Police Headquarters. He left before the wind picked up. He's outrunning the storm and will be there within the hour. You can contact him from the bridge if you like. We have high-powered radios there."

India appraised the technicians. "Thank you for assisting our guests," she told Jennifer and Lars, dismissing them.

Guests? What happened to *non-competent individuals?*

India suggested Hal be taken to the medical bay where he could be treated whilst restrained, shackled to the bed. Cooper and Georgie agreed.

"And Electron?" she asked as Whyte and Georgie led Hal towards the medical bay.

"We're heading back," India told them, her face stern. "It'll be dawn by the time we get into port. I've asked for two cabins to be prepared for you with towels and some dry clothes. They're crew uniforms, but they'll fit. If you need sea sickness medication, I'd suggest taking it now. We're in for a bumpy night."

Cooper swallowed. Another night on board. She glanced at Whyte as he passed, saw his lips twitch in a half-smile. He leant in, whispering something for her ears only.

CHAPTER 49

THE STORM'S TANTRUM HAD abated, leaving behind a crisp, clear morning with icy pavements and swirls of frost on car windscreens. The Uber dropped Cooper outside HQ. Her car was still at the Royal Victoria Infirmary. She'd had time to pop home, shower, change, and kiss her baby before returning to the station.

Cooper pushed through the doors. Her breath caught in her throat as she spotted Whyte across the lobby. Their eyes met, but they didn't speak. He was still wearing the white polo shirt and dark utility trousers he'd been given by the crew, having escorted Hal straight from Electron.

In the interview suite, Singh sat ramrod straight in a pinstripe ensemble. He offered her a wrapped sweet from his pocket.

"Sugar helps the brain, you know," he said.

Cooper declined. "My brain's fine, thank you, Daljit."

Liar.

The door opened. Having been checked over by the station doctor, Hal shuffled in, flanked by two officers, his feet dragging across the floor. His clothes were clean, but everything else about him screamed defeat. The bandage on his leg. The pallor of his skin. The haunted look in his eyes. Cooper carefully observed him as he lowered himself into the chair. Each movement seemed to cost him. Good. She hoped he felt the weight of what he'd done.

Cooper leaned forward, pitching her voice low and gentle. "You look tired, Hal."

He crossed his arms over his chest. A barrier.

"We just want the truth," Cooper continued, her hands resting on the table. Open. Inviting. "You said you didn't want this to happen, didn't you? You said you didn't mean for it to happen. All of this – it's spiralled out of control, hasn't it?"

Hal chewed the inside of his cheek, but she caught the glimmer of something in his eyes. "It doesn't have to end badly for you," she pressed. "Tell us what happened. Maybe we can help."

The silence stretched. Cooper held her breath, watching for any crack in Hal's defences.

"We know about Scotland, Hal. Your DNA flagged the report. We know you're tied to eco-terrorism."

Come on, you bastard. Break.

Hal's shoulders sagged.

"Jude..." His voice cracked. "He figured it out. After everything, he pieced it all together."

Cooper leaned further in. "What did he figure out, Hal?"

"I messed up. I didn't delete the last message."

Cooper waited.

Hal's words came in fragments, each one a struggle. "He knew I leaked the data about the bird deaths. When— When he knew I'd done that, he wondered what else I'd leaked. He suspected I was the one who gave the protesters North Star's coordinates."

Cooper remembered reading Jude's statement about how he didn't understand how the protesters had found them out there. The wind farm was still under construction. It wasn't on any charts. Even if the protestors had checked the notices for mariners, they still shouldn't have found the vessel in that thick fog. North Star's transmitter was broken; they were essentially invisible.

"It was my fault," Hal whispered. "I told them where to find us. If I hadn't—"

"Violet might still be alive," she finished.

Hal shuddered, sobbing, tears dripping onto the table.

"How did Jude react when he found out?" Cooper asked, keeping her tone even.

Hal's laugh was hollow. "How do you think?"

"I think he'd be really fucking pissed off." The shift in Cooper's tone shocked Hal into sitting back and meeting her eye. "He faced a tribunal, Hal. He almost lost his job. He had to live under the shadow of Violet Sinclair's death every day since it happened. He had PTSD. Nightmares. Depression."

"He turned to drink," added Singh. "Engaged in self-destructive behaviour. Pushed his friends away, had an affair."

"What happened after he found the message?" Cooper asked, rubbing her neck.

"He lost it," Hal continued, his voice cracking, his hands trembling on the table. "He came at me in a blind rage. Said I was to blame. That Violet died because of me. I... I panicked," he whispered. "There was a scalpel in the first aid kit on the bridge. I just... grabbed it."

A jolt went through Cooper. The first aid kit. Her mind flashed to India and Gray using that same kit to treat Hal, to try and resuscitate Jude. The murder weapon had been there the entire time.

"I didn't mean to... but he kept coming. I felt cornered. I was scared he was going to kill me," Hal said, his words tumbling out. "The blade... it just slid in so easily. It cut deep. Suddenly, Jude was on the floor, bleeding out." His eyes met Cooper's, pleading. "I didn't mean for it to go that far. I just... I couldn't stop."

His remorse seemed genuine. Cooper stood, feeling agitated by the hard plastic seat. "It all happened so quickly? You weren't thinking? You felt threatened? You acted in self-defence?"

Hal nodded eagerly, but Cooper cut him off. "Bullshit."

The little colour Hal had drained instantly from his face. "No. No. I was scared. Jude was mad. Completely mad. I was scared for my life."

"That might be true," Cooper said. "I can believe that. Can you believe that, DI Singh?"

Singh pondered for a moment. "Yes. I can believe that, DCI Cooper."

Hal smiled at Singh.

"Do you believe this man acted in self-defence?"

"Absolutely not."

Hal's smile abruptly disappeared.

"And why might that be, DI Singh?"

"The boots, DCI Cooper."

Hal paled further, fussing with his glasses, shifting in his chair. "I panicked. I swear I just panicked. I knew I was in trouble, so I grabbed a pair of boots and turned the scalpel on myself."

"If that's true, why was none of Jude's blood found outside of the bridge?"

Cooper waited for an answer, but none came.

"It's because you stole the boots – Cliff Longacre's boots – *before* attacking Jude. That's not self-defence, Hal. That's premeditated. You didn't panic; you made a plan. You told us you'd left the bridge to get your glasses case and when you came back someone was attacking the captain. I think you left the bridge to find yourself an alibi. You saw Cliff leave his cabin with Kay and, knowing his cabin was unoccupied, helped yourself to his boots. You left, stole the boots, returned, killed Jude, then walked around the scene, framing an innocent man."

Cooper's voice increased in volume, maddened by the man's deception. He'd fooled them all. Fooled VāyuVolt into hiring him. Fooled the media into believing the distorted data. Fooled the doctors. Fooled her.

Cooper slammed her hand on the desk. Singh jumped almost as much as Hal did. "Then you hid the damn boots where you thought we wouldn't find them and turned the scalpel on yourself, framing Cliff for not one attack but two."

Cooper hovered over the table, pouring herself a glass of water with shaking hands. "I'll give you extra points for commitment, though, Hal. You didn't half do a number on yourself. That's not easy."

She dragged her seat back, its legs squealing against the floor. She sat, stared at the snivelling man in front of her. "When I met you in the hospital, you called yourself – and I quote – *a fucking coward*. Sounds about right, don't you think, DI Singh?"

"I wouldn't use such colourful language," Singh said, unwrapping a sweet. "But yes, it's an apt description of Mr Simpson here."

"And why is that, DI Singh?"

Singh chewed, then swallowed. "Because Mr Simpson had every chance to put this right, but every time, he doubled down on his lies. Firstly, he wore Mr Longacre's boots. Then he lied and gave the description of the broad, six-foot-something man with blond hair poking out of a balaclava. A man who had a motive because Captain Jude had previously reported him to HR."

"Then there's the knife," Cooper said, staring down at Hal. "You lied again, telling us it was a small kitchen knife. I showed you pictures of the knives we found onboard, and you chose

339

one from Kay Longacre's kitchen. We wasted time and money running tests on it. We wasted time and money interviewing innocent people. Now we're wasting time chatting to you. You've confessed to killing Jude, and I have plenty of evidence to rule out your self-defence bullshit."

Tears continued to flow down Hal's face. He wiped at them, gasping for air, holding his ribs where his stitches were.

Singh methodically folded the sweet wrapper into a perfect square. "Innocent people who act in self-defence don't check themselves out of hospital and arrange to flee the country under the cover of darkness. I should probably inform you that police in Denmark are currently questioning members of Terra Nostra. Does that name mean anything to you?"

Another chance to come clean. He shook his head.

"They're a small but well-organised eco-activism group flagged for sabotaging infrastructure and threatening officials," Singh said. "Curious how you claim ignorance, yet they had a boat fueled and ready to leave Aahus Harbour with a map of Odin's Gale on board. Must just be a coincidence."

Hal looked up, saw the sarcasm written all over Singh's face and averted his eyes, muttering in panicked sobs about how he wouldn't survive jail.

Cooper felt no pity for him. "You could have done good things, Hal. Could have tried to save the world in ethical and legal ways, like VāyuVolt. But you didn't. Your tree spiking alone cost over a hundred people their jobs. Your subterfuge resulted in Violet's death and Jude's mental health problems. Until you killed him, of course. You are a coward, Hal Simpson, and I am charging you with the murder of Captain Jude McDermott."

CHAPTER 50

THE LOW WINTER SUN illuminated the hospital ward, its rays refracting off the glass, casting weak beams across a pale blue tiled floor. Keaton thought the space felt too clean, too orderly, as if it were unaffected by the bedlam they'd all endured.

She shifted on the stiff mattress, wincing due to the ache of being still for so long. The discomfort was worth it to see the team gathered around. Whyte stood next to Martin. Boyd sat on the end of his bed, looking lovingly at her boyfriend with big puppy-dog eyes. They were worse than teenagers. Singh was next to Keaton, reading the various greeting cards on her bedside table. Cooper stood by the window, watching the bare trees sway in the wind.

Once suitably propped up in bed, Keaton gave a loud "Ahem" and brandished a copy of the Evening Chronicle. "I appreciate you all coming along to gawk at us invalids..."

Cooper turned from the window. "Glad to see your charm hasn't been affected, Keaton."

"Takes more than a failed Gordon Ramsay with a God complex to knock that out of me," she retorted. "But enough about me." She placed the paper on her lap, unfolded it with a dramatic flourish, and read the bold headline. *"Newcastle's Finest: Off-Duty Detective's Daring Rescue at Restaurant."*

Boyd blushed but Keaton continued. "Our wee Saffron is bloody famous. Now, I know you don't like to be more than ten feet from that handsome beau of yours, but come on over here."

Boyd, head bowed and uncomfortable, moved to Keaton's bedside, turning increasingly crimson as Keaton read every word of the article.

"DC Saffron Boyd's quick thinking and bravery saved lives, Detective Chief Superintendent Howard Nixon was quoted as saying. Her actions exemplify the dedication of our police force."

Keaton smirked and slapped Boyd on the shoulder. "Look at you," she said, her tone teasing but sincere, glancing at Boyd's bandaged hands resting awkwardly on her lap. "You got a compliment out of Nixon; they're as rare as hen's teeth, you know? But seriously, talk about the hero of the hour. You've come a long way, Saff. Didn't think you had it in you."

Boyd's cheeks flushed further. "Just doing my job," she mumbled.

Keaton snorted. *My arse.* Classic Boyd, always downplaying her achievements. But there was no denying the quiet pride in the younger woman's eyes. Maybe this would finally give her the confidence boost she needed.

Keaton drifted back to the newspaper. *"Jeremy Knox has been charged with the attempted murder of detectives Paula Keaton – the most bad ass detective in the country – and Oliver Martin – her daft little side kick—"*

"It does not say that!" Scoffed Martin.

"May as well do. Anyway... bla bla bla... *Knox will also face a charge for producing a biological toxin contrary to section one of the Biological Weapons Act 1974."*

Keaton paused on a photograph between the sixth and seventh paragraphs. Nestled between talk of Boyd's heroics was a photo of April Davis.

Her ex.

Keaton's heart didn't skip a beat. Her stomach didn't clench. There was no pang of loss or lingering resentment. Nothing.

"Well, I'll be damned," she muttered.

Boyd leaned in. "What is it?" she asked quietly.

Keaton tapped the photo. "Guess I'm finally over her."

Boyd nudged her. "That's... good, right?"

"Bloody brilliant," Keaton grinned. "Consider me officially moving on."

Martin was still gazing longingly at Boyd. It was enough to make a person puke – even if they hadn't been poisoned.

"He's lucky to have you, you know?"

"He has both of us," Boyd said.

They shared a quiet laugh, a moment of understanding passing between the two women who were as different as night and day but united by their care for the same man.

The moment was broken by Whyte stretching languidly, his joints popping. "You two are about to be discharged," he said, nodding at Keaton and Martin. "And we all need a drink – or six – after that mess. What do you say?"

Boyd lit up. "Hell, yes!" She turned to Singh. "You coming?"

Singh dipped his head and returned the cards to the table in a neat pile. "I know an excellent coffee shop nearby. They do an espresso that will send you to the moon."

Whyte groaned. "No offence, but I need hard liquor. Something that burns going down."

"Agreed," Boyd nodded fiercely. "Though maybe less *burny*. I've had enough of hot oil for a lifetime. The Hancock's a five-minute walk from here."

Keaton and Martin exchanged a rueful glance. "Yeah, we'll come along," said Keaton, "but as much as I'd love to join in with the binge drinking, we're on a hospital-controlled diet. No beer. No coffee. Just bland beige food."

Martin winced as he shifted in bed. "We're not allowed anything stronger than water for the next few days. Doctor's orders." He turned to Cooper who was still standing apart from the group. "You'll join us, won't you, boss?"

She shook her head. "I'm heading home. It's been a long couple of days."

No one pressed further.

THE HANCOCK PUB WAS lively, as it always seemed to be. Close enough to the universities and the RVI to attract students, doctors, and professors alike, the pub was a mishmash of old-school charm and contemporary ease. The bar stretched wide, its surface stained from countless spilled pints, with brass taps gleaming under the light of a red neon sign depicting the pub's name.

Boyd breathed in the heady mix of hops, fried food and roasted meats while waiting for the bartender to pour her pint. A hint of cigarette smoke lingered from the outside terrace, where the rest of the group were seated, allowing Keaton and Martin some fresh air after their days confined to the hospital ward. She followed the smell to a bench and a long, black picnic table, exhaling heavily as she dropped onto the wooden seat. Her pint sloshed slightly, threatening to soak her bandaged hands. She brought it to her lips and took a long, satisfying gulp.

"I needed this," she muttered, setting the glass down with a thud.

Across from her, Keaton glared at her pint of water as though it were a warm pot of urine. "Tell me about it."

Martin looked equally displeased, tracing lazy shapes in the condensation forming on the glass. Only Singh looked happy with his glass of H2O.

Whyte stared at the untouched triple whiskey in front of him, fingers drumming on the table as though it were a piano. The amber liquid gleamed in the dim light of a patio heater as he swirled it around the glass.

"Drinking for three?" Boyd asked.

"Drinking to forget," he answered, picking up the glass and downing half of it in one. "What a week."

WHILE WHYTE DRANK TO forget and Boyd drank to drown her adrenaline, Cooper pulled up at the end of Latimer Terrace. She undid her seatbelt and walked the remaining distance, her mind drifting between the camaraderie she'd left behind at the hospital and the promise of home ahead.

The sight that greeted her made her pause mid-step. Framed in the warm glow of their living room window were her boyfriend, her mother, and her children. Julie was telling a story that had Tina in fits of giggles. Atkinson cleared the table of dinner plates with one hand, holding Danny with the other.

A tableau of domesticity that should have filled her with unalloyed joy.

But it didn't. Not entirely.

The moment she stepped inside, a whirlwind of raven-black hair and giggles crashed into her. Tina was in her Shark's uniform, fresh home from practice. "Mum, you need to hear Grandma's story about how she accidentally crashed a wedding in Lanzarote; I nearly wet myself laughing."

Cooper put an arm around her daughter. Tina was taller than she was now. "How was training?"

"Tiring. Did you really get stuck on that turbine during the storm? Was it scary?"

Atkinson appeared in the hallway, their son cradled against his chest. His smile was easy, warm. "Welcome home."

Cooper let go of Tina to kiss Danny, then Atkinson. "Yes, and yes," she told Tina.

The comforting scent of home – a mix of Danny's baby lotion and the faintest hint of dinner lingering in the air. It brought Cooper a sense of belonging she'd been craving for days. The smell wrapped around her like a blanket she didn't deserve.

Atkinson looked more relaxed than he had in weeks, his fitted t-shirt hugging his slim frame, the casual way his glasses were askew. She met his eyes, genuine happiness bubbling up inside her.

"It's good to be back," she said.

But underneath, a current of guilt tugged at her. The memory of another pair of eyes, another set of lips...

"Everything alright?" Atkinson asked.

She thought of Hal Simpson, and how he'd managed to fool her and everyone around him. If he could do it, so could she. She could act her way out of this. She forced a smile. "Just exhausted. The case, the ship, Paula and Oliver..."

Atkinson handed her Danny, and she smiled at her little bundle of cuteness. She swore he'd grown even since that morning.

"Why don't you put him to bed," he suggested. "Have ten minutes with the little tinker. I'll reheat dinner."

"I'll run you a bath," said Tina, tucking her hair behind her ear and heading for the stairs.

Julie stuck her head around the doorframe. "And I'll pour you a drink, darling. God knows you must need it."

With every step Cooper took up the stairs she felt the case slip into her memories, filed away until she needed to appear in court to give evidence against Hal Simpson. She laid Danny in his crib, her heart swelling as his tiny hand wrapped around her thumb. She sang him a lullaby and listened to him make the sweetest noises as he drifted asleep. Downstairs, there was another fit of laughter – her family safe and happy. It was a sound so pure and innocent it brought tears to her eyes.

The kiss had been a moment, a fleeting escape from the demands of being a detective and a working mum. But so was this. This moment right here. Her baby was healthy, her daughter had a bright future and her mother was adapting to life as a widow.

Atkinson tiptoed into the room, holding a plate of reheated pizza. "Pizza delivery for the world's greatest detective."

She laughed. "You have the wrong house."

"Oh, is that so? I'll just take this elsewhere, shall I?" he joked.

"Don't you dare." She removed her thumb from Danny's grip and took a slice, feeling grateful for it all. She could never give herself fully to them. She would always have one foot in the world of crime and the chaos of policing. But for now, this was where Cooper belonged. These were the people who mattered.

DCI Cooper will return.

- Message from the Author -

Hello, crime fiction fans,

Thank you for joining DCI Erica Cooper on her latest investigation in *The Bridge*, the eighth instalment of the series.

I hope you found the voyage with Cooper as riveting as I found writing it. If so, I would be immensely grateful if you could share your thoughts with a review on Amazon or Goodreads. Your support not only helps Cooper's stories reach new audiences but also fuels my continued passion for storytelling.

Before you go, I'd like to share with you some of the real-life events, news, and experiences which inspired Cooper's voyage into the North Sea and Odin's Gale.

The idea for the main plot, particularly the chilling detail of the boots that never left the bridge, was inspired by the 2011 Lululemon murder case. A retail worker brutally murdered her colleague inside a Maryland yoga apparel store and then staged the scene to look like a violent robbery. The murderer walked around the crime scene in a pair of men's size 14 Reeboks before hiding them within the store. She was sentenced to life for first-degree murder.

The subplot involving Oliver Martin and the Whatsapp group also draws from various real-life cases of officers dismissed over inappropriate messages, highlighting the consequences of our digital interactions. To read more, you can search for *Whatsapp* on policeconduct.gov.uk.

As well as being a scene in *The Bridge*, Barter Books, Alnwick is the location that ignited my passion for crime fiction and, consequently, writing crime fiction. I've written myself into this scene, quietly hoping for a cameo if Cooper ever transitions from page to screen. Did you spot me reading the PJ Tracy thriller?

This book was penned during a significant chapter of my life – while living on a boat. Sailing from North Shields to Gibraltar, I've passed numerous wind farms and SOVs and experienced the vast isolation of the sea. I feel this perspective enriched the maritime elements of the story, from the solitude of the sea to the solidarity among the crew. You can read more on my blog at betsybaskerville.com.

Speaking of wind farms, *The Bridge* addresses the contentious issue of renewable energy. While showcasing the ecological benefits, like artificial reefs supporting marine life, I also touch on the challenges, such as the impact on bird populations. However, technology is continuously improving, and innovations such as radar-based detection systems can now monitor migratory or endangered birds, shutting down turbines when a risk of collision is detected.

This brings us to Electron, the cutting-edge, fully-electric service vessel at the centre of *The Bridge*. Electron is a little ahead of her time, but boats such as this are on the horizon (pardon the pun). Damen Shipyards Group is developing fully electric SOVs, crew transfer vessels and tugs, which will be able to charge via substations (like in *The Bridge*) or directly from turbines or other vessels. I look forward to sailing past one in the coming seasons! I will have my camera ready.

For the latest updates, behind-the-scenes peeks, and more, please visit my website, betsybaskerville.com, where you can sign up for my newsletter. You can also connect with me on Facebook (B Baskerville - Author).

Your engagement and feedback are what make writing truly rewarding.

Thank you for your continued support.

Warmest regards, B x

- BE SOCIABLE -

Facebook: B Baskerville - Author

Twitter: B_ _Baskerville

Instagram: B_Baskerville_Author

Newsletter: You can subscribe to the B
Baskerville newsletter using the form on
BetsyBaskerville.com. You'll mainly hear from
me when I have something to share, such as a
pre-order going live, a new book release or sale etc.

- ABOUT THE AUTHOR -

B WAS BORN AND raised in Gosforth, Newcastle and is an alumnus of "Gossy High." Surprisingly, her academic journey led her to Sunderland University, where she studied sport and exercise development, a far cry from the creative writing path she would later tread.

Life took her to charming North Shields, a place that would become a source of inspiration for her writing. The local beaches and the bustling Fish Quay infused her work with a unique coastal flavour.

In a personal plot twist, in spring 2023, B and her husband embarked on an adventure by moving onto a boat, accompanied by their naughty Welsh terrier. Together, they sailed an impressive 1600 nautical miles, circumnavigating the UK's breathtaking coastline.

In 2024 they decided to continue the adventure by sailing south along the coasts of France, Spain, Portugal and Gibraltar.

Away from the keyboard, or the helm, B enjoys reading, weight training, exploring new places, yoga, walking said naughty Welsh terrier, and drinking copious amounts of tea.

- Also By B Baskerville -

The DCI Cooper Series:
Cut The Deck
Rock, Paper, Scissors
Roll The Dice
Northern Roulette
Hide & Seek
Finders Keepers
The House Always Wins
The Bridge

Stand Alones:
The Only Weapon In The Room
Dead In The Water

Milton Keynes UK
Ingram Content Group UK Ltd.
UKHW031159041224
3332UKWH00004B/300